MELBOURNE HOUSE.

THE OLD IRISH TOMB.

Melbourne House, Vol. I.

MELBOURNE HOUSE.

BY THE

AUTHOR OF THE "WIDE, WIDE WORLD."

"Even a child is known by his doings, whether his work be pure, and whether it be right."—PROV. XX. 11.

VOL. I.

NEW YORK:
ROBERT CARTER & BROTHERS,
530 BROADWAY.
1865.

Stereotyped by Smith & McDougal, 82 & 84 Beekman St.
Printed by E. O. Jenkins, 20 North William St.

MELBOURNE HOUSE.

CHAPTER I.

A LITTLE girl was coming down a flight of stairs that led up from a great hall, slowly letting her feet pause on each stair, while the light touch of her hand on the rail guided her. The very thoughtful little face seemed to be intent on something out of the house, and when she reached the bottom, she still stood with her hand on the great baluster that rested on the marble there, and looked wistfully out of the open door. So the sunlight came in and looked at her; a little figure in a white frock and blue sash, with the hair cut short all over a little round head, and a face not only just now full of some grave concern, but with habitually thoughtful eyes and a wise little mouth. She did not seem to see the sunlight which poured all over her, and lit up a wide, deep hall, floored with marble, and opening at the other end on trees and flowers, which shewed the sunlight busy there too. The child lingered wistfully. Then crossed the hall, and went into a matted, breezy, elegant room, where a lady lay luxuriously on a couch, playing with a book and a leaf-cutter. She could not be *busy* with anything in that attitude. Nearly all that was to be seen was a flow of lavender silk flounces, a rich slipper at rest on a cushion, and a dainty little cap with roses on a head too much at ease to rest. By the side of the lavender silk stood the little white dress, still and preöccupied as before—a few minutes without any notice.

"Do you want anything, Daisy?"

"Mamma, I want to know something."

"Well, what is it?"

"Mamma"—Daisy seemed to be engaged on a very puzzling question—"what does it mean to be a Christian?"

"*What?*" said her mother, rousing herself up for the first time to look at her.

"To be a Christian, mamma?"

"It means, to be baptized and go to church, and all that," said the lady, turning back to her book.

"But mamma, that isn't all I mean."

"I don't know what you mean. What has put it into your head?"

"Something Mr. Dinwiddie said."

"What absurd nonsense! Who is Mr. Dinwiddie?"

"You know him. He lives at Mrs. Sandford's."

"And where did he talk to you?"

"In the little school in the woods. In his Sunday-school. Yesterday."

"Well, it's absurd nonsense, your going there. You have nothing to do with such things. Mr. Randolph?——"

An inarticulate sound, testifying that he was attending, came from a gentleman who had lounged in and was lounging through the room.

"I won't have Daisy go to that Sunday-school any more, down there in the woods. Just tell her she is not to do it, will you? She is getting her head full of the most absurd nonsense. Daisy is just the child to be ruined by it."

"You hear, Daisy," said Mr. Randolph, indolently, as he lounged finally out of the room by an open window; which, as did all the windows in the room, served for a door also. By the door by which she had entered, Daisy silently withdrew again, making no effort to change the resolution of either of her parents. She knew it would be of no use; for excessively indulgent as they both were in general, whenever they took it upon them to exercise authority, it was unflinchingly done. Her father would never even hear a supplication to reconsider a judgment, especially if pronounced at the desire of her mother. So Daisy knew.

It was a disappointment, greater than anybody thought or would have guessed, that saw her. She went out to the large porch before the door, and stood there, with the same thoughtful look upon her face, a little cast down now. Still she did not shed tears about the matter, unless one time when Daisy's hand went up to her brow rather quick, it was to get rid of some improper suggestion there. More did not appear, either before or after the sudden crunching of the gravel by a pair of light wheels, and the coming up of a little Shetland pony, drawing a miniature chaise.

"Hollo, Daisy! come along; he goes splendidly!"

So shouted the driver, a boy somewhat bigger than Daisy.

"Where are you going?"

"Anywhere—down to the church, if you'll be quick. Never mind your hat!"

He waited, however, while Daisy dashed into the house and out again, and then stepped into the low chaise beside him. Then the eager intimation was given to the pony, which set off as if knowing that impatience was behind him. The smooth, wide, gravelled road was as good and much better than a plank flooring; the chaise rolled daintily on under the great trees; the pony was not forgetful, yet ever and anon a touch of his owner's whip came to remind him, and the fellow's little body fairly wriggled from side to side in his efforts to get on.

"I wish you wouldn't whip him so!" said Daisy, "he's doing as well as he can."

"What do girls know about driving!" was the retort from the small piece of masculine science beside her.

"Ask papa," said Daisy quietly.

"Well, what do they know about horses, any how!"

"I can *see*," said Daisy, whose manner of speech was somewhat slow and deliberate, and in the choice of words, like one who had lived among grown people. "I can observe."

"See that, then!"—And a cut, smarter than ordinary, drove the pony to his last legs, namely, a gallop. Away they went; it was but a short-legged gallop after all; yet they passed along swiftly over the smooth gravel road. Great, beautiful trees overshadowed the ground on either side with their long arms; and underneath, the turf was mown short, fresh and green. Sometimes a flowering bush of some sort broke the general green with a huge spot of white or red flowers; gradually those became fewer, and were lost sight of; but the beautiful grass and the trees seemed to be unending. Then a gray rock here and there began to shew itself. Pony got through his gallop, and subsided again to a waddling trot.

"This whip's the real thing," said the young driver, displaying and surveying it as he spoke; "that is a whip now, fit for a man to use."

"A man wouldn't use it as you do," said Daisy. "It is cruel."

"That's what *you* think. I guess you'd see papa use a whip once in a while."

"Besides, you came along too fast to see anything."

"Well, I told you I was going to the church, and we hadn't time to go slowly. What did you come for?"

"I suppose I came for some diversion," said Daisy with a sigh.

"Ain't Loupe a splendid little fellow?"

"Very; I think so."

"Why, Daisy, what ails you? there is no fun in you to-day. What's the matter?"

"I am concerned about something. There is nothing the matter."

"Concerned about Loupe, eh!"

"I am not thinking about Loupe. O Ransom! stop him; there's Nora Dinwiddie; I want to get out."

The place at which they were arrived had a little less the air of carefully kept grounds, and more the look of a sweet wild wood; for the trees clustered thicker in patches, and grey rock, in large and in small quantities, was plenty about among the trees. Yet still here was care; no unsightly underbrush or rubbish of dead branches was anywhere to be seen; and the greensward, where it spread, was shaven and soft as ever. It spread on three sides

THE CHURCH BY THE WINTERGREENS.

around a little church, which, in green and gray, seemed almost a part of its surroundings. A little church, with a little quaint bell-tower and arched doorway, built after some old, old model; it stood as quietly in the green solitude of trees and rocks, as if it and they had grown up together. It was almost so. The walls were of native greystone in its natural roughness; all over the front and one angle the American ivy climbed and waved, mounting to the tower; while at the back, the closer clinging Irish ivy covered the little "apse," and creeping round the corner, was advancing to the windows, and promising to case the first one in a loving frame of its own. It seemed that no carriage-road came to this place, other than the dressed gravelled path which the pony-chaise had travelled, and which made a circuit on approaching the rear of the church. The worshippers must come humbly on foot; and a wicket in front of the church led out upon a path suited for such. Perhaps a public road might be not far off, but at least here there was no promise of it. In the edge of the thicket, at the side of the church, was the girl whose appearance Daisy had hailed.

"I sha'n't wait for you," cried her brother, as she sprang down.

"No—go—I don't want you,"—and Daisy made few steps over the greensward to the thicket. Then it was,—"O Nora! how do you do? what are you doing?"—and "O Daisy! I'm getting wintergreens." Anybody who has ever been nine, or ten, or eleven years old, and gone in the woods looking for wintergreens, knows what followed. The eager plunging into the thickest of the thicket; the happy search of every likely bank or open ground in the shelter of some rock; the careless, delicious straying from rock to rock, and whithersoever the bank or the course of the thicket might lead them. The wintergreens sweet under foot, sweet in the hands of the children, the whole air full of sweetness. Naturally their quest led them to the thicker and wilder grown part of the wood; prettier there, they declared it to be, where the ground became broken, and there were ups and downs, and rocky dells and heights, and to turn a corner was to come upon something new. They did not note nor care where they went, intent upon business and pleasure together, till they came out suddenly upon a little rocky height, where a small spot was shaded with cedars and set with benches around and under them. The view away off over the tops of the trees to other heights and hills in the distance was winningly fair, especially as the sun shewed it just now in bright, cool light and shadow. It was getting near sundown.

"Look where we are!" cried Nora, "at the Sunday-school!"

Daisy seated herself without answering.

"I think," went on Nora, as she followed the example, "it is the very prettiest place for a Sunday-school that there ever was."

"Have you been in other Sunday-schools?" asked Daisy.

"Yes, in two."

"What were they like?"

"O they were in a church, or in some sort of a room. I like being out of doors best; don't you?"

"Yes, I think so. But was the school just like this in other things?"

"O yes; only once I had a teacher who always asked us what we thought about everything. I didn't like that."

"What you thought about everything?" said Daisy.

"Yes; every verse and question, she would say, 'What do you think about it?' and I didn't like that, because I never thought anything."

Whereat Daisy fell into a muse. Her question recurred to her; but it was hardly likely, she felt, that her little companion could enlighten her. Nora was a bright, lively, spirited child, with black eyes and waves of beautiful black hair; neither at rest; sportive energy and enjoyment in every motion. Daisy was silent.

"What is supposed to be going on here?" said a stronger voice behind them, which brought both their heads round. It was to see another head just making its way up above the level of their platform; a head that looked strong and spirited as the voice had sounded; a head set with dark hair, and eyes that were too full of light to let you see what colour they were. Both children came to their feet, one saying, "Marmaduke!" the other, "Mr. Dinwiddie!"

"What do two such mature people do when they get together? I should like to know," said the young man as he reached the top.

"Talking, sir," said Daisy.

"Picking wintergreens," said the other, in a breath.

"Talking! I dare say you do. If both things have gone on together, like your answers," said he, helping himself out of Nora's stock of wintergreens,—"you must have had a basket of talk."

"*That* basket isn't full, sir," said Daisy.

"My dear," said Mr. Dinwiddie, diving again into his sister's, "that basket never is; there's a hole in it somewhere."

"You are making a hole in mine," said Nora, laughing. "You sha'n't do it, Marmaduke; they're for old Mrs. Holt, you know."

"Come along, then," said her brother; "as long as the baskets are not full the fun isn't over."

And soon the children thought so. Such a scrambling to new places as they had then; such a harvest of finest wintergreens as they all gathered together; till Nora took off her sun-bonnet to serve for a new basket. And such joyous, lively, rambling talk as they had all three, too; it was twice as good as they had before; or as Daisy, who was quiet in her epithets, phrased it, "it was *nice*." By Mr. Dinwiddie's help they could go faster and further than they could alone; he could jump them up and down the rocks, and tell them where it was no use to waste their time in trying to go.

They had wandered, as it seemed to them, a long distance—they knew not whither—when the children's exclamations suddenly burst forth, as they came out upon the Sunday-school place again. They were glad to sit down and rest. It was just sundown, and the light was glistening, crisp and clear, on the leaves of the trees and on the distant hill-points. In the west a mass of glory that the eye could not bear was sinking towards the horizon. The eye could not bear it, and yet every eye turned that way.

"Can you see the sun?" said Mr. Dinwiddie.

"No, sir,"—and "No, Marmaduke."

"Then why do you look at it?"

"I don't know!" laughed Nora; but Daisy said: "Because it is so beautiful, Mr. Dinwiddie."

"Once when I was in Ireland," said the gentleman, "I was looking, near sunset, at some curious old ruins. They were near a very poor little village where I had to pass the night. There had been a little chapel or church of some sort, but it had crumbled away; only bits of the walls were standing, and in place of the floor there was nothing but grass and weeds, and one or two monuments that had been under shelter of the roof. One of them was a large square tomb in the middle of the place. It had been very handsome. The top of it had held two statues, lying there with hands upraised in prayer, in memory of those who slept beneath. But it was so very old—the statues had been lying there so long since the roof that sheltered them was gone, that they were worn away so that you could only just see that they had been statues; you could just make out the remains of what had been the heads and where the hands had been. It was all rough and shapeless now.*

"What had worn the stone so?" asked Daisy.

"The weather—the heat and the cold, and the rain, and the dew."

"But it must have taken a great while?"

"A very great while. Their names were forgotten—nobody knew whose monument or what church had been there."

* See frontispiece.

"More than a hundred years?" asked Nora.

"It had been many hundred."

"O Duke!"

"What's the matter? Don't you believe that people died many hundred years ago?"

"Yes; but ——"

"And they had monuments erected to them, and they thought their names would live forever; but these names were long gone, and the very stone over their grave was going. While I sat there, thinking about them, and wondering what sort of people they were in their lifetime,—the sun, which had been behind a tree, got lower, and the beams came striking across the stone and brightening up those poor old worn heads and hands of what had been statues. And with that the words rushed into my head, and they have never got out since,—"*Then* shall the righteous shine forth as the sun in the kingdom of their Father."

"When, Mr. Dinwiddie?" said Daisy, after a timid silence.

"When the King comes!" said the young man, still looking off to the glowing west,—"the time when he will put away out of his kingdom all things that offend him. You may read about it, if you will, in the thirteenth chapter of Matthew, in the parable of the tares."

He turned round to Daisy as he spoke, and the two looked steadily into one another's faces; the child wondering very much what feeling it could be that had called an additional sparkle into those bright eyes the moment before, and brought to the mouth, which was always in happy play, an expression of happy rest. He, on his part, queried what lay under the thoughtful, almost anxious, search of the little one's quiet grey eyes.

"Do you know," he said, "that you must go home? The sun is almost down."

So home they went—Mr. Dinwiddie and Nora taking care of Daisy quite to the house. But it was long after sundown then.

"What has kept you?" her mother asked, as Daisy came in to the tea-table.

"I didn't know how late it was, mamma."

"Where have you been?"

"I was picking wintergreens with Nora Dinwiddie."

"I hope you brought me some," said Mr. Randolph.

"O I did, papa; only I have not put them in order yet."

"And where did you and Nora part?"

"Here, at the door, mamma."

"Was she alone?"

"No, ma'am—Mr. Dinwiddie found us in the wood, and he took her home, and he brought me home first."

Daisy was somewhat of a diplomatist. Perhaps a little natural reserve of character might have been the beginning of it, but the habit had certainly grown from Daisy's experience of her mother's somewhat capricious and erratic views of her movements. She could not but find out that things which to her father's sense were quite harmless and unobjectionable, were invested with an unknown and unexpected character of danger or disagreeableness in the eyes of her mother; neither could Daisy get hold of any chain of reasoning by which she might know beforehand what would meet her mother's favour and what would not. The unconscious conclusion was, that reason had little to do with it; and the consequence, that without being untrue, Daisy had learned to be very uncommunicative; about her thoughts, plans, or wishes. To her mother, that is; she was more free with her father, though the habit, once a habit, asserted itself everywhere. Perhaps, too, among causes, the example of her mother's own elegant manner of shewing truth only as one shews a fine picture,—in the best light,—might have had its effect. Daisy's diplomacy served her little on the present occasion.

"Daisy!" said her mother, "look at me." Daisy fixed her eyes on the pleasant, handsome, mild face. "You are not to go anywhere in future where Mr. Dinwiddie is. Do you understand?"

"If he finds you lost out at night, though," said Mr. Randolph a little humorously, "he may bring you home."

Daisy wondered and obeyed, mentally, in silence; making no answer to either speaker. It was not her habit either to shew her dismay on such occasions, and she shewed none. But when she went up an hour later to be undressed for bed, instead of letting the business go on, Daisy took a Bible and sat down by the light and pored over a page that she had found.

The woman waiting on her, a sad-faced mulatto, middle-aged and respectable looking, went patiently round the room, doing or seeming to do some trifles of business, then stood still and looked at the child, who was intent on her book.

"Come, Miss Daisy," said she at last, "wouldn't you like to be undressed?"

The words were said in a tone so low they were hardly more than a suggestion. Daisy gave them no heed. The woman stood with dressing gown on her arm and a look of habitual endurance upon her face. It was a singular face, so set in its lines of enforced patience, so unbending. The black eyes were bright enough, but without the help of the least play of those fixed lines, they expressed nothing. A little sigh came from the lips at last, which also was plainly at home there.

"Miss Daisy, it's gettin' very late."

"June, did you ever read the parable of the tares?"

"The what, Miss Daisy?"

"The parable about the wheat and the tares in the Bible—in the thirteenth chapter of Matthew?"

"Yes, ma'am,"—came somewhat dry and unwillingly from June's lips, and she moved the dressing-gown on her arm significantly.

"Do you remember it?"

"Yes, ma'am,—I suppose I do, Miss Daisy—"

"June, when do you think it will be?"

"When will what, Miss Daisy?"

"When the 'Son of Man shall send forth his angels, and they shall gather out of his kingdom all things that offend and them which do iniquity, and shall cast them into a furnace of fire; there shall be wailing and gnashing of teeth. Then shall the righteous shine forth as the sun in the kingdom of their Father.' It says, 'in the end of this world'—did you know this world would come to an end, June?"

"Yes, Miss Daisy ——"

"When will it be, June?"

"I dont know, Miss Daisy."

"There won't be anybody alive that is alive now, will there?"

Again unwillingly the answer came: "Yes, ma'am. Miss Daisy, hadn't you better ——"

"How do you know, June?"

"I have heard so—it's in the Bible—it will be when the Lord comes."

"Do you like to think of it, June?"

The child's searching eyes were upon her. The woman half laughed, half answered, and turning aside, broke down and burst into tears.

"What's the matter, June?" said Daisy, coming nearer and speaking awedly; for it was startling to see that stony face give way to anything but its habitual formal smile. But the woman recovered herself almost immediately, and answered as usual: "It's nothing, Miss Daisy." She always spoke as if everything about her was "nothing" to everybody else.

"But, June," said Daisy tenderly, "why do you feel bad about it?"

"I shouldn't, I s'pose," said the woman desperately, answering because she was obliged to answer; "I hain't no right to feel so—if I felt ready."

"How can one be ready, June? that is what I want to know. Aren't you ready?"

"Do, don't, Miss Daisy!—the Lord have mercy upon us!" said June under her breath, wrought up to great excitement, and unable to bear the look of the child's soft grey eyes. "Why don't ye ask your papa about them things? he can tell ye."

Alas, Daisy's lips were sealed. Not to father or mother would she apply with any second question on this subject. And now she must not ask Mr. Dinwiddie. She went to bed, turning the matter all over and over in her little head.

CHAPTER II.

For some days after this time, Mrs. Randolph fancied that her little daughter was less lively than usual; she "moped," her mother said. Daisy was not moping, but it was true she had been little seen or heard; and then it was generally sitting with a book in the Belvidere or on a bank under a rose-bush, or going out or coming in with a book under her arm. Mrs. Randolph did not know that this book was almost always the Bible, and Daisy had taken a little pains that she should not know, guessing somehow that it would not be good for her studies. But her mother thought Daisy was drooping; and Daisy had been a delicate child, and the doctor had told them to turn her out in the country and "let her run;" therefore it was that she was hardly ever checked in any fancy that came into her head. But therefore it was partly, too, that Mrs. Randolph tried to put books and thinking as far from her as she could.

"Daisy," she said one morning at the breakfast-table, "would you like to go with June and carry some nice things down to Mrs. Parsons?"

"How, mamma?"

"How what? Do speak distinctly."

"How shall I go, I mean?"

"You may have the carriage. I cannot go, this morn ing or this afternoon."

"O papa, mayn't I take Loupe and drive there myself?"

If Daisy had put the question at the other end of the table, there would have been an end of the business, as she knew. As it was, her father's "yes" got out just before her mother's "no."

"Yes she may," said Mr. Randolph—"no harm. John, tell Sam that he is to take the black pony and go with the pony-chaise whenever Miss Daisy drives. Daisy, see that he goes with you."

"Well," said Mrs. Randolph, "you may do as you like, but I think it is a very unsafe proceeding. What's Sam?—he's a boy."

"Safe enough," said Mr. Randolph. "I can trust all three of the party; Daisy, Loupe, and Sam. They all know their business, and they will all do it."

"Well!—I think it is very unsafe," repeated Mrs. Randolph.

"Mamma," said Daisy, when she had allowed a moment to pass—"what shall I take to Mrs. Parsons."

"You must go and see Joanna about that. You may make up whatever you think will please her or do her good. Joanna will tell you."

And Mrs. Randolph had the satisfaction of seeing that Daisy's eyes were lively enough for the rest of breakfast-time, and her colour perceptibly raised. No sooner was breakfast over than she flew to the consultation in the housekeeper's room.

Joanna was the housekeeper, and Mrs. Randolph's right hand; a jewel of skill and efficiency; and as fully satisfied with her post and power in the world, at the head of Mr. Randolph's household, as any throned emperor or diademed queen; furthermore, devoted to her employers as though their concerns had been, what indeed she reckoned them, her own.

"Mrs. Randolph didn't say anything to me about it," said this piece of capability,—"but I suppose it isn't hard to manage. Who is Mrs. Parsons? that's the first thing."

"She's a very poor old woman, Joanna; and she is obliged to keep her bed always; there is something the matter with her. She lives with a daughter of hers who takes care of her, I believe; but they haven't much to live upon, and the daughter isn't smart. Mrs. Parsons hasn't anything fit for her to eat, unless somebody sends it to her."

"What's the matter with her? ain't she going to get well?"

"No, never—she will always be obliged to lie on her bed as long as she lives; and so, you see, Joanna, she hasn't appetite for coarse things."

"Humph!" said Joanna. "Custards won't give it to her. What does the daughter live upon?"

"She does washing for people; but of course that don't give her much. They are very poor, I know."

"Well, what would you like to take her, Miss Daisy?"

"Mother said you'd know."

"Well, I'll tell you what *I* think—sweetmeats ain't good for such folks. You wait till afternoon, and you shall have a pail of nice broth and a bowl of arrowroot with wine and sugar in it; that'll hearten her up. Will that do?"

"But I should like to take something to the other poor woman, too."

"How are you going?"

"In my pony-chaise—I can take anything."

Joanna muttered an ejaculation. "Well then, Miss Daisy, a basket of cold meat wouldn't come amiss, I suppose."

"And some bread, Joanna?"

"The chaise won't hold so much."

"It has got to hold the basket," said Daisy in much glee, "and the bread can go in. And, Joanna, I'll have it ready at half-past four o'clock."

There was no air of moping about Daisy, when, at half-past four she set off from the house in her pony-chaise, laden with pail and basket and all she had bargained for. A happier child was seldom seen. Sam, a capable black

LOUPE.

boy, was behind her on a pony not too large to shame her own diminutive equipage; and Loupe, a good-sized Shetland pony, was very able for more than his little mistress was going to ask of him. Her father looked on, pleased, to see her departure; and when she had gathered up her reins, leaned over her and gave her with his kiss a little gold piece to go with the pail and basket. It crowned Daisy's satisfaction; with a quiet glad look and word of thanks to her father, she drove off.

The pony waddled along nicely, but as his legs were none of the longest, their rate of travelling was not precisely of the quickest. Daisy was not impatient. The afternoon was splendid, the dust had been laid by late rains, and Daisy looked at her pail and basket with great contentment. Before she had gone a quarter of a mile from home, she met her little friend of the wintergreens. Nora sprang across the road to the chaise.

"O Daisy, where are you going?"

"I am going to carry some things for mamma, to a house."

"All alone?"

"No, Sam is there to take care of me."

Nora looked back at the black pony, and then at Daisy. "Isn't it nice!" she said, with a sort of half-regretful ad miration.

"It's as nice as a fairy tale," said Daisy. "I'm just as good as a princess, you know, Nora. Don't you want to go, too? Do come."

"No, I musn't—there are people coming to tea. Mrs. Linwood, and Charles and Jane—I wish I could go! How far is it, Daisy?"

"About five miles. Down beyond Crum Elbow, a good nice way; but I shan't go through Crum Elbow."

"It's so splendid!" sighed Nora. "Well, good-bye. I can't go."

On went the pony. The roads were good and pleasant, leading through farm fields and here and there a bit of wood, but not much. It was mostly open country, cultivated by farmers; and the grain fields not yet ripe, and the grass fields not yet mown, looked rich and fair and soft in bright colours to Daisy's eyes, as the afternoon sun shone across them and tree shadows lay long over the ground. For trees there were, a great many, growing singly about the fields and fences, and some of them very large and fine. Daisy was not so busy with her driving but that she could use her eyes about other things. Now and then she met a farm wagon, or a labourer going along the road. The men looked at her curiously and pleasantly, as if they thought it a pretty sight; but once Daisy, passing a couple of men together, overheard one say to the other:

"It's Randolph's folks—they stick themselves up considerable——"

The tone of the voice was gruff and coarse, and Daisy marvelled much in her little mind what had displeased the man in her or in "Randolph's folks." She determined to ask her father. "Stick ourselves up?" said Daisy thoughtfully—"we *never* do!"

So she touched the pony, who was falling into a very leisurely way of trotting, and in good time came to Mrs. Parsons' door.

Daisy went in. The daughter was busy at some ironing in the outer room; she was a dull, lack-lustre creature, and though she comprehended the gifts that had been brought her, seemed hardly to have life enough to thank the donor. *That* wasn't quite like a fairy tale, Daisy thought. No doubt this poor woman must have things to eat, but there was not much fun in bringing them to her Daisy was inclined to wonder how she had ever come to marry anybody with so lively a name as Lark. But before she got away, Mrs. Lark asked Daisy to go in and see her mother, and Daisy, not knowing how to refuse, went in as requested.

What a change! Another poor room to be sure, very poor it looked to Daisy; with its strip of rag carpet on the floor, its rush-bottomed chairs, and paper window-shades; and on the bed lay the bed-ridden woman. But with such a nice pleasant face; eyes so lively and quiet, smile so contented, brow so calm, Daisy wondered if it could be she that must lie there always and never go about again as long as she lived. It had been a matter of dread to her to see anything so disagreeable; and now it was not disagreeable. Daisy was fascinated. Mrs. Lark had withdrawn.

"Is your mother with you, dear?"

"No ma'am, I came alone. Mamma told me to ask Mrs. Parsons if there is anything she would like to have, that mamma could do for her."

"Yes; if you would come in and see me sometimes," said the old lady, "I should like it very much."

"Me?" said Daisy.

"Yes. I don't see young faces very often. They don't care to come to see an old woman."

"I should like to come," said Daisy, "very much, if I could do anything; but I must go now, because it will be late. Good-bye, ma'am."

Daisy's little courtesy it was pleasant to see, and it was

so pleasant altogether that Mrs. Parsons had it over and over in her thoughts that day and the next.

"It's as nice as a fairy tale," Daisy repeated to herself, as she took her seat in the chaise again and shook up her reins. It was better than a fairy tale really, for the sunshine coming between the trees from the sinking sun, made all the world look so beautiful that Daisy thought no words could tell it. It was splendid to drive through that sunlight. In a minute or two more she had pulled up her reins short, and almost before she knew why she had done it or whom she had seen, Mr. Dinwiddie stood at her side. Here he was. She must not go where he was; she had not; he had come to her. Daisy was very glad. But she looked up in his face now without speaking.

"Ha! my stray lamb," said he, "whither are you running?"

"Home, sir," said Daisy meekly.

"Do you know you have run away from me?"

"Yes, Mr. Dinwiddie."

"How came that?"

"It was unavoidable, sir," said Daisy, in her slow, old-fashioned way. But the bright eye of the young man saw that her eye fell and her face clouded over; it was not a slight nor a chance hindrance that had been in her way, he was sure.

"Then you don't mean to come to me any more?"

It was a dreadful question, but Mr. Dinwiddie's way of speaking was so clear and quick and business-like, and he seemed to know so well what he was talking about, that the answer was forced from Daisy. She looked up and said, "No, sir." He watched the soft thoughtful face that was raised towards him.

"Then if this is the last time we are to talk about it, Daisy, shall I look for you among those that will 'shine as the sun' in the Lord's kingdom?"

"O sir,—Mr. Dinwiddie,"—said Daisy, dropping her

reins and rising up, "that is what I want to know about. Please tell me!"

"Tell you what?" said Mr. Dinwiddie, gathering up the reins.

"Tell me how to do, sir, please."

"What have you done, Daisy?"

"Nothing, sir—only reading the Bible."

"And you do not find it there?"

"I find a great deal, sir; but I don't quite understand —I don't know how to be a Christian."

Daisy thought it might be her last chance; she was desperate, and spoke out.

"Do you love the Lord Jesus, Daisy?"

"I don't know, Mr. Dinwiddie."

"You know how he loves you? You know what he has done for you?"

"Yes—I know—"

"He died to save you from death and sin. He will do it if you trust him. Now what he wants is that you should love him and trust him. 'Let the little children come to me,' he said a great while ago, and says now. Daisy, the good Lord wants you to give him your heart."

"But suppose, Mr. Dinwiddie——"

"Yes. What?"

"Suppose I can't. I don't know how."

"Do you want to do it?"

"Yes, sir. Indeed I do."

"Very well; the Lord knows just what your difficulty is; you must apply to him."

"Apply to him?" said Daisy.

"Ask him."

"How, sir?"

"Pray to him. Tell the Lord your trouble, and ask him to make it all right for you. Did you never pray to him?"

"No, sir—not ever."

"My lamb," said Mr. Dinwiddie, "he will hear you, if you never prayed to him before. I will shew you the word of his promise." And he opened a pocket-Bible and found the place of these words which he gave Daisy to read. "'*I will put a new spirit within you; and I will take the stony heart out of their flesh, and will give them an heart of flesh; that they may walk in my statutes, and keep mine ordinances, and do them: and they shall be my people, and I will be their God.*' Now is that what you want, Daisy?"

"Yes, sir; only I don't know how."

"Never mind; the Lord knows. He will make it all right, if only you are willing to give yourself to be his little servant."

"I will give him all I have got, sir," said Daisy, looking up.

"Very well; then I will shew you one thing more—it is a word of the Lord Jesus. See—'*If ye love me, keep my commandments.*' Now I want you to keep those two words, and you can't remember where to find them again—I must let you take this book with you." And Mr. Dinwiddie folded down leaves in the two places.

"But Mr. Dinwiddie,"—said Daisy softly—"I don't know when I can get it back to you again, sir."

"Never mind—keep it, and when you don't want it, give it to some poor person that does. And remember, little one, that the good Lord expects his servants to tell him their troubles and to pray to him every day."

"Thank you, sir!" was Daisy's deep ejaculation.

"Don't thank me. Now will your pony get you home before dark?"

"O yes, Mr. Dinwiddie! Loupe is lazy, but he can go, and I will make him."

The chaise went off at a swift rate accordingly, after another soft grateful look from its little driver. Mr. Dinwiddie stood looking after it. Of a certain woman of Thyatira it is written that "the Lord opened her heart, that she attended to the things which were spoken." Surely, the gentleman thought, the same had been true of his late little charge. He went thoughtfully home. While Daisy, not speculating at all, in her simplicity sat thinking that she was the Lord's servant; and rejoiced over and over again that she had for her own and might keep the book of her Lord's commandments. There were such things as Bibles in the house, certainly, but Daisy had never had one of her own. That in which she had read the other night and which she had used to study her lessons for Mr. Dinwiddie, was one belonging to her brother, which he was obliged to use at school. Doubtless Daisy could also have had one for the asking; she knew that; but it might have been some time first; and she had a certain doubt in her little mind that the less she said upon the subject the better. She resolved her treasure should be a secret one. It was right for her to have a Bible; she would not run the risk of disagreeable comments or commands by in any way putting it forward. Meanwhile she had become the Lord's servant! A very poor little beginning of a servant she thought herself; nevertheless in telling Mr. Dinwiddie what she had, it seemed to Daisy that she had spoken aloud her oath of allegiance; and a growing joy in the transaction and a growing love to the great Saviour who was willing to let her be his servant, filled her little heart. She just knew that the ride home was lovely, but Daisy's mind was travelling a yet more sunshiny road. She was intelligent in what she had done. One by one Mr. Dinwiddie's lessons had fallen on a willing and open ear. She knew herself to be a sinner and lost; she believed that the Lord Jesus would save her by his death; and it seemed to her the most natural and reasonable and pleasant thing in the world, that the life for which his blood had been shed, should be given to him. "If ye love me, keep my commandments." "I wonder," thought Daisy, "what they are."

CHAPTER III.

"WHAT sort of an expedition did you have, Daisy?" her father asked at breakfast next morning. Company the evening before had prevented any talk about it.

"O very good, papa! It was as good as a fairy tale."

"Was it?" said Mr. Randolph. "I wonder what pitch of excellence that is. I don't remember ever finding a fairy tale very good to me."

"Did you ever read any, papa?"

"I don't know! Were you not tired with your long drive?"

"O no, papa!"

"Would you like to go again?"

"Yes papa, very much."

"You may go as often as you like—only always let Sam be along."

"Did you find out what Mrs. Parsons wants?" said Mrs. Randolph.

"No, mamma—she did not look as if she wanted anything, except to see me. And yet she is very poor, mamma."

At this speech Mr. Randolph burst into a round laugh, and even Mrs. Randolph seemed amused.

"Did she *look* as if she wanted to see you, Daisy?"

"Papa, I think she did," said Daisy colouring; "she said so at any rate; but I could not find out what else she would like."

"Daisy, I think she shewed very good taste," said Mr.

Randolph, drawing his little daughter into his arms; "but it would be safe to take something else with you when you go."

"Your birthday is next week, Daisy," said her mother; "and your aunt Gary and your cousins will be here. What would you like to have, to celebrate the day?"

"I don't know, mamma," said Daisy, returning her father's kisses.

"You may have what you please, if you will think and tell me."

"Mamma, may I talk to Nora Dinwiddie about it?"

"Nonsense! What for?"

"Only to consult, mamma."

"Consult Ransom. He would be a much better help to you."

Daisy looked sober and said nothing.

"Why not?" said Mr. Randolph. "Why not consult your brother?"

"Papa," said Daisy slowly, "Ransom and I do not understand each other."

"Don't you," said her father laughing; "what is the cause of that, Daisy?"

Daisy was not very willing to answer, but being pressed by both father and mother she at length spoke. "I think, papa, it is because he understands so many other things."

Mr. Randolph was excessively amused. "Ransom!"—he called out to the hall.

"Please, papa, don't!" said Daisy.

"Ransom!—come here.—What is this? your sister says you do not understand her."

"Well, papa," said Ransom, an exceedingly handsome and bright-looking boy and a great pet of his mother,—"there are things that are not deep enough to be understood."

Daisy's lips opened eagerly and then closed again.

"Girls always use magnifying glasses where themselves

are concerned!" went on Ransom, whose dignity seemed to be excited.

"Hush, hush!" said his father,—"take yourself off, if you cannot maintain civility. And your mother does not like fishing-tackle at the breakfast-table—go! I believe," he said as Ransom bounded away, "I believe conceit is the normal condition of boyhood."

"I am sure," said Mrs. Randolph, "girls have enough of it—and women too."

"I suppose it would be rash to deny that," said Mr. Randolph. "Daisy, I think *I* understand you. I do not require so much depth as is necessary for Ransom's understanding to swim in."

"If you do not deny it, it would be well not to forget it," said Mrs. Randolph; while Daisy still in her father's arms was softly returning his caresses.

"What shall we do on your birthday, Daisy?" said her father without seeming to heed this remark.

"Papa, I will think about it. Mamma, do you like I should talk to Nora about it?"

"By all means!" said Mr. Randolph; "send for her and hold a grand council. Your mother can have no objection."

Daisy did not feel quite so sure of that; but at any rate she made none, and a messenger was sent to ask Nora to come that afternoon. All the morning Daisy was engaged with her mother, going to make a visit to some friends that lived a long way off. It was not till the afternoon was growing cool and pleasant that she was released from dinner and dressing and free to go with her Bible to her favourite reading place;—or rather one of her favourites; a garden seat under a thick oak. The oak stood alone on a knoll looking over a beautiful spread of grassy sward that sloped and rolled away to a distant edge of thicket. Other noble trees dotted the ground here and there; some fine cattle shewed their red and white heads, standing or lying about in the shade. Above the distant thicket, far,

far away, rose the heads of great blue mountains. The grass had just been mown, in part; and a very sweet smell from the hay floated about under the trees around the house. Daisy's tree however was at some distance from the house. In the absolute sweet quiet, Daisy and her Bible took possession of the place. The Bible had grown a wonderful book to her now. It was the book of the commandments of the Great King whose servant she felt herself. Now every word would tell her of something she must do, or not do; all sweet to Daisy; for she felt she loved the King, and his commandments were good to her. This time she got very much interested in the twenty-fifth chapter of Matthew, in the parable of the talents. But she wished she could have had Mr. Dinwiddie to tell her a little better exactly what it meant. Some of its meaning she understood; and remembering Mr. Dinwiddie's words, she prayed with clasped hands and a very earnest little heart, that the Lord would "make her know what all her talents were and help her to make good use of them." Then Daisy went on studying.

In the midst of her studies, a light step bounded down through the shrubbery from the house, and Daisy had hardly raised her head when Nora was at her side. There was room for her on the seat, and after a glad greeting the children sat down together, to talk much joyful talk and tell childish news, in the course of which Daisy's perplexities came out, for which she had wanted Nora's counsel. She explained that she could have precisely what she chose, in the way of merry-making for her birthday. Daisy spoke about it seriously, as a weighty and important matter; and so Nora took it up, with a face of great eagerness.

"You can have *just* what you like, Daisy?" Daisy nodded. "O what have you thought of, Daisy?"

"What would be nicest, Nora?"

"I'll tell you what *I* should have—I should have a party."

"A party!"

"Yes, that is what *I* should have."

"I never thought of that. Who would you ask, Nora? I thought of a pic-nic; and of a great journey to Schroeder's Mountain;—that would be nice;—to spend the whole day, you know."

"Yes, that would be nice: but I should have a party. O there are plenty to have. There is Kitty Marsden."

"I don't know Kitty Marsden, much"—said Daisy.

"And Ella Stanfield."

"I like Ella Stanfield"—said Daisy sedately.

"And there are the Fishes."

"I don't like Mrs. Fish's children very well;—when Alexander and Ransom get together, they make—a great deal of disturbance!"

"O we needn't mind their disturbance," said Nora; and she went on discussing the plan and the advantages of the party. Suddenly Daisy broke in with a new subject. "Nora, you know the story of the servants with the talents, in the New Testament?"

"Yes—" said Nora with open eyes; "I know."

"Do you know what it means?—the talents, I mean; of course I know what the rest means; but do you know what the talents are? Is it just money?—because then you and I have very little indeed; and all the servants had something."

"Why Daisy, what made you think of that just now? we were talking about the party."

"I have been thinking of it all the while," said Daisy. "I was reading it—do you know what it means, Nora?"

"But we were talking about the party!" said Nora.

"Yes, but I want to understand this; and then we will go on about the party. If *you* know what it means."

"I have heard Duke explain it," said Nora, unwillingly coming to the graver subject.

"Well, what does he say it is? the talents, you know."

2*

"Duke says it is everything anybody has. Not money, *everything*—Now don't you think we can make up a nice party?"

"Everything, Nora? Just wait a little—I want to know about this. What do you mean by 'everything'?"

"Are you studying for Sunday-school, Daisy? that isn't the lesson."

"No," said Daisy sorrowfully; "if I was, I could ask Mr. Dinwiddie. That's why I want you to help me, Nora; so think and tell me what he said."

"Well, *that*," said Nora, "he said that; he said the talents meant everything God has given people to work with for him."

"What could they work with besides money?" said Daisy.

"Why *everything*, Duke says; all they've got; their tongues and their hands and their feet, and all they know, and all their love for people; and even the way we do things, our studies and all, Marmaduke says. What do you want to know for, Daisy?"

"I was thinking about it," answered Daisy evasively. "Wait a minute, Nora,—I want to write it down, for fear I should forget something."

"What *are* you going to do?" exclaimed Nora. "Are you going to teach a class yourself?"

Daisy did not answer, while she was writing down with a pencil what Nora had said and making her repeat it for that purpose. When she had done she looked a little dubiously off towards the woods, while Nora was surprised and disappointed into silence.

"I think perhaps I ought to tell you——" was Daisy's slow conclusion. "I want to know what this means, that I may do it, Nora."

"*Do* it?"

"Yes," said Daisy turning her quiet eyes full upon her companion— I want to try to please God. I love the Lord Jesus."

Nora was very much confounded, and looked at Daisy as if a gap in the ground had suddenly separated them.

"So," Daisy went on, "as I have talents to use, I want to know what they are, for fear I shouldn't use them all. I don't understand it yet, but I will think about it. Now we will go on about the party if you like."

"But Daisy——" said Nora.

"What?"

"Are you in earnest?"

"Certainly I am in earnest," said Daisy gravely. "What makes you ask me? Don't you think your brother is in earnest?"

"Marmaduke! oh yes,—but—you never told me of it before."

"I didn't know it till yesterday," said Daisy simply, "that I loved the Lord Jesus; but I know I do now, and I am very glad; and I am going to be his servant."

Her little face was very sweet and quiet as she looked at her little neighbour and said these words; but Nora was utterly confounded, and so nearly dismayed that she was silent; and it was not till several invitations in Daisy's usual manner had urged her, that she was able to get upon the subject of the party again and to discuss it with any spirit. The discussion then did not come to any determination. Daisy was at least lukewarm in her fancy for that mode of spending her birthday; and separate plans of pic-nics and expeditions of pleasure were taken up and handled, sure to be thrown aside by Nora for the greater promise and splendour of the home entertainment. They broke up at last without deciding upon anything, except that Nora should come again to talk about it, and should at all events have and give her share in whatever the plan for the day might be.

Perhaps Daisy watched her opportunity, perhaps it came; but at all events she seized the first chance that she saw to speak with her father in private. He was sauntering out the next morning after breakfast. Daisy joined him, and they strolled along through the grounds, giving here and there directions to the gardener, till they came near one of the pleasant rustic seats, under the shade of a group of larches.

"Papa, suppose we sit down here for a moment and let us look about us."

"Well, Daisy,"—said her father, who knew by experience what was likely to follow.

"Papa," said Daisy as they sat down, "I want to ask you about something."

"What is it?"

"When I was in the chaise, driving Loupe the other day, papa, I heard something that I could not understand."

"Did you?"

"It was two men that passed me on the road; I heard one say to the other as I went by, that it was your carriage, and then he said that 'Randolph's folks were a good deal *stuck up*;'—what did he mean, papa?"

"Nothing of any consequence, Daisy."

"But why did he say it, papa?"

"Why do you want to know?"

"I did not understand it nor like it, papa; I wanted to know what he meant."

"It is hardly worth talking about, Daisy. It is the way those who have not enough in the world are very apt to talk of others who are better off than themselves."

"Why, papa?"

"They were poor men, I suppose, weren't they?"

"Yes papa—working men."

"That class of people, my dear, are very apt to have a grudge against the rich."

"For what, papa?"

"For being able to live better than they do."

"Why papa! do poor people generally feel so?"

"Very often, I think. They do not generally speak it out aloud."

"Then papa," said Daisy speaking slowly, "how do you know? What makes you think they feel so?"

Her father smiled at her eagerness and gravity. "I see it, Daisy, when they do not speak it. They shew it in various ways. Besides, I know their habit of talking among themselves."

"But papa, that is very bad."

"What?"

"That poor people should feel so. I am sure rich people are their best friends."

Her father stroked her head fondly, and looked amused. "They don't believe that, Daisy."

"But *why* don't they believe it, papa?" said Daisy growing more and more surprised.

"I suppose," said Mr. Randolph rising, "they would be better satisfied if I gave them my horses and went afoot."

A speech which Daisy pondered and pondered and could make nothing of. They walked on, Mr. Randolph making observations and giving orders now and then to workmen. Here a man was mowing under the shrubbery; there the gardener was setting out pots of greenhouse flowers; in another place there were holes digging for trees to be planted. Daisy went musing on while her father gave his orders, and when they were again safe out of hearing she spoke. "Papa, do you suppose Michael and Andrew and John, and all your own people, feel so about you?"

"I think it is likely, Daisy. I can't hope to escape better than my neighbours."

"But, papa, they don't look so, nor act so?

"Not before me. They do not wish to lose their places."

"Papa,—couldn't something be done to make them feel better?"

"Why Daisy," said her father laughing, "are you going to turn reformer?"

"I don't know what that is, papa."

"A thankless office, my dear. If you could make all the world wise, it would do, but fools are always angry with you for trying it."

The conversation ended and left Daisy greatly mystified. Her father's people not liking him?—the poor having ill will against the rich, and a grudge against their pleasant things?—it was very melancholy! Daisy thought about it a great deal that day; and had a very great talk on the subject with Nora, who without a quarter of the interest had much more knowledge about it than Daisy. She had been with her brother sometimes to the houses of poor children, and she gave Daisy a high-coloured picture of the ways of living in such houses and the absence of many things by Daisy and herself thought the necessaries of life. Daisy heard her with a lengthening face, and almost thought there was some excuse for the state of feeling her father had explained in the morning. The question however was too long a one for Daisy; but she arrived at one conclusion, which was announced the next morning at the breakfast-table. Mrs. Randolph had called upon her to say what was determined upon for the birthday.

"Papa," said Daisy, "will there be a great plenty of strawberries next week?"

"Yes, I believe so. Logan says the vines are very full. What then?"

"Papa, you gave me my choice of what I would have for Wednesday."

"Yes. Is it my strawberry patch?"

"Not for myself, papa. I want you to have a great table set out of doors somewhere, and give a feast to all your work people."

"Daisy!" exclaimed Mrs. Randolph. "I never heard anything so ridiculous in all my life!"

Daisy waited with downcast eyes for her father to speak. He was not in a hurry.

"Would that give you pleasure, Daisy?"

"Yes, papa."

"Did Nora Dinwiddie put that scheme in your head?" asked Mrs. Randolph.

"She didn't like it at all, mamma. I put it into her head."

"Where did you get it?"

Daisy looked troubled and puzzled, and did not answer till her father said "Speak." Then nestling up to him with her head on his breast, a favourite position, she said, "I got it from different sources, I think, papa."

"Let us hear, for instance."

"I think, partly from the Bible, papa—and partly from what we were talking of yesterday."

"I wish you would shew me where you found it in the Bible. I don't remember a strawberry feast there."

"Do you mean it in earnest, papa?"

"Yes."

Daisy walked off for a Bible—not her own—and after some trouble found a place which she shewed her father; and he read aloud, "When thou makest a dinner or a supper, call not thy friends nor thy brethren, neither thy kinsmen, nor thy rich neighbours; lest they also bid thee again, and a recompense be made thee. But when thou makest a feast, call the poor, the maimed, the lame, the blind; and thou shalt be blessed; for they cannot recompense thee; for thou shalt be recompensed at the resurrection of the just." Mr. Randolph closed the book and laid it on the table, and drew his little daughter again within his arms.

"That child is in a way to get ruined!" said Mrs. Randolph energetically.

"But Daisy, our work people are not lame or blind—how will they do?" said her father.

"They are poor, papa. I would like to have the others too, but we can't have everybody."

Mr. Randolph kissed the little mouth that was lifted so near his own, and went on.

"Do you think then it is wrong to have our friends and neighbours? Shall we write to your aunt and cousins, and Gary McFarlane and Capt. Drummond, to stay away?"

"No, papa," said Daisy smiling, and her smile was very sweet,—"you know I don't mean that. I would like to have them all; but I would like the feast made for the other people."

"You will let the rest of us have some strawberries?"

"If there are enough, papa. For that day, I would like the other people to have them."

Mr. Randolph seemed to find something as sweet as strawberries in Daisy's lips.

"It is the very most absurd plan I ever heard of!" repeated her mother.

"I am not sure that it is not a very good thing," remarked Mr. Randolph.

"Is it expected that on that day we are to do without servants in the house, and wait upon ourselves? or are we expected to wait upon the party!"

"O mamma," said Daisy, "it isn't the servants—it's only the out-of-door people."

"How many will there be, Daisy?" said her father; "have you numbered them up?"

"Not yet, papa. There is Logan, and Michael, and Mr. Stilton, and the two under-gardeners——"

"And four hay-makers."

"Hay-makers, papa?"

"Yes—there will be four of them in the fields next week. And there is the herdsman and boy."

"And there is old Patrick at the gate. That is all, papa."

"And are the ladies of all these families to be invited?"

"Papa! What do you think?"

"I have no doubt there will be strawberries enough."

"But I am afraid there would be too many children.

Logan has six, and Michael has four, and I believe the herdsman has some; and there are four at the Lodge. And Mr. Stilton has two."

"What shall we do with them, Daisy?"

"Papa, we can't have them. I should like to have the men and their wives come, I think, and send some strawberries home to the children. Wouldn't that do best?"

"Admirably. And you can drive over to Crum Elbow and purchase some suitable baskets. Take the chaise and Sam. I expect you to arrange everything. If you want help, come and consult me."

"If mamma will tell Joanna—— ?" said Daisy looking somewhat doubtfully towards the other end of the table.

"I have nothing to do with it," said Mrs. Randolph. "I have no knowledge how to order such parties. You and Joanna may do what you please."

Daisy's eye went to her father.

"That will do, Daisy," said he. "You and Joanna can manage it. You may have carte-blanche."

The earliest minute that she knew Joanna could attend to her, found Daisy in the housekeeper's room. Joanna was a tall, rather hard-featured woman, with skill and capacity in every line of her face however, and almost in every fold of her gown. She heard with a good deal of astonishment the project unfolded to her, and to Daisy's great delight gave it her unqualified approbation.

"It's a first-rate plan," said Joanna. "Now I like that. The men won't forget it. Where are you going to have the table set, Miss Daisy?"

"I don't know yet, Joanna. In some pretty, shady place, under the trees."

"Out of doors, eh!" said Joanna. "Well, I suppose that'll be as good a way as any. Now what are you going to have, Miss Daisy? what do you want of me?"

"Mamma and papa said I was to arrange it with you."

Joanna sat down and folded her arms to consider the matter.

"How many will there be?"

"I counted," said Daisy. "There will be about seven teen, with their wives, you know."

"Seventeen, wives and all?" said Joanna. "You'll have to get the carpenter or Mr. Stilton to make you a table."

"Yes, that's easy," said Daisy; "but Joanna, what shall we have on it? There will want to be a good deal, for seventeen people; and I want it handsome, you know."

"Of course," said Joanna, looking as if she were casting up the Multiplication Table—"it'll have to be that, whatever else it is. Miss Daisy, suppose you let me manage it—and I'll see and have it all right. If you will give orders about the strawberries, and have the table made."

"I shall dress the table with flowers, Joanna."

"Yes—well—" said Joanna,—"I don't know anything about flowers; but I'll have the cake ready, and everything else."

"And tea and coffee, Joanna?"

"Why I never thought of that!—yes, to be sure, they'll want something to drink—who will pour it out, Miss Daisy?"

"I don't know. Won't you, Joanna?"

"Well—I don't know—" said the housekeeper, as if she were afraid of being taken on too fast by her little counsellor—"I don't know as there's anything to hinder, as it's your birthday, Miss Daisy."

Away went Daisy delighted, having secured just what she wanted. The rest was easy. And Daisy certainly thought it was as promising an entertainment as she could have devised. It gave her a good deal of business. The table, and the place for the table, had to be settled with Mr. Stilton, and the invitations given, and many particulars settled; but to settle them was extremely pleasant, and Daisy found that every face of those concerned in the invitations wore a most golden glow of satisfaction when the thing was understood. Daisy was very happy. She hoped, besides the pleasantness of the matter, it would surely incline the hearts of her father's workpeople to think kindly of him.

CHAPTER IV.

It happened that one cause and another hindered Daisy from going to Crum Elbow to fetch the strawberry-baskets, until the very Tuesday afternoon before the birthday. Then everything was right; the pony chaise before the door, Sam in waiting, and Daisy just pulling her gloves on, when Ransom rushed up. He was flushed and hurried.

"Who's going out with Loupe?"

"I am, Ransom."

"You can't go, Daisy—I'm going myself."

"You cannot, Ransom. I am going on business. Papa said I was to go."

"He couldn't have said it! for he said I might have the chaise this afternoon and that Loupe wanted exercise. So! I am going to give him some. He wouldn't get it with you."

"Ransom," said Daisy trembling, "I have got business at Crum Elbow, and I must go, and you must not."

"Fiddlesticks!" said Ransom, snapping his fingers at her. "Business! I guess you have. Girls have a great deal of business! Here Sam—ride round mighty quick to Mr. Rush's and tell Hamilton to meet me at the cross road."

And without another word to Daisy, Ransom sprang into the chaise, cracked his whip over Loupe's head and started him off in a very ungraceful but very eager waddling gallop. Daisy was left with one glove on and with a spirit thoroughly disordered. A passionate child she was not, in outward manner at least; but her feelings once roused were by no means easy to bring down again. She was exceedingly offended, very much disturbed at missing her errand, very sore at Ransom's ill-bred treatment of her. Nobody was near; her father and mother both gone out; and Daisy sat upon the porch with all sorts of resentful thoughts and words boiling up in her mind. She did not believe half of what her brother had said; was sure her father had given no order interfering with her proceedings; and she determined to wait upon the porch till he came home and so she would have a good opportunity of letting him know the right and the wrong of the case. Ransom deserved it, as she truly said to herself. And then Daisy sorrowed over her lost expedition, and her missing strawberry baskets. What should she do? for the next morning would find work enough of its own at home, and nobody else could choose the baskets to please her. Ransom deserved——!

In the midst of the angry thoughts that were breaking one over the other in Daisy's mind, there suddenly came up the remembrance of some words she had read that day or the day before. "*Lord, how oft shall my brother sin against me and I forgive him? till seven times? Jesus saith unto him, I say not unto thee, until seven times, but until seventy times seven.*" This brought Daisy up short; her head which had been leaning on her hands suddenly straightened itself up. What did those words mean? There could be no doubt, for with the question came the words in the Lord's Prayer which she knew well, but had never felt till then. Forgive Ransom out and out?—say nothing about it?—not tell her father, nor make her grievance at all known to Ransom's discomfiture?—Daisy did not want to yield. He *deserved* to be reproved and ashamed and made to do better. It was the first time that a real conflict had come up in her mind between wrong and right; and now that she clearly saw what was right, to her surprise she did not want to do it! Daisy saw both facts. There was a power in her heart that said, No, I will not forgive, to the command from a greater power that bade her do it. Poor Daisy! it was her first view of her enemy; the first trial that gave her any notion of the fighting that might be necessary to overcome him. Daisy found she could not overcome him. She was fain to go, where she had just begun to learn she might go, "to the Strong for strength." She ran away from the porch to her room, and kneeled down and prayed that the King would give her help to keep his commandments. She was ashamed of herself now; but so obstinate was her feeling of displeasure against her brother, that even after she thought she had forgiven him Daisy would not go downstairs again nor meet him nor her father, for fear she should speak words that she ought not, or fail of a perfectly gentle and kind manner.

But what to do about her baskets? A bright and most business-like thought suddenly came into her head. The breakfast hour was always late; by being a little earlier than usual she could have plenty of time to go to Crum Elbow and return before the family were assembled. Splendid! Daisy went down the back stairs and gave her orders in such a way that they should not reach Ransom's ear. If not put on the alert he was sure to be down to breakfast last of anybody. So Daisy went to bed and to sleep with her mind at rest.

It was so pleasant when she came out at half past six the next morning, that Daisy almost thought it was the prettiest time of all. The morning air smelt so fresh, with the scent of the trees and flowers coming through the dew; and the light was so cool and clear, not like the hot glow of later hours, that Daisy felt like dancing for very gladness. Then it was such a stroke of business to go to Crum Elbow before breakfast!

The pony and the chaise came up presently, and Sam and the black pony, all right, and every one of them looking more brisk and fresh than usual. And off they went; under the boughs of the dew-bright trees, where the birds seemed to be as glad as Daisy, to judge by the songs they were singing; and by and by out from the beautiful grounds of Melbourne, into the road. It was pleasanter there, Daisy thought, than she had ever seen it. The fields looked more gay in that clear early light, and the dust was kept down by the freshness in the air. It was delightful; and Loupe never went better. Daisy was a very good little driver, and now the pony seemed to understand the feeling in her fingers and waddled along at a goodly rate.

Crum Elbow was not a great many miles off, and in due time they reached it. But Daisy found that other people kept earlier hours than her father and mother at Melbourne. She saw the farmers were getting to work as she went on; and in the houses of the village there were signs that everybody was fully astir to the business of the day. It was a scattering village; the houses and the churches stood and called to each other across great spaces of fields and fences between; but just where the crossing of two roads made a business point, there was a little more compactness. There was the baker's, and the post-office, and two stores and various other houses, and a blacksmith's shop. Up to the corner where the principal store stood, came the pony and his mistress, and forthwith out came Mr. Lamb the storekeeper, to see what the little pony chaise wanted to take home; but Daisy must see for herself, and she got out and went into the store.

"Baskets," said Mr. Lamb. "What sort of baskets?"

"Baskets to hold strawberries—little baskets," said Daisy.

"Ah! strawberry baskets. That, ma'am, is the article."

Was it? Daisy did not think so. The storekeeper

had shewed her the kind of baskets commonly used to hold strawberries for the market; containing about half a pint. She remarked they were not large enough.

"No, ma'am? They are the kind generally used—regular strawberry baskets—we have sold 'em nearly all out, but we've got a few left."

"They are not large enough, nor pretty enough," repeated Daisy.

"They'll look pretty when they get the strawberries in them," said the storekeeper with a knowing look at her. "But here's a kind, ma'am, are a little neater—may be you would like these—What do you want, child?"

There had come into the store just after Daisy a little poor-looking child, who had stood near, watching what was going on. Daisy turned to look at her as Mr. Lamb's question was thrown at her over the counter, in a tone very different from his words to herself. She saw a pale, freckled, pensive-faced little girl, in very slim clothing, her dress short and ragged, and feet bare. The child had been looking at her and her baskets, but now suddenly looked away to the shopkeeper.

"Please, sir, I want——"

"There! stop," said Mr. Lamb; "don't you see I'm busy. I can't attend to you just now; you must wait.—Are these baskets better, ma'am?" he said coming back to Daisy and a smooth voice.

Daisy felt troubled, but she tried to attend to her business. She asked the price of the baskets.

"Those first I shewed you, ma'am, are three pence apiece—these are sixpence. This is quite a tasty basket," said Mr. Lamb, balancing one on his forefinger. "Being open, you see, it shews the fruit through. I think these might answer your purpose."

"What are those?" said Daisy pointing to another kind.

"Those, ma'am, are not strawberry baskets."

"But please let me see one.—What is the price?"

"These fancy baskets, ma'am, you know, are another figure. These are not intended for fruit. These are eighteen pence apiece, ma'am."

Daisy turned the baskets and the price over. They were very neat! they would hold as many berries as the sixpenny ones, and look pretty too, as for a festival they should. The sixpenny ones were barely neat—they had no gala look about them at all. While Daisy's eye went from one to the other, it glanced upon the figure of the poor, patient, little waiting girl who stood watching her. "If you please, Mr. Lamb," she said, "will you hear what this little girl has to say?—while I look at these."

"What do you want, child?"

The answer came very low, but though Daisy did not want to listen she could not help hearing.

"Mother wants a pound of ham, sir."

"Have you brought the money for the flour?"

"No, sir—mother'll send it."

"We don't cut our hams any more," said the storekeeper. "Can't sell any less than a whole one—and that's always cash. There! go child—I can't cut one for you."

Daisy looked after the little ragged frock as it went out of the door. The extreme mystery of some people being rich and some people poor, struck her anew, and perhaps something in her look as it came back to the storekeeper made him say,

"They're very poor folks, Miss Randolph—the mother's sickly, and I should only lose my money. They came and got some flour of me yesterday without paying for it—and it's necessary to put a stop to that kind of thing at once. Don't you think that basket'll suit, ma'am?"

Baskets? and what meant those words which had been over and over in Daisy's mind for the few days past?—"Whatsoever ye would that men should do to you, do ye even so to them." Her mind was in great confusion.

"How much does a ham cost, Mr. Lamb?"

"Sixteen pence a pound, ma'am," said the storekeeper rather drily, for he did not know but Daisy was thinking a reproof to him.

"But how many pounds are there in a ham?"

"Just as it happens, ma'am—sometimes twenty, and from there down to ten."

"Then how much does a whole ham cost?" said Daisy, whose arithmetic was not ready.

"A ham of fifteen pounds, ma'am, would be about two dollars and forty cents."

Daisy stood looking at the baskets, and thinking how much money she would have over if she took the sixpenny ones. She wanted twenty baskets; she found that the difference of price between the plain and the pretty would leave her twenty shillings in hand. Just enough! thought Daisy,—and yet, how could she go to a strange house and offer to give them a ham? She thought she could not. If she had known the people; but as it was——Daisy bought the pretty baskets and set off homewards.

"Whatsoever ye would that others should do to you, do ye even so to them"—Daisy could see nothing along the road but those words. "That is my King's command to me—and those poor people have got no breakfast. If I was in that little girl's place, I would *like* to have it given to me. But those other baskets—would they do?—I could make them do somehow—Nora and I could dress them up with greens and flowers!"——

The pony chaise stopped. Sam came up alongside.

"Sam, take those baskets back to the store. I am going back there."

Round came the chaise, and in five minutes more they were at the Crum Elbow corner again, for Daisy's heart-burning had not let her go far. Mr. Lamb was exceedingly mystified, as it was very unusual for young ladies like this one to come buying whole hams and riding off with them. However he made no objections to the exchange, being a gainer by ten cents; for Daisy had asked for a ham of fifteen pounds. Then Daisy enquired the way to the girl's house, and her name, and set off in a new direction. It was not far; a plain little brown house, with a brown gate a few yards from the door. Daisy got out of the chaise and opened the gate, and there stood still and prayed a little prayer that God would help her not to feel foolish or afraid when she was trying to do right. Then she went up to the door and knocked. Somebody said in a very uninviting tone of voice, "Come in!"

It was hard for Daisy; she had expected that somebody would open the door, but now she must go in and face all that was there. However, in she went. There was a poor room to be sure, with not much in it. A woman was taking some hot bread, just baked, out of a little cooking stove. Daisy saw the little girl standing by; it was the right place.

"Well!" said the woman looking up at Daisy from her stove oven—"what is it?" She looked pale and unhappy, and her words were impatient. Daisy was half afraid.

"I am Daisy Randolph"—she began gently.

"Go on," said the woman, as Daisy hesitated.

"I was in Mr. Lamb's store just now, when your little girl came to buy some ham."

"Well!—what then?"

"Mr. Lamb said he would not cut any, and she was obliged to go without it."

"Well, what have you to do with all that?"

"I was sorry she was disappointed," said Daisy more steadily; "and as Mr. Lamb would not cut one for her I have brought a whole one—if you will please accept it. It is at the gate, because the boy could not leave the horses."

The woman set her bread on the floor, left the oven door open, and rose to her feet.

"What did you tell her, Hephzibah?" she said in a threatening voice.

"I didn't tell her nothing," said the girl hurriedly—"I never spoke to her."

"How did she know what you came for?"

"I was so near," said Daisy bravely, though she was afraid, "that I couldn't help hearing."

"Well what business was it of yourn?" said the woman turning upon her. "If we are poor, we don't throw it in anybody's face; and if you are rich, you may give charity to those that ask it. *We* never asked none of you—and don't want it."

"I am not rich," said Daisy gently, though she coloured and her eyes were full of tears;—"I did not mean to offend you; but I thought you wanted the ham, and I had money enough to get it. I am very sorry you won't have it."

"Did Mr. Lamb tell you we were beggars?"

"No, not at all."

"Then what put into your head to come bringing a ham here? who told you to do it?"

"Nobody told me," said Daisy. "Yes there did, though. The Lord Jesus Christ told me to do it, ma'am."

"What do you mean?" said the woman, suddenly sobering as if she was struck.

"That's all, ma'am," said Daisy. "He had given me the money to buy the ham, and I heard that your little girl wanted it. And I remembered his commandment, to do to others what I would like they should do to me—I didn't mean to offend you."

"Well I ain't offended," said the woman. "I s'pose you didn't mean no harm; but we have some feelings as well as other folks. Folks may work, and yet have feelings. And if I could work, things would be well enough; but I've been sick, miss, and I can't always get work that I would like to do—and when I can get it, I can't always do it," she added with a sigh.

Daisy wanted to go, but pity held her fast. That poor, pale, ragged child, standing motionless opposite her! Daisy didn't venture to look much, but she saw her all the same.

"Please keep the ham this time!" she broke out bravely—"I won't bring another one!"

"Did nobody send you?" said the woman eyeing her keenly.

"No," said Daisy, "except the Lord Jesus—he sent me."

"You're a kind little soul!" said the woman, "and as good a Christian as most of 'em I guess. But I won't do that. I'd die first!—unless you'll let me do some work for you and make it up so." There was relenting in the tone of these last words.

"O that will do," said Daisy gladly. "Then will you let your little girl come out and get the ham? because the boy cannot leave the horses. Good bye, Mrs. Harbonner."

"But stop!" cried the woman—"you hain't told me what I am to do for you."

"I don't know till I get home and ask there. What would you like to do?"

"My work is tailoring—I learnt that trade; but beggars mustn't be choosers. I can do other things—plain sewing, and washing, and cleaning, and dairy work; anything I *can* do."

Daisy said she would bring her word, and at last got off; without her ham and in glee inexpressible. "They will have some for breakfast," she said to herself; for there had been something in little Hephzibah's eye as she received the great ham in her arms, that went through and through Daisy's heart and almost set her to crying. She was *very* glad to get away and to be in the pony chaise again driving home, and she almost wondered at her own bravery in that house. She hardly knew herself; for true it was, Daisy had considered herself as doing work not of her own choosing while she was there; she felt in her Master's service, and so was bold where for her own cause she would have shrunk away. "But they have got something for breakfast! I think mine will be good when I get it," said Daisy.

Daisy however fell into a great muse upon the course of her morning's experience. To do as she would be done by, now seemed not quite so easy as she had thought; since it was plain that her notions and those of some other people were not alike on the subject. How *should* she know what people would like? When in so simple a matter as hunger, she found that some would prefer starving to being fed. It was too deep a question for Daisy. She had made a mistake, and she rather thought she should make more mistakes; since the only way she could see straight before her was the way of the command and the way of duty therefore; and she was very much inclined to think, besides, that in that way her difficulties would be taken care of for her. It had been so this morning. Mrs. Harbonner and she had parted on excellent terms—and the gleam in that poor child's eyes!—

CHAPTER V.

Daisy was so full of her thoughts that she never perceived two gentlemen standing at the foot of the hall steps to receive her. Not till Loupe in his best style had trotted up the road and stopped, and she had risen to throw down her reins. Then Daisy started a little. One gentleman touched his cap to her, and the other held out his hands to help her to alight.

"You are just in time for breakfast, Miss Randolph. Is that the coach that was made out of a pumpkin?"

Daisy shook hands with the other gentleman and made no answer.

"I had always heard," went on the first, "that the young ladies at the North were very independent in their habits; but I had no idea that they went to market before breakfast."

"Sam," said Daisy, "take the baskets to Joanna."

"What is in the baskets?—eggs?—or butter?—or vegetables? Where do you go to market?"

"To New York, sir," said Daisy.

"To New York! And have you come from there this morning? Then that is certainly also the pony that was once a rat! it's a witchcraft concern altogether."

"No sir," said Daisy, "I don't go to market."

"Will you excuse me for remarking, that you just said you did?"

"No sir,—I didn't mean that *I* went."

"How are gentlemen to understand you, in the future experience of life, if you are in the habit of saying what you do not mean?"

"I am not in the habit of it," said Daisy, half laughing, for she knew her questioner. He was a handsome young man, with a grave face and manner through all his absurd speeches; dressed rather picturesquely; and altogether a striking person in Daisy's eyes. To her relief, as they reached the hall her mother appeared.

"Come in to breakfast, Gary—Daisy, run and get yourself ready."

And Daisy went, in great glee on various accounts. When she came down, everybody was at table; and for a little while she was permitted to eat her breakfast in peace. Daisy felt wonderfully happy. Such a pleasant breakfast, for the talk among the elders went on very briskly; such pleasant work done already, such pleasant work to do all through the day; nothing but joy seemed to be in the air.

"And what did you get at market, Daisy?" suddenly asked the gentleman whom her mother called "Gary."

"I went to buy baskets," said Daisy concisely.

"What else did you get at market?"

"I didn't go to market, sir."

"She told me she did"—said Mr. Gary looking at her father.

"Did you buy anything else, Daisy?" said her father carelessly.

"Papa," said Daisy colouring, "Mr. McFarlane asked me, I thought, where we went to market, and I told him New York. I did not mean that *I* went myself."

"Didn't you get anything but baskets?" said Mr. McFarlane mischievously.

"Papa," said Daisy making a brave push, "if I only spend what you give me for my birthday, don't you think it would be considerate in Mr. McFarlane not to ask me any more?" But this speech set the gentlemen to laughing.

"Daisy, you make me curious," said her father. "Do you think it would be inconsiderate in *me* to ask?"

"Papa, I think it would."

"Answer, Daisy, directly, and don't be ridiculous," said her mother.

Daisy's face clouded, coloured, and the tears came into her eyes.

"Answer, Daisy, since it is put so," said her father gravely.

"I bought a ham, papa."

But the shout that was raised at this was so uproarious that Daisy was almost overcome. She would certainly have made her escape, only she knew such a thing would not be permitted. She sat still, and bore it as well as she could.

"The baskets held eggs, no doubt," said Capt. Drummond, the other gentleman.

"Roast potatoes would be better for your Irish friends, Daisy," said McFarlane. "Ham and eggs is good for the Yankees. It would be the best plan to make a fire out of doors and let each one cook for himself, according to his country. How do you expect to please everybody?"

"Come here, Daisy," said her father kindly, and he put his arm round her and kissed her; "did you have money enough for your ham and your other purchases too?"

"Plenty, papa," said Daisy gratefully.

"And why didn't you go yesterday afternoon, as I thought you intended?" Daisy's and Ransom's eyes met.

"Papa, it was a great deal pleasanter this morning than it would have been then; I never had such a nice ride."

"And what do you want done now? Is your table ready?"

"It will be ready—Mr. Stilton is getting it ready."

"Who is invited, Daisy?" inquired Mr. McFarlane. "Do you intend to receive any except those who are not your friends?"

"I don't think those of a different class had better come," said Daisy.

"Daisy is quite right," said Mrs. Randolph.

"Do you not intend to shew yourself?" said her husband, with some meaning.

"I? No! Certainly not. At her age, since you choose to indulge Daisy in her whim, she may do what she pleases."

Was this what the man meant by Randolph's people being "stuck up?" Daisy looked grave, and her father bade her run away and attend to her preparations.

Even then she went slowly and a little puzzled, till she reached the housekeeper's room; and there the full beauty of the occasion burst upon her. Such nice things as Joanna was making ready!

Daisy ran off at full speed to Logan to get a supply of greens and flowers to trim her baskets. Nora was coming to help her and be with her all day, and arrived just in time. With aprons and baskets full, the two children sought a hidden spot on the bank under the trees, and there sat down, with strawberry baskets in one heap and the sprigs and leaves to dress them in another.

"Now throw off your hat," said Daisy. "It's shady enough, and you'll feel cooler. Now Nora, how shall we do?—You try one and I'll try one; that will be best; and then we can see. I want them to look very pretty, you know; and they are to be filled with strawberries to send home to the children; if we make them very nice they will go on the table, I think, and help dress it up."

For a time there was comparative silence, while the little hands turned and twisted the mosses and bits of larch and cedar and hemlock in and out of the openings of the baskets. It was not found easy at first to produce a good effect; hands were unused to the work; and Nora declared after half an hour she believed the baskets would look best plain, just as they were. But Daisy would not give up. She grew very warm indeed with the excitement of her efforts, but she worked on. By and by she succeeded in dressing a basket so that it looked rich with green; and then a bit or two of rosebuds or heath or bright yellow everlasting made the adornment gay and pretty enough. It was taken for a model; and from that time tongues and fingers worked together, and heat was forgotten.

"Isn't this pleasant!" exclaimed Daisy at length, dropping her work into her lap. "Isn't it just as pleasant as it can be, Nora?"

"Yes," said Nora, working away.

"Just see the river—it's so smooth. And look up into the leaves;—how pretty they are!—and every one of them is trembling a little; not one of them is still, Nora. How beautiful the green is, with the sun shining through! Wouldn't you like to be a bird up there?"

"No," said Nora; "I'd rather be down here."

"I think it would be nice to be a bird," said Daisy; "it must be pleasant up in those branches—only the birds don't know anything, I suppose. What do you think heaven must be like, Nora ?"

"Daisy, you're so funny. What makes you think about heaven ?"

"Why, you know," said Daisy slowly, "I expect to go there. Why shouldn't I think about it ?"

"But you won't go there till you die," said Nora.

"I don't see what that has to do with my thinking about it. I shall die, some time."

"Yes, but Daisy, don't be so queer. You are not going to die now."

"I don't know about that," said Daisy ; "but I like to think of heaven. Jesus is there. Isn't it pleasant, Nora, that he can see us always, and knows what we are doing ?"

"Daisy, Marmaduke said he wished you would invite him to your party."

The turn Nora wished to give to Daisy's thoughts took effect for the moment. It was grievous ; to wish so much for her friend and to have him join in the wish, and all in vain. But, characteristically, Daisy said nothing. She was only silent a moment.

"Nora, did you ever hear Mr. Dinwiddie say that poor people disliked rich people ?"

"No. They don't dislike *him*, I know."

"Is Mr. Dinwiddie rich too ?"

"Of course he is," said Nora.

"I shouldn't think anybody would dislike him," said Daisy ; "but then he never seemed like rich people." She went into a muse about it.

"Well, he is," said Nora. "He has got as much money as he wants, I know."

"Nora, you know the parable of the servants and the talents ?"

"Yes."

"Are you one of the good servants ?"

Nora looked up very uneasily. Daisy's face was one of quiet inquiry. Nora fidgeted.

"Daisy, I wish you would be like yourself, as you used to be, and not talk so."

"But are you, Nora?"

"No, I don't suppose I am! I couldn't do much."

"But would you like to have the King say to you what he said to the servant who had one talent and didn't do anything?"

"Daisy, I don't want to have you talk to me about it," said Nora, a little loftily. "I have got Marmaduke to talk to me, and that's as much as I want."

"*I* mean to be one of them!" said Daisy gently. "Jesus is the king; and it makes me so glad to think of it!—so glad, Nora. He is my king, and I belong to him; and I *love* to give him all I've got; and so would you, Nora. I only want to find out all I have got, that I may give it to him."

Nora went on very assiduously with the covering of the baskets, and Daisy presently followed her example. But the talk was checked for a little.

"Nora, Jesus is *your* king, though," said Daisy again. "He made everything, and he made you; and he *is* your king. I wish you would be his servant too."

Daisy was greatly astonished at the effect of this speech; for Nora without speaking arose, left her baskets and greens on the ground, and set off from the spot with an air that said she did not mean to return to it. Daisy was too bewildered to speak, and only looked after her till she was too far to be recalled.

What was the matter? Greatly puzzled and dismayed, she tried to find a possible answer to this question. Left alone on her birthday in the midst of her business, by her best friend,—what could have brought about so untoward a combination of circumstances? Daisy could not understand it; and there was no time to go after Nora to get an understanding. The baskets must be finished. Luckily there did not much remain to be done, for Daisy was tired. As soon as her work was out of her hand, she went to see about the success of her table. It was done; a nice long, neat table of boards, on trestles; and it was fixed under a beautiful grove of trees, on the edge of a bank from which the view over the grounds was charming. Mr. Stilton was just gathering up his tools to go away, and looked himself so smiling and bright that Daisy concluded there was reason to hope her party was going to be all right; so with fresh spirit she went in to her own dinner.

After that it was busy times. The long table was to be spread with a table-cloth, and then the cups and plates in proper number and position, leaving the places for the baskets of strawberries. It was a grave question whether they should be arranged in a pyramid, with roses filling the spaces, or be distributed all round the table. Daisy and Joanna debated the matter, and decided finally on the simpler manner; and Logan dressed some splendid bouquets for the centre of the table instead. Daisy saw that the maids were bringing from the house pretty china dishes and cups; and then she ran away to get dressed herself. Just as this was almost done she saw her mother driving off from the house with several gentlemen in her party. It suddenly struck Daisy, who was to do the honours of the strawberry feast? She ran down stairs to find her father; she could not find him, he was out; so Daisy went to see that the setting the table was going on all right, and then came and planted herself in the library, to wait for Mr. Randolph's coming in. And while she waited eagerly, she began to think about its being her birth-day.

"Nine years old," thought Daisy; "there isn't much of my life passed. Perhaps, if I live a good while, I may do a great deal to serve the Lord. I wonder if I know all the things I can do now! all my 'talents'? I am afraid of missing some of them for not knowing. Everything I have, Mr. Dinwiddie said,—so Nora said,—is a talent of some sort or other. How strange Nora was to-day! But I suppose she will come and tell me what was the matter. Now about the talents—I wish papa would come! This birth-day was one talent, and I thought it would be a good thing if papa's people could be made to know that he is not 'stuck up,' if he is rich,—but if neither he nor mamma come out to speak to them at all, I wonder what they will think?"

Daisy ran out again to view the table. Yes, it was looking very handsome. Joanna was there herself, ordering and directing; and china and glass, and flowers, and silver, made a very brilliant appearance, though none of the dishes were on the table as yet.

"But who is going to pour out the coffee and the tea, Joanna?" said Daisy. "Aren't you going to dress and come and do it for me?"

"La! Miss Daisy, I don't see how I can. I expect the best plan will be to have you do it yourself. That will give the most satisfaction, I guess."

"Joanna! I don't know how."

"Yes, you do, Miss Daisy; you'll have the coffee urn, and all you have to do is to turn the faucet, you know; and Sam will wait upon you, and if you want tea poured out he can lift it for you. It'll taste twice as good to all the party if you do it."

"Do you think so, Joanna?"

"I don't want to think about it," said Joanna; "I know without thinking."

"But, Joanna, I can't reach the things."

"I'll have a high seat fixed for you. I know what you want."

Daisy stood watching; it was such a pleasure to see Joanna's nice preparations. And now came on the great dishes of strawberries, rich and sweet to the eye and the smell; and then handsome pitchers filled with milk and ice-water, in a range down the table. Then came great fruit cakes and pound cakes, superbly frosted and dressed with strawberries and rosebuds; Joanna had spared no pains. Great store of sliced bread and butter too, and plates of ham and cold beef, and forms of jelly. And when the dressed baskets of strawberries were set in their places all round the table, filling up the spaces, there was a very elegant, flowery, and sparkling appearance of a rich feast. Why was not Nora there?—and with the next thought Daisy flew back to the library to find her father. He was found.

"Oh papa," she said gently, though she had rushed in like a little summer wind, "are you going to come to the feast?"

"What for, my dear?"

"Papa, they will all like it; they will be pleased."

"I think they will enjoy themselves better without me."

"Papa, I am *sure* they would be pleased."

"I should only make it a constraint for them, Daisy. I do not think they will want anything but the strawberries —especially if *you* look at them."

"But mamma is not here to speak to them either, papa."

"You think somebody must speak to them, eh? I don't think I can make speeches, Daisy," said Mr. Randolph, stretching himself at ease in a chaise longue. "But perhaps I may step down and look at them by and by, my dear."

There was no more to be done, Daisy knew. She went slowly off over the grounds, meditating whether the people would be satisfied with so very at-arms'-length an entertainment. Would *this* draw the poor nearer to the rich? or the rich nearer to the poor? Daisy had an instinctive, delicate sense of the want, which she set herself to do the best her little self could to supply. "Whatsoever ye would that men should do to you"—that sweet and most perfect rule of high breeding was moving her now; and already the spirit of another rule, which in words she did not yet know, was beginning to possess her heart in its young discipleship; she was ready "to do good to all men, even as she had opportunity."

She went slowly back to the table. Nobody come yet. Joanna was there, putting some last touches. Suddenly a new idea struck Daisy, as she saw what a long table it was.

"Joanna—there must be somebody else to wait. Sam can never do it all."

"He'll have to. James is busy, and Hiram. Sam's all that can be spared; and that's as much as ever."

"But I must have more, Joanna. Can't some of the maids come?"

"To wait?—they wouldn't, Miss Daisy."

"Yes they would, Joanna. You must make them, Joanna. Send Maria and Ophelia down here, and I'll tell them what I want of them. And quick, Joanna; and don't you tell them, please, what I want."

"I hope you'll grow up to marry the President, some day," said Joanna, walking off; "you could help him if he got puzzled!"

Poor Daisy almost felt as if she had the affairs of a nation on her hands, when she saw Mr. and Mrs. Stilton, dressed in their best, coming near through the trees. But the spirit of kindness was so thoroughly at work in Daisy, that it made her reception of her guests just what it ought to be, and she was delighted a few minutes after to see that their eyes were kindling with gratification. Logan looked at the table as if he had some right to take an interest in it; the hay-makers were open-mouthed; the women in a flutter of ribands and propriety; and the various people who had come upon the ground with doubtful expectancy, sat down to table proud and gay. It was a pretty sight! and prettier was the sight of little Daisy perched up at one end of the board and with tremulous fingers filling cups of coffee and ordering cups of tea.

"Miss Daisy," said Mrs. Stilton, "it's too much trouble foı you to fill all them cups—sha'n't I come there, and take the responsibility? if you would delegate me."

Gladly Daisy agreed, slipped off her high chair, and saw Mrs. Stilton's full portly figure take the place. But Daisy's labours were not ended. She saw one of the Irish labourers sitting with his eyes straight before him and nothing on his plate for them to look at. Daisy went round. It was her feast; she felt she must do the honours.

"Will you have a cup of coffee?" said a soft little voice at the man's elbow. He started.

"Ach!—Sure Miss, I wouldn't be troublesome."

"It's no trouble. Will you have some tea or some coffee?"

"'Dade, sorrow a drop ever I tuk of ary one of 'em but the one time, plase yer ladyship. It's too good for me, sure; that's why it don't agree wid me, Miss."

Very much puzzled by the confidential little nod with which this information was communicated, Daisy yet felt she could not give up the matter.

"Then what will you have?—some ham? or some strawberries?"

"Sure I'll do very well, niver fear, plase yer ladyship; don't trouble yerself. The angels wouldn't want something purtier to eat, than what we have, Miss!"

Daisy gave up in despair and charged Sam to see that the man had his supper. Then without asking any more questions she carried a cup of coffee down the table to a meek-looking old woman who likewise seemed to be in a state of bewilderment. It was the mother of Michael the gate-keeper. She started a little too, as Daisy's hand set down her cup, and half rose from her chair.

"Blessings on ye, for a dear little lady! It's a wonder

to see the likes of you. The saints above bless the hand and the fut that wasn't above doing that same! and may ye always have plenty to wait on ye, and the angels of heaven above all!"

"Sit down, Mrs. Sullivan," said Daisy. "Do you like coffee?"

"Do I like it! It's better to me nor anything else in the worruld, when it wouldn't be a sup o' summat now and thin, if I'd have the rheumatiz."

"A sup of what?"

"Medicine, dear, medicine that I take whin the doctor says it's good for me. May you niver know the want of it, nor of anything in the wide worruld! and niver know what it is to be poor!"

Daisy managed to get the old woman to eat, supplying her with various things, every one of which was accepted with—"Thank you, Miss," and "Blessings on ye!" and turning away from her at last, saw her handmaids approaching from the house. The girls, however disposed to stand upon their dignity, could not refuse to do what their little mistress was doing; and a lively time of it they and Daisy had for the next hour, with all the help Sam and Mrs. Stilton could give them. Daisy saw that strawberries and cream, cake and coffee, were thoroughly enjoyed; she saw too that the honour of being served off silver and china was duly felt. If her father had but come out to say a kind word! but he did not come. His little substitute did all a substitute could do; and at last when everybody seemed in full tide of merrymaking, she stole away that they might have no constraint upon it. Before she had got far, she was startled by a noise behind her, and looking round saw that all the tableful had risen to their feet. The next instant there was a great shout. Daisy could not imagine what they were doing, but she saw that they were all looking at her. She came back a step or two. Now there was another shout greater than the other; the women flourished handkerchiefs, the men waved their arms above their heads. "Long life to ye!" "Good luck to ye forever!" "Blessings on ye for a lady!" "Many thanks to ye, Miss Daisy!" "May ye niver want as good!" "Hurra for the flower of Melbourne!"—Shouts various and confused at last made Daisy comprehend they were cheering *her*. So she gave them a little courtesy or two, and walked off again as fast as she thought it was proper to go.

She went home and to the library, but found nobody there; and sat down to breathe and rest; she was tired. Presently Ransom came in.

"Hallo, Daisy!—is nobody here?"

"No."

"Have you seen your things yet?"

"My things?—what things?"

"Why your *things*—your birthday things. Of course you haven't or you'd know. Never mind, you'll know what I mean by and by. I say, Daisy——"

"What?"

"You know when papa asked you this morning why you didn't go yesterday to Crum Elbow?——"

"Yes."

"Why didn't you tell him?"

Daisy hesitated. Ransom was cutting a pencil vigorously, but as she was silent he looked up.

"Why didn't you tell him? did you tell him *afterwards?*"

"Why no, Ransom!"

"Well why didn't you?—that's what I want to know. Didn't you tell anybody?"

"No, of course not."

"Why didn't you, then?"

"Ransom——" said Daisy doubtfully.

"What? I think you're turned queer."

"I don't know whether you'd understand me."

"Understand *you!* That's a good one! I couldn't understand *you!* I should rather like to have you try."

"Well, I'll tell you," said Daisy.

"Just do."

"Ransom, you know who the Lord Jesus Christ is."

"I used to; but I have forgotten."

"Oh Ransom!"

"Come, go ahead, and don't palaver."

"I am his servant," said Daisy; "and he has bid me do to other people what I would like to have them do to me."

"He has bid you! What do you mean?"

"You know what I mean. It is in the Bible."

"What's in the Bible?"

"*That;*—that I must do to other people what I would like to have them do to me."

"And I suppose you thought I wouldn't like to have you tell? Well you're out, for I don't care a shot about it—there! and you may tell just as fast as you're a mind to."

"Oh Ransom! you know——"

"What do I know?"

"It's no matter," said little Daisy checking herself.

"Go ahead, and finish! What is the use of breaking off? That's the way with girls;—they don't know how to speak English. You may just as well say the whole of something ugly, as the half of it."

If Daisy was tempted to comply with the request, she did not give way to the temptation; for she was silent; and in a mood less pleasant than her own apparently, Ransom took himself out of her presence. Left alone, Daisy presently curled herself down on a couch, and being very tired fell asleep.

CHAPTER VI.

Daisy slept on, until a bustle and sounds of voices and laughter in the hall, and boots clattering over the marble and up the staircase, at last found their way into her ears.

The riding party had got home. Daisy sat up and rubbed her eyes and looked out.

The sun was low, and shining from the western mountains over the tops of all the trees. It was certainly near dinner-time; the cool glittering look of the light on the trees and shrubs could not be earlier than that. What had become of the strawberry feast? It seemed like a dream. Daisy shook off the remains of her sleep and hurried out by one of the glass doors to go and see. She ran down to the bank where the table was spread. It was a feast over. The company were gone, so were the baskets of strawberries; yes, and the very bouquets of flowers had been taken away. That was a sign of pleasure. Nothing was left but the disordered table. Daisy hoped the people had had a good time, and slowly went back towards the house. As she came near the library window she saw her father, standing in it.

"Well, Daisy?"

"Well, papa."

"How has the feast gone off?"

"I don't know, papa. There's nothing left but the boards and the cups and saucers."

Mr. Randolph sat down and drew his little daughter up to his side.

"Have you enjoyed it, Daisy?"

"Yes, papa—I have enjoyed it pretty well."

"Only pretty well!—for your birthday! Do you think now you made a good choice, Daisy?"

"Yes, sir—I think I did."

"What has been wanting? I am afraid your ham did not figure on the board, if it is so empty?"

Daisy did not answer, but her father watching her saw something in her face which made him pursue the subject.

"Did it?"

"No, papa," said Daisy, colouring a little.

"How was that?"

"Joanna arranged everything that was to go on the table."

"And left the ham out of the question? It seems to me that was a mistake, though I am not much of a housekeeper. Why was that?"

"Papa," said Daisy, "do you think I would make a wrong use of a ham?"

Mr. Randolph laughed. "Why Daisy, unless you are a finished economist, that might be. Do you mean that I am not to know the particular use made of this ham?"

"Papa, I wish you would not desire to know!"

But Daisy's face was too much in earnest. "I think I cannot grant that request," said her father. "You must tell me."

Daisy looked distressed. But she dared not evade the order, though she feared very much what might come of it.

"I didn't buy the ham for the party, papa."

"Then for what?"

"I bought it, papa, for a little girl who was going without her breakfast. She came to Mr. Lamb's to buy ham, and she had no money, and he wouldn't let her have any."

"And what became of your baskets?"

"O I got them, papa; I got cheaper ones; and Nora and I dressed them with greens. I had money enough."

Mr. Randolph took his little daughter on his knee and softly put down his lips to kiss her.

"But Daisy, after all, why did you not go to Crum Elbow yesterday afternoon, as you meant to do?"

"Papa, this morning did better, for it was pleasanter."

"Do you call that an answer?" said Mr. Randolph, who was still softly kissing her.

"Papa, if you would be so *very* good as not to ask me that?"

"I am not good at all, Daisy. I ask,—and I mean to know."

Daisy was in trouble. No entreaty was worth a straw after that. She was puzzled how to answer.

"Papa," she ventured, "I don't like to tell you, because Ransom would not like I should."

"Ransom's pleasure must give way to mine, Daisy."

"He wanted the pony-chaise," said Daisy, looking very downcast.

"And you gave it him?"

"No, sir."

"What then? Daisy," said Mr. Randolph bringing her head round to face him, "tell me what I want to know without any more questions."

"He took the chaise, papa,—that was all,—so I went this morning."

"Ransom knew you wanted it?"

"Yes, sir."

"Then Daisy, tell me further, why you did not give me this information when I asked about your drive this morning at breakfast?"

"Papa, I thought Ransom would not like to have it told."

"Were you afraid he would revenge himself in any way if you did?"

"O no, papa! not at all."

"Then what moved you to silence?"

"Why papa, I did not want to trouble Ransom. I was afraid you would be displeased with him perhaps, if I told."

"Were you not displeased when he took the chaise?"

"Yes, papa," said Daisy softly.

"And had your displeasure all gone off by this morn ing?"

"Yes, sir."

Mr. Randolph was not quite satisfied. There was no doubting Daisy; but he had reasons of his own for knowing that she had not said to him quite all that she had confessed to her brother. He would have liked the whole confession; but did not see how he could get at it just now. He took a little gold piece out of his pocket and quietly slipped it into Daisy's hand.

"Papa! what is this for?"

"For your poor woman, if you like. You can send it to her by Sam."

"O thank you, papa! But papa, she won't take it so—she will not take the least thing without working to pay for it."

"How do you know?"

"She told me so, papa."

"Who told you so?"

"The poor woman—Mrs. Harbonner."

"Where did you see her?"

"I saw her at her house, papa."

"Why did you go to her house?"

"To take her the ham, sir."

"And she told you she wouldn't have anything without doing work for it—eh?"

"Yes, papa—she wouldn't even take the ham any other way."

"What work did you engage her to do, Daisy?"

"I thought Joanna could find her some, papa."

"Well, let Joanna manage it. You must not go there

again, nor into any strange house, Daisy, without my leave. Now go and get ready for dinner, and *your* part of your birthday."

Daisy went very soberly. To see Mrs. Harbonner and her daughter again, and to do them all sorts of good, had been a dream of hers, ever since the morning. Now this was shut off. She was very sorry. How were the rich to do good to the poor, if they never came together? A question which Daisy thought about while she was dressing. Then she doubted how her feast had gone; and she had been obliged to tell of Ransom. Altogether, Daisy felt that doing good was a somewhat difficult matter, and she let June dress her in very sober silence. Daisy was elegantly dressed for her birthday and the dinner. Her robe was a fine beautifully embroidered muslin, looped with rose ribbands on the shoulder and tied with a broad rose-coloured sash round the waist. There was very little rose in Daisy's cheeks, however; and June stood and looked at her when she had done, with mingled satisfaction and dissatisfaction.

"You've tired yourself to-day, Miss Daisy, with making that party for the men!" she said.

"Have you done? Now June, will you go away, please, and leave me my room for a few minutes?"

"Yes, Miss Daisy—but it's most time for you to go down."

June went, and Daisy locked her doors, and dropped on her knees by her little bed. How was she to know what was right to do? and still more, how was she to do it wisely and faithfully? Little Daisy went to her stronghold, and asked for help; and that she might know what her talents were.

"Miss Daisy," said the voice of June at the door, "you are wanted in the library."

Down went Daisy in a hurry. There was her father;

and there also, to her great surprise, were Nora and Mr. Dinwiddie !

"I have brought Nora to make her peace with you, Daisy," said Mr. Dinwiddie. "I found her in great trouble because, she said, you were offended with her. Will you love her again ?"

Daisy put her arms round Nora, who looked a little ashamed, and gave her a very peaceful and reassuring kiss. The gentlemen both smiled at her action. It was too graceful to need the aid of words.

"My mission is successful," said Mr. Dinwiddie.

"But I was not offended the least bit, Mr. Dinwiddie," said Daisy.

"I believe it; but Nora thought you had so much reason, that she would not come alone to make her apology."

The young man looked towards Mr. Randolph, whose attention was just then taken by somebody who had come to him on business. He waited.

"Won't you sit down, Mr. Dinwiddie ?" said Daisy.

"I must go."

"But I want to ask you a question, sir."

Mr. Dinwiddie sat down.

"Mr. Dinwiddie," said Daisy with a grave face, "what are my talents ?"

"What is the question, Daisy ? I do not understand."

"You know, sir—one servant had ten and another had five. What are my talents ?"

"I do not know."

"But how can I tell, Mr. Dinwiddie ?"

Then the young man's eyes glowed, as Daisy had a few times seen them do before. "Ask the Lord, Daisy. See what his word tells you to do."

"But Mr. Dinwiddie, I am little; I can't do much."

"*You* cannot do anything. But Jesus can use you, to do what he pleases,—if you will be his little servant.—Give me that spoon, Nora."

"But Marmaduke——"

"Yes—I know," said her brother. He took from Nora's hand and unfolded from its wrapping-paper a very curious thing, which he told Daisy was an Egyptian spoon. He did not give her time to look at it, only he held it so that she saw what it was.

"You see that spoon, Daisy. It cannot do anything. But in your hand it might carry drops of comfort to somebody's lips."

Daisy looked earnestly at the spoon, then at the bright eyes that were fixed on her; and taking his meaning, she smiled, a bright, satisfied smile. It satisfied Mr. Dinwiddie too. He wrapped up the spoon again, handed it to Nora, and rose up to make his adieus to Mr. Randolph.

"Daisy," whispered Nora, "this spoon is for you. Will you take it for my birthday present? Marmaduke says it is very handsome. It is his—he gave it to me to give to you."

"It is very, very old," said Mr. Dinwiddie coming to Daisy. "It was found in an old Egyptian tomb, and was made and put there perhaps before the Israelites came out of Egypt. Good bye!"

He took Daisy's hand with a strong, kindly grasp, and went away with his little sister just as the dinner-bell rang. Daisy had not time to look at her present. She held it tight, and went in to dinner with it in her hand.

Daisy did not generally dine with her father and mother. To-day was a great exception to the rule. Even to-day she was not expected to eat anything till the dessert came on; she had had her dinner; so she had the more time for other things. Her place was by her mother; Capt. Drummond on the other side, and Gary McFarlane opposite. Then her aunt, Mrs. Gary, had arrived, just an hour before dinner; and she and her children and one or two other friends filled the table, and the talking and laughing went round faster than the soup. Daisy looked and listened, very much pleased to see her aunt and cousins, and amused; though as usual in her quiet fashion she gave no sign of it.

"How did that party come off, Daisy?" said Mr. Gary McFarlane.

"What party?" said Mrs. Gary.

"Daisy's birthday entertainment."

"Daisy invited all the gardeners and haymakers to take supper and strawberries with her, Aunt Gary," said Ransom.

"What is that?" said Mrs. Gary, looking to her sister.

"Ransom has stated the matter correctly."

"Gardeners and haymakers! What was that for, Daisy?"

"I thought it would give them pleasure, aunt Gary,—" said Daisy.

"Give *them* pleasure! of course, I suppose it would; but are we to give everybody pleasure that we can? At that rate, why not invite our footmen and chambermaids too? Why stop?"

"I suppose that will be the next thing," said Mrs. Randolph. "Daisy, you must not eat that cheese."

"What's Daisy's notion?" said Mrs. Gary, appealing to her brother-in-law.

"A child's notion," said Mr. Randolph. "The worst you can say of it is, that it is Arcadian."

"How did it go off, Daisy?" said Gary McFarlane.

"I don't know," said Daisy. "I think it went off pretty well."

"How did the hob-nails behave themselves?"

"They had lots of things to eat," said Ransom. "I don't believe we shall have any strawberries for a day or two ourselves."

"Did you give them strawberries?" said Mrs. Gary.

"A tableful," said Ransom; "and baskets and baskets to take home."

"Something new,—" said Mrs. Gary, eating her salad.

"But how did the company behave?" said Mr. McFarlane.

"I saw no behaviour that was not proper," Daisy answered gravely. She thought as much could not be said of the present company, seeing that servants were present.

"What have you there, Daisy?" said her mother.

"It is a birthday present, mamma. It is an Egyptian spoon."

"An Egyptian spoon! Where did you get it?"

"Mr. Dinwiddie—I mean, Nora gave it to me"

"What about Mr. Dinwiddie?"

"Nothing, mamma."

"Then why did you speak his name?"

"I don't know. He brought Nora to see me just now."

"Where did you see him?"

"In the library."

"Mr. Randolph"—said the lady—"did Mr. Dinwiddie call to see you?"

"He did me that honour," said Mr. Randolph; "but I think primarily his visit was to Daisy."

"Who is Mr. Dinwiddie?" said Mrs. Gary, seeing a contraction in her sister's brow. "It's a Virginian name."

"He is a fanatic," said Mrs. Randolph. "I don't know what else he is."

"Let us see the fanatic's spoon," said Gary McFarlane. "Egyptian, is it, Daisy? Curious, upon my word!"

"Beautiful!" said Capt. Drummond, taking the spoon in his turn across the table. "Beautiful! This is a nice piece of carving—and very old it undoubtedly is. This is the lotus, Daisy—this stem part of the spoon; and do you see, in the bowl here is the carving of a lake, with fish in it?"

"Is it?" said Daisy; "and what is a *lotus*, Capt. Drummond?"

"If you will put me in mind to-morrow, privately, I will tell you about it," said he.

"Let me look at that, Capt. Drummond," said Mrs. Gary.—"Why, here's a duck's head at the end of the handle. What a dear old thing! Who is this Mr. Dinwiddie, pray?"

"The duck's bill makes the spoon, aunt Gary," said Daisy.

"If you asked me *what* he is, I have told you," said Mrs. Randolph.

"He is a young man, of good family I believe, spending the summer with a neighbour of ours who is his relation," Mr. Randolph answered.

"What is he a fanatic about?"

This question did not get an immediate answer; the conversation diverged, and it was lost. Daisy's spoon made the round of the company. It was greatly admired, both from its oddness and from the beauty of its carving.

"Daisy, I will buy this spoon of you," said her aunt.

Daisy thought not; but she said, "With what, aunt Gary?"

"With anything you please. Do you set a high value on it? What is it worth?"

Daisy hesitated; and then she said, "I think it is worth my regard, aunt Gary!"

She could not guess why there was a general little laugh round the table at this speech.

"Daisy, you are an original," said Mrs. Gary. "May I ask, why this piece of old Egypt deserves your regard?"

"I think anything does, aunt Gary, that is a gift," Daisy said, a little shyly.

"If your first speech sounded forty years old, your second does not," said the lady.

"Arcadian again, both of them," Mr. Randolph remarked.

"You always take Daisy's part," said the lady briskly. But Mr. Randolph let the assertion drop.

"Mamma," said Daisy, "what is an original?"

"Something your aunt says you are. Do you like some of this *biscuit*, Daisy?"

"If you please, mamma. And mamma, what do you mean by a fanatic?"

"Something that I will not have you," said her mother, with knitting brow again.

Daisy slowly eat her biscuit-glacé and wondered. Wondered what it could be that Mr. Dinwiddie was and that her mother was determined she should not be.

Mr. Dinwiddie was a friend of poor people—was that what her mother meant? He was a devoted, unflinching servant of Christ;—"so will I be," said Daisy to herself; "so I am now; for I have given the Lord Jesus all I have got, and I don't want to take anything back. Is that what mamma calls being a fanatic?"—Daisy's meditations were broken off; for a general stir round the table made her look up.

The table was cleared, and the servants were bringing on the fruit; and with the fruit they were setting on the table a beautiful old fashioned silver épergne, that was never used but for great occasions. Generally it was adorned with fruit and flowers; to-day it was empty, and the attendants proceeded to arrange upon it very strange looking things; packages in white paper, books, trinkets, what not; and in the middle of all a little statuette of a Grecian nymph, which was a great favourite of Daisy's. Daisy began to guess that the épergne had something to do with her birthday. But the nymph?—perhaps she came there by her beauty to dignify this use made of the stately old thing. However, she forgot all about fanatics and Mr. Dinwiddie for the present. The looks and smiles of the company were unmistakable. Who would speak first?

"How are you to reach the épergne, Daisy?" said her father.

"Shall I be the medium?" said Mrs. Gary. "These things are to travel up to Daisy, I suppose."

"I will represent the rolling stock of this road, and undertake to carry parcels safely," said Mr. McFarlane. "Any message with the goods, Mrs. Gary?"

"I believe they carry their own message with them," said the lady;—"or else I don't see what is the use of these little white tickets. Where shall I begin, Mr. Randolph?"

"I do not think the order of proceedings will be criticised, provided it does not delay," said Daisy's father.

"Then transmit this, Gary."

"Literary freight"—said Gary McFarlane, handing over to Daisy a little parcel of books. Five or six little volumes, in pretty binding—Daisy looked eagerly to see what they might be. "Marmion"—"The Lady of the Lake"—Scott's Poetical Works.

"O thank you, papa!" said Daisy, looking delighted.

"Not me," said Mr. Randolph. "I am not to be thanked."

"There's no name in them—" said Daisy.

"That's Preston's gift," said her aunt. Preston was Daisy's oldest cousin; a fine boy of sixteen.

"I like it so much, Preston!" said Daisy, sending a grateful look down the table to where he sat.

"Is Daisy fond of poetry?" inquired Mr. McFarlane with a grave look.

"Very fond," Mrs. Randolph said.

"Dangerous taste!" said Gary. "What is this new consignment?"

"Something valuable—take care of it."

"To be taken with care—right side up," said Gary, putting before Daisy by a stretch of his long arm a little paper covered package. Daisy's cheeks were beginning to grow pink. She unfolded the package.

A little box—then white cotton—then a gold bracelet.

"Mamma?—" said Daisy instantly. Mrs. Randolph stooped and kissed her.

"It's beautiful, mamma!" Daisy spoke very earnestly; however her face did not shew the light of pleasure which the first gift had called into it.

"How did you know so well?" said Mr. McFarlane. "Mrs. Randolph, I am afraid you are not literary. Now Daisy, exercise your discernment upon that."

It was a little box containing a Chinese puzzle, with the plans and keys belonging to it.

"Where do you think *that* comes from?"

Daisy looked up. "I think—perhaps—from *you*, Mr. McFarlane."

"Do you think I am anything like a puzzle?"

"I think—perhaps—you mean to be,"—Daisy said innocently. But a shout from the whole tableful answered to this chance hit. Daisy didn't know what they could mean.

"I have done!" said Gary. "I have got more than my match. But I know who will plague people worse than a puzzle, if she gets well educated. There's a pair of gloves, you little fencer."

It was a nice little thick pair of riding or driving gloves; beautifully made and ornamented. These came from Eloïse, Daisy's other cousin. Mrs. Gary had brought her two beautiful toilet bottles of Bohemian glass. Daisy's end of the table was growing full.

"What is this?" said Mrs. Gary, taking from the épergne a sealed note directed to Daisy.

"That is Ransom's present. Give her mine first," said Mr. Randolph.

"Which is yours? I don't see anything more."

"That little Proserpine in the middle."

"*This?* Are you going to give this to Daisy? But why is she called Proserpine? I don't see."

"Nor I," said Mr. Randolph, "only that everything must have a name. And this damsel is supposed to have been carrying a basket, which might easily have been a basket of flowers, I don't see how the statement could be disproved. And Daisy is fonder of the little nymph, I believe, than any one else in the house."

"O papa! thank you," exclaimed Daisy, whose eyes sparkled. "I like to have her *very* much!"

"Well, here she goes," said Mrs. Gary. "Hand her over. You have a variety, Daisy. Chinese playthings and Grecian art."

"*Some* modern luxury," said Gary McFarlane. "Just a little."

"Egyptian art, too," said Capt. Drummond.

"O where's my spoon?" cried Daisy. "Has papa got it?"

"Here is Ransom's present," said her aunt, handing the note. "Nobody knows what it is. Are we to know?"

Daisy opened and read, read over again, looked very grave, and finally folded the note up in silence.

"What is it?" said her aunt.

Daisy hesitated, wishing, but in doubt if she would be permitted to keep it to herself. Her father answered for her.

"It is all of Ransom's part, share, and possession in a certain small equipage known about these premises; the intent and understanding being, that henceforth the pony carriage and pony are Daisy's sole property, and to be by her used and appropriated without any other person's interference whatever."

"But, papa—" Ransom began.

"I think it is a very poor arrangement, Mr. Randolph," said Ransom's mother. "Daisy cannot use the pony half enough for his good."

"She will make more use of him now," said Mr. Randolph.

Ransom looked very glum. His mother rose, with the ladies, and went to the drawing-room.

CHAPTER VII.

A day or two after the birthday, it happened that Capt. Drummond was enjoying the sunshine in a way that gentlemen like to enjoy it; that is, he was stretched comfortably on the grass under the shade of some elm trees, looking at it. Perhaps it was not exactly the sunshine that he was enjoying, but the soft couch of short grass, and the luxurious warm shadow of the elms, and a little fanciful breeze which played and stopped playing, and set the elm trees all a flutter and let them be still, by turns. But Capt. Drummond was having a good time there, all by himself, and lying at length in a most lazy luxurious fashion; when he suddenly was "ware" of a fold of white drapery somewhere not very far from his left ear. He raised himself a little up, and there to be sure, as he had guessed, was Daisy. She was all alone too, and standing there looking at him.

Now Capt. Drummond was a great favourite of Daisy's. In the first place he was a handsome fellow, with a face which was both gentle and manly; and his curly light-brown hair and his slight well-trimmed moustache set off features that were pleasant for man or woman to look upon. Perhaps Daisy liked him partly for this, but I think she had other reasons. At any rate, there she stood looking at him.

"Can you command me, Daisy?" said the young officer.

"Are you at leisure, Capt. Drummond?"

"Looks like it!" said the gentleman rousing himself. "What shall I give you? a camp-chair? or will you take the—O! that is a better arrangement."

For Daisy had thrown on the ground a soft shawl for a carpet, and took her place upon it beside Capt. Drummond, who looked at her in a pleased kind of way.

"Are you quite at leisure, Capt. Drummond?"

"Gentlemen always are—when ladies' affairs are to be attended to."

"Are they?" said Daisy.

"They ought to be!"

"But I am not a lady."

"What do you call yourself?"

"I don't know," said Daisy gravely. "I suppose I am a little piece of one."

"Is that it?" said Capt. Drummond laughing. "Well, I will give you as large a piece of my leisure as you can make use of—without regard to proportions. What is on hand, Daisy?"

"Capt. Drummond," said Daisy with a very serious face,—"do soldiers have a very hard time?"

"Not always. Not when they are lying out under the trees at Melbourne, for example."

"But I mean, when they are acting like soldiers?"

He was ready with a laughing answer again, but seeing how earnest Daisy's face was, he controlled himself; and leaning on his elbow, with just a little smile of amusement on his face, he answered her.

"Well, Daisy—sometimes—they do."

"How, Capt. Drummond?"

"In a variety of ways."

"Will you please tell me about it?"

He looked up at her. "Why, Daisy, what makes you curious in the matter? Have you a friend in the army?"

"No other but you," said Daisy.

"That is a kind speech. To reward you for it, I will tell you anything you please. What is the question, Daisy?"

"I would like to know in what way soldiers have a hard time?"

"Well, Daisy, to begin with, a soldier can't do what he has a mind."

"Not about anything?"

"Well—no; not unless he gets leave. I am only at Melbourne now because I have got leave; and I must go when my leave is up. A soldier does not belong to himself."

"To whom does he belong?'

"To his commander! He must go and come, do or not do things, just as his General bids him; and ask no questions."

"Ask no questions?" said Daisy.

"No; only do what he is ordered."

"But why mayn't he ask questions?"

"That isn't his business. He has nothing to do with the reason of things; all he has got to do is his duty. The *reason* is his General's duty to look after."

"But suppose he had a very good General—then that wouldn't be much of a hardship," said Daisy.

"Well, that is a very material point," said the Captain. "*Suppose* he has a good General—as you say; that would make a great difference, certainly."

"Is that all, Capt. Drummond?"

"Not quite all."

"What else?"

"Well, Daisy, a soldier, even under a good General, is often ordered to do hard things."

"What sort of things?"

"What do you think," said the Captain lolling comfortably on the green bank, "of camping out under the rain-clouds—with no bed but stones or puddles of mud and wet leaves—and rain pouring down all night, and hard work all day; and no better accommodations for week in and week out?"

"But Capt. Drummond!" said Daisy horrified, "I thought soldiers had tents?"

"So they do—in fine weather—" said the Captain. "But just where the hardest work is to do, is where they can't carry their tents."

"Couldn't that be prevented?"

"I'm afraid not."

"I should think they'd get sick?"

"*Think* they would! Why they do, Daisy, by hundreds and hundreds. What then? A soldier's life isn't his own; and if he has to give it up in a hospital instead of on the field, why it's good for some other fellow."

So this it was, not to belong to oneself! Daisy looked on the soldier before her who had run, or would run, such risks, very tenderly; but nevertheless the child was thinking her own thoughts all the while. The Captain saw both things.

"What is the 'hard work' they have to do?" she asked presently.

"Daisy, you wouldn't like to see it."

"Why, sir?"

"Poor fellows digging and making walls of sand or sods to shelter them from fire—when every now and then comes a shot from the enemy's batteries, ploughs up their work, and knocks over some poor rascal who never gets up again. That's one kind of hard work."

Daisy's face was intent in its interest; but she only said, "Please go on."

"Do you like to hear it?"

"Yes, I like to know about it."

"I wonder what Mrs. Randolph would say to me?"

"Please go on, Capt. Drummond!"

"I don't know about that. However, Daisy, work in the trenches is not the hardest thing—nor living wet through or frozen half through—nor going half fed—About the hardest thing I know, is in a hurried retreat to be obliged to leave sick and wounded friends and poor fellows to fall into the hands of the enemy. That's hard."

"Isn't it hard to fight a battle?"

"You would not like to march up to the fire of the enemy's guns, and see your friends falling right and left of you—struck down?"

"Would you?" said Daisy.

"Would I what?"

"Don't *you* think it is hard, to do that?"

"Not just at the time, Daisy. It is a little tough afterwards, when one comes to think about it. It is hard to see fellows suffer too, that one cannot help."

Daisy hardly knew what to think of Capt. Drummond. His handsome pleasant face looked not less gentle than usual, and *did* look somewhat more sober. Daisy concluded it must be something about a soldier's life that she could not understand, all this coolness with which he spoke of dreadful things. A deep sigh was the testimony of the different feelings of her little breast. Capt. Drummond looked up at her.

"Daisy, women are not called to be soldiers."

Daisy passed that.

"Have you told me all you can tell me, Capt. Drummond?"

"I should not like to tell you all I could tell you."

"Why? Please do! I want to know all about soldiers."

He looked curiously at her. "After all," he said, "it is not so bad as you think, Daisy. A good soldier does not find it hard to obey orders."

"What sorts of orders does he have to obey?"

"All sorts."

"But suppose they were wrong orders?"

"Makes no difference."

"*Wrong* orders?"

"Yes," said Capt. Drummond, laughing. "If it is something he can do, he does it; if it is something he can't do, he loses his head trying."

"Loses his head, sir?"

"Yes—by a cannon ball; or his heart, by a musket ball; or maybe he gets off with losing a hand or a leg; just as it happens. That makes no difference, either." He watched Daisy as he spoke, seeing a slight colour rise in her cheeks, and wondering what made the child's quiet grey eyes look at him so thoughtfully.

A SOLDIER.

"Capt. Drummond, is he ever told to do anything he *can't* do?"

"A few years ago, Daisy, the English and the French were fighting the Russians in the Crimea. I happened to be there on business, and I saw some things. An order was brought one day to an officer commanding a body of cavalry—you know what cavalry is?"

"Yes, I know."

"The order was brought in—Hallo! what's that?"

For a voice was heard shouting at a little distance, "Drummond!—Ho, Drummond! Where are you?"

"It's Mr. McFarlane!" said Daisy. "He'll come here. I'm very sorry."

"Don't be sorry," said the Captain. "Come,—let us disappoint him. He can't play hide and seek."

He jumped up and caught Daisy's willing hand, with the other hand caught up her shawl, and drew her along swiftly under cover of the trees and shrubbery towards the river, and away from the voice they heard calling. Daisy half ran, half flew, it seemed to her; so fast the strong hand of her friend pulled her over the ground. At the edge of the bank that faced the river, at the top of a very steep descent of a hundred feet or near that, under a thick shelter of trees, Capt. Drummond called a halt and stood listening. Far off, faint in the distance, they could still hear the shout,

"Drummond!—where are you? Hallo!"

"We'll go down to the river," said the Captain; "and he is too lazy to look for us there. We shall be safe. Daisy, this is a retreat—but it is not a hardship, is it?"

Daisy looked up delighted. The little face so soberly thoughtful a few minutes ago was all bright and flushed. The Captain was charmed too.

"But we can't get down there,"—said Daisy, casting her eye down the very steep pitch of the bank.

"That is something," said the Captain, "with which as a soldier you have nothing to do. All you have to do is to obey orders; and the orders are that we charge down hill."

"I shall go head first, then," said Daisy, "or over and over. I couldn't keep my feet one minute."

"Now you are arguing," said the Captain; "and that

shews insubordination, or want of discipline. But we have got to charge, all the same; and we'll see about putting you under arrest afterwards."

Daisy laughed at him, but she could not conceive how they should get to the bottom. It was very steep and strewn with dead leaves from the trees which grew thick all the way. Rolling down was out of the question, for the stems of the trees would catch them; and to keep on their feet seemed impossible. Daisy found however that Capt. Drummond could manage what she could not. He took hold of her hand again; and then—Daisy hardly believed it while she was doing it,—but there she was, going down that bank in an upright position; not falling nor stumbling, though it is true she was not walking neither. The Captain did not let her fall, and his strong hand seemed to take her like a feather over the stones and among the trees, giving her flying leaps and bounds down the hill along with him. How *he* went and kept his feet remained always a marvel to Daisy; but down they went, and at the bottom they were in a trifle of time.

"Do you think he will come down there after us?" said the Captain.

"I am sure he won't," said Daisy.

"So am I sure. We are safe, Daisy. Now I am your prisoner and you are my prisoner; and we will set each other at any work we please. This is a nice place."

Behind them was the high, steep, wooded bank, rising right up. Before them was a little strip of pebbly beach, and little wavelets of the river washing past it. Beyond lay the broad stream, all bright in the summer sunshine, with the great blue hills rising up misty and blue in the distance. Nothing else; a little curve in the shore on each side shut them in from all that was above or below near at hand.

"Why this is a fine place," repeated the Captain. "Were you ever here before?"

"Not in a long time," said Daisy. "I have been here with June."

"June! Aren't we here with June now?"

"*Now!*—O I don't mean the month—I mean mamma's black June," said Daisy laughing.

"Well that is the first time I ever heard of a black June!" muttered the Captain. "Does she resemble her name or her colour?"

"She isn't much like the month of June," said Daisy. "I don't think she is a very cheerful person."

"Then I wouldn't come here any more with her—or anywhere else."

"I don't," said Daisy. "I don't go with her, or with anybody else—much. Only I go with Sam and the pony."

"Where's Ransom? Don't he go with you?"

"O Ransom's older, you know; and he's a boy."

"Ransom don't know his advantages. This is pleasant, Daisy. Now let us see. What were you and I about?"

"You were telling me something, Capt. Drummond."

"What was it? O I know. Daisy, you are under arrest, you know, and sentenced to extra duty. The work you are to perform, is to gather as many of these little pebbles together—these white ones—as you can in five minutes."

Daisy went to work; so did the Captain; and very busy they were, for the Captain gathered as many pebbles as she did. He made her fetch them to a place where the little beach was clean and smooth, and in the shadow of an overhanging tree they both sat down. Then the Captain throwing off his cap, began arranging the white pebbles on the sand in some mysterious manner—lines of them here and lines of them there—whistling as he worked. Daisy waited with curious patience; watched him closely, but never asked what he was doing. At last he stopped, looked up at her, and smiled.

"Well!—" he said.

"What is it all, Capt. Drummond?"

"This is your story, Daisy."

"My story!"

"Yes. Look here—these rows of white stones are the Russians;—these brown stones are the English," said he, beginning to marshal another set into mysterious order some distance from the white stones. "Now what shall I do for some guns?"

Daisy in a very great state of delight began to make search for something that would do to stand for artillery; but Capt. Drummond presently solved the question by breaking some twigs from the tree overhead and cutting them up into inch lengths. These little mock guns he distributed liberally among the white stones, pointing their muzzles in various directions; and finally drew some lines in the sand which he informed Daisy were fortifications. Daisy looked on; it was better than a fairy tale.

"Now Daisy, we are ready for action. This is the battle of Balaklava; and these are part of the lines. An order was brought to an officer commanding a body of cavalry stationed up here—you know what cavalry is?"

"Yes, I know."

"The order was brought to him to charge upon the enemy down *there*,—in a place where he could do no good and must be cut to pieces;—the enemy had so many guns in that place and he had so few men to attack them with. The order was a mistake. He knew it was a mistake, but his General had sent it—there was nothing for him to do but to obey. So he charged."

"And his men?"

"Every one. They knew they were going to their death—and everybody else knew it that saw them go—but they charged!"

"Did you see it, Capt. Drummond?"

"I saw it."

"And did they go to their death?" said Daisy, awe-stricken, for Captain Drummond's look said that he was thinking of something it had been grave to see.

"Why yes. Look here, Daisy—here were cannon; there were cannon; there were more cannon; cannon on every side of them but one. They went into death they knew, when they went in there."

"How many of them went there?"

"Six hundred."

"Six hundred!—were they *all* killed?"

"No. There were a part of them that escaped and lived to come back."

Daisy looked at the pebbles and the guns in profound silence.

"But if the officer knew the order was a mistake, why must he obey it?"

"That's a soldier's duty, Daisy. He can do nothing but follow orders. A soldier can't know, very often, what an order is given for; he cannot judge; he does not know what his General means to accomplish. All he has to think of is to obey orders; and if every soldier does that, all is right."

What was little Daisy thinking of? She sat looking at her friend the Captain. He was amused.

"Well, Daisy—what do you think? will it do? Do you think you will stand it and be a soldier?"

Daisy hesitated a good deal, and looked off and on at the Captain's face. Then she said very quietly, "Yes."

"You will!" he said. "I wish you would join my branch of the service. Suppose you come into my company?"

"Suppose you join mine?"

"With all my heart!" said the Captain laughing; "if it is not inconsistent with my present duties. So you have enlisted already? Are you authorized to receive recruits?"

Daisy shook her head and did not join in his laugh.

"Honestly, Daisy, tell me true; what did you want to know about soldiers for? I have answered you; now answer me. I am curious."

Daisy did not answer, and seemed in doubt.

"Will you not honour me so far?"

Daisy hesitated still, and looked at the Captain more than once. But Capt. Drummond was a great favourite, and had earned her favour partly by never talking nonsense to her; a great distinction.

"I will tell you when we get back to the house," she said,—"if you will not speak of it, Capt. Drummond."

The Captain could get no nearer his point; and he and Daisy spent a good while longer by the river-side, erecting fortifications and studying the charge of the Light brigade.

CHAPTER VIII.

THE Captain was not able to claim Daisy's promise immediately. On their return to the house he was at once taken up with some of the older people, and Daisy ran off to her long delayed dinner.

The next day in the course of her wanderings about the grounds, which were universal, Daisy came upon her cousin Preston. He sat in the shade of a clump of larches under a great oak, making flies for fishing; which occupation, like a gentlemanly boy as he was, he had carried out there where the litter of it would be in nobody's way. Preston Gary was a very fine fellow; about sixteen, a handsome fellow, very spirited, very clever, and very gentle and kind to his little cousin Daisy. Daisy liked him much, and was more entirely free with him perhaps than with any other person in the family. Her seeing him now was the signal for a joyous skip and bound which brought her to his side.

"O Preston, are you going fishing?"

"Perhaps—if I have a good day for it."

"When?"

"To-morrow."

"Who's going with you?"

"Nobody, I reckon. Unless you want to go, Daisy."

"O Preston, may I go with you? Where are you going?"

"Daisy, I'm bound for the Hillsdale woods, back of Crum Elbow—they say there are first-rate trout streams there; but I am afraid you can't go so far."

"O I can go anywhere, Preston! with Loupe, you know. You're going to ride, aren't you?"

"Yes, but Loupe! What shall we do with Loupe? You see, I shall be gone the whole day, Daisy—it's likely. You'd get tired."

"Why we could find somewhere to put Loupe—Sam could take care of him. And I should like to go, Preston, if you think I would not frighten the fish."

"O if Sam's going along, that is another matter," said Preston. "*You* frighten the fish, Daisy! I don't believe you can do that for anything. But I won't let you get into mischief."

So it was settled, and Daisy's face looked delighted; and for some time she and Preston discussed the plan, the fish, and his flies. Then suddenly Daisy introduced another subject.

"Preston, where is the Crimea?"

"The Crimea!" said Preston.

"Yes; where the English and the French were fighting with the Russians."

"The Crimea! Why Daisy, don't you know where it is? You'll find it in the Black Sea somewhere."

Daisy hesitated.

"But Preston, I don't know where the Black Sea is."

"Why Daisy, what has become of your geography?"

"I never had much," said Daisy humbly, and looking serious;—"and lately mamma hasn't wanted me to do anything but run about."

"Well, if you take the map of Europe, and set out from the north of Russia and walk down, you'll find yourself in the Crimea after a while. Just hold that, Daisy, will you?"

Daisy held the ends of silk he put in her fingers; but while he worked, she thought. Might it not be possible that a good knowledge of geography might have something to do with the use or the improvement of her *talents?*

And if a knowledge of geography, why not also a knowledge of history, and of arithmetic,—and of everything! There could not be a reasonable doubt of it. What would Preston be,—what would Mr. Dinwiddie or Capt. Drummond be,—if they knew nothing? And by the same reasoning, what would Daisy Randolph be? What could she do with her talents, if she let them lie rusty with ignorance? Now this was a very serious thought to Daisy, because she did not like study. She liked knowledge right well, if she could get it without trouble, and if it was entertaining knowledge; but she did not think geography at all entertaining, nor arithmetic. Yet—Daisy forgot all about Preston's artificial flies, and her face grew into a depth of sobriety.

"Preston—" she began slowly,—"is it hard?"

"Not just that," said Preston, busy in finishing a piece of work,—"it is a little ticklish to stroke this into order—but it isn't hard, if you have the right materials, and know how."

"O no—I don't mean flies—I mean geography."

"Geography!" said Preston. "O you are at the Crimea yet, are you? I'll shew it to you, Daisy, when we go in."

"Preston, is the use of geography only to know where places are?"

"Well, that's pretty convenient," said Preston. "Daisy, just look for that bunch of grey silk—I had it here a minute ago."

"But Preston, tell me what *is* the use of it?"

"Why, my dear little Daisy—thank you!—you'd be all abroad without it."

"All abroad!" exclaimed Daisy.

"It comes to about that, I reckon. You wouldn't understand anything. How can you? Suppose I shew you my pictures of the North American Indians—they'll be as good as Chinese to you, if you don't know geography."

Daisy was silent, feeling puzzled.

"And," said Preston, binding his fly, "when you talk of the Crimea you will not know whether the English came from the east or the west, nor whether the Russians are not living under the equator and eating ripe oranges."

"Don't they eat oranges?" said Daisy seriously. But that question set Preston off into a burst of laughter, for which he atoned as soon as it was over by a very gentle kiss to his little cousin.

"Never mind, Daisy," he said; "I think you are better without geography. You aren't just like everybody else —that's a fact."

"Daisy," said Capt. Drummond, coming upon the scene, "do you allow such things?"

"It is Preston's manner of asking my pardon, Capt. Drummond," Daisy answered, looking a little troubled, but in her slow, womanly way. The Captain could not help laughing in his turn.

"What offence has he been guilty of?—tell me, and I will make him ask pardon in another manner. But Daisy, do you reckon such a liberty no offence?"

"Not if I am willing he should take it," said Daisy. The Captain seemed much amused.

"My dear little lady!" he said, "it is good for me you are not half a score of years wiser. What were you talking about the Crimea?—I heard the word as I came up."

"I asked Preston to shew it to me on the map—or he said he would."

"Come with me and I'll do it. You shouldn't ask anybody but me about the Crimea."

So getting hold affectionately of Daisy's hand, he and she went off to the house. No one was in the library. The Captain opened a large map of Russia; Daisy got up in a chair, with her elbows on the great library table, and leaned over it, while the Captain drew up another chair and pointed out the Crimea and Sebastopol, and shewed the course by which the English ships had come, for Daisy took care to ask that. Then, finding so earnest a listener, he went on to describe to her the situation of other places on the Peninsula, and the character of the country, and the severities of the climate in the region of the great struggle. Daisy listened, with her eyes varying between Capt. Drummond's face and the map. The Black Sea became known to Daisy thence and forever.

"I never thought geography was so interesting!" she remarked with a sigh, as the Captain paused. He smiled.

"Now Daisy, you have something to tell me," he said.

"What?" said Daisy, looking up suddenly.

"Why you wanted to know about soldiers—don't you remember your promise?"

The child's face all changed; her busy, eager, animated look. became on the instant thoughtful and still. Yet changed, as the Captain saw with some curiosity, not to lesser but to greater intentness.

"Well, Daisy?"

"Capt. Drummond, if I tell you, I do not wish it talked about."

"Certainly not!" he said suppressing a smile, and watched her while she got down from her chair and looked about among the book-shelves.

"Will you please put this on the table for me?" she said—"I can't lift it."

"A Bible!" said the Captain to himself. "This is growing serious." But he carried the great quarto silently and placed it on the table. It was a very large volume, full of magnificent engravings, which were the sole cause and explanation of its finding a place in Mr. Randolph's library. He put it on the table and watched Daisy curiously, who disregarding all the pictures turned over the leaves hurriedly, till near the end of the book; then stopped, put her little finger under some words, and turned to him. The Captain looked and read—over the little finger—

"Thou therefore endure hardness, as a good soldier of Jesus Christ."

It gave the Captain a very odd feeling. He stopped and read it two or three times over.

"But Daisy!"—he said.

"What, Capt Drummond?"

"What has this to do with what we were talking about?"

"Would you please shut this up and put it away, first?"

The Captain obeyed, and as he turned from the book-shelves Daisy took his hand again, and drew him, child-fashion, out of the house and through the shrubbery. He let her alone till she had brought him to a shady spot, where under the thick growth of magnificent trees a rustic seat stood, in full view of the distant mountains and the river.

"Where is my answer, Daisy?" he said, as she let go his hand and seated herself.

"What was your question, Capt. Drummond?"

"Now you are playing hide and seek with me. What have those words you shewed me,—what have they to do with our yesterday's conversation?"

"I would like to know," said Daisy slowly, "what it means, to be a good soldier?"

"Why?"

"I think I have told you," she said.

She said it with the most unmoved simplicity. The Captain could not imagine what made him feel uncomfortable. He whistled.

"Daisy, you are incomprehensible!" he exclaimed, and catching hold of her hand, he began a race down towards the river. Such a race as they had taken the day before. Through shade and through sun, down grassy steeps and up again, flying among the trees as if some one were after them, the Captain ran; and Daisy was pulled along with him. At the edge of the woods which crowned the river bank, he stopped and looked at Daisy who was all flushed and sparkling with exertion and merriment.

"Sit down there!" said he, putting her on the bank and throwing himself beside her. "Now you look as you ought to look!"

"I don't think mamma would think so," said Daisy panting and laughing.

"Yes, she would. Now tell me—do you call yourself a soldier?"

"I don't know whether there can be such little soldiers," said Daisy. "If there can be, I am."

"And what fighting do you expect to do, little one?"

"I don't know," said Daisy. "Not very well."

"What enemies are you going to face?"

But Daisy only looked rather hard at the Captain and made him no answer.

"Do you expect to emulate the charge of the Light Brigade, in some tilt against fancied wrong?"

Daisy looked at her friend; she did not quite understand him, but his last words were intelligible.

"I don't know," she said meekly. "But if I do it will not be because the order is a *mistake*, Capt. Drummond."

The Captain bit his lip. "Daisy," said he, "are you the only soldier in the family?"

Daisy sat still, looking up over the sunny slopes of ground towards the house.

The sunbeams shewed it bright and stately on the higher ground; they poured over a rich luxuriant spread of greensward and trees, highly kept; stately and fair; and Daisy could not help remembering that in all that domain, so far as she knew, there was not a thought in any heart of being the sort of soldier she wished to be. She got up from the ground and smoothed her dress down.

"Capt. Drummond," she said with a grave dignity that

was at the same time perfectly childish too,—"I have told you about myself—I can't tell you about other people."

"Daisy, you are not angry with me!"

"No sir."

"Don't you sometimes permit other people to ask your pardon in Preston Gary's way?"

Daisy was about to give a quiet negative to this proposal, when perceiving more mischief in the Captain's face than might be manageable, she pulled away her hand from him, and dashed off like a deer. The Captain was wiser than to follow.

MELBOURNE HOUSE.

Later in the day, which turned out a very warm one, he and Gary McFarlane went down again to the edge of the bank, hoping to get if they could a taste of the river breeze. Lying there stretched out under the trees, after a little while they heard voices. The voices were down on the shore. Gary moved his position to look.

"It's that child—what under the sun is she doing! I beg pardon for naming anything warm just now, Drummond—but she is building fortifications of some sort, down there."

Capt. Drummond came forward too. Down below them, a little to the right, where a tiny bend in the shore made a spot of shade, Daisy was crouching on the ground apparently very busy. Back of her a few paces was her dark attendant, June.

"There's energy," said Gary. "What a nice thing it is to be a child and play in the sand!"

The talk down on the shore went on; June's voice could scarcely be heard, but Daisy's words were clear—"Do, June! Please try." Another murmur from June, and then Daisy—"Try, June—do, please!" The little voice was soft, but its utterances were distinct; the words could be heard quite plainly. And Daisy sat back from her sand-work, and June began to sing something. *What*, it would have been difficult to tell at the top of the bank, but then Daisy's voice struck in. With no knowledge that she had listeners, the notes came mounting up to the top of the bank, clear, joyous and strong, with a sweet power that nobody knew Daisy's voice had.

"Upon my word, that's pretty!" said the Captain.

"A pretty thing, too, faith," said Gary. "Captain, let's get nearer the performers. Look out, now, and don't strike to windward."

They went, like hunters, softly down the bank, keeping under shelter, and winding round so as to get near before they should be seen. They succeeded. Daisy was intent upon her sand-work again, and June's back was towards them. The song went on more softly; then in a chorus Daisy's voice rang out again, and the words were plain.

"Die in the field of battle,
Die in the field of battle,
Die in the field of battle,
Glory in your view."

"Spirited!" whispered Gary.

"I almost think it is a Swedish war song," said the Captain. "I am not sure."

"Miss Daisy!"—said June—"the gentlemen—"

Daisy started up. The intruders came near. On the ground beside her lay an open map of Europe; in the sand before her she had drawn the same outlines on a larger scale. The shore generally was rough and pebbly ; just in this little cove there was a space of very fine sand, left wetted and adhesive by the last tide. Here the battle of Inkermann had been fought, and here Daisy's geography was going on. Capt. Drummond, who alone had the clue to all this, sat down on a convenient stone to examine the work. The lines were pretty fairly drawn, and Daisy had gone on to excavate to some depth the whole area of the Mediterranean and Black Seas, and the region of the Atlantic to some extent; with the course of the larger rivers deeply indented.

"What is all this gouging for, Daisy?" he said. "You want water here now, to fill up."

"I thought when the tide came, Capt. Drummond, I could let it flow in here, and see how it would look."

"It's a poor rule that don't work both ways," said the Captain. "I always heard that 'time and tide wait for no man;' and we won't wait for the tide. Here Gary—make yourself useful—fetch some water here; enough to fill two seas and a portion of the Atlantic Ocean."

"What shall I bring it in, if you please?"

"Anything!—your hands, or your hat, man. Do impossibilities for once. It is easy to see you are not a soldier."

"The fates preserve me from being a soldier under you!" said Gary—"if that's your idea of military duty What are *you* going to do while I play Neptune in a bucket?"

"I am going to build cities and raise up mountains. Daisy, suppose we lay in a supply of these little white stones, and some black ones——"

While this was done, and Daisy looked delighted, Mr. McFarlane seized upon a tin dipper which June had brought, and filled it at the river. Capt. Drummond carefully poured out the water into the Mediterranean, and opened a channel through the Bosphorus and Dardanelles, which were very full of sand, into the Black Sea. Then he sent Gary off again for more, and began placing the pebbles.

"What is that for, Capt. Drummond?" asked Daisy.

"These are the Alps—white, as they should be, for the snow always lies on them."

"Is it so cold there?"

"No,—but the mountains are so high. Their tops are always cold, but flowers grow down in the valleys. These are very great mountains, Daisy."

"And what are those black ones, Capt. Drummond?"

"This range is the Pyrenees—between France and Spain;—they are great too, and beautiful. And here go the Carpathians—and here the Ural mountains,—and these must stand for the Apennines."

"Are they beautiful too?"

"I suppose so—but I can't say, never having been there. Now what shall we do for the cities? As they are centres of wealth, I think a three-cent piece must mark them. Hand over, Gary; I have not thrips enough. There is St. Petersburg—here is Constantinople—here is Rome—now here is Paris. Hallo! we've no England! can't leave London out. Give me that spoon, Daisy—" and the Captain, as he expressed it, went to work in the trenches. England was duly marked out, the channel filled, and a bit of silver planted for the metropolis of the world.

"Upon my word!" said Gary,—"I never knew geography before. I shall carry away some ideas."

"Keep all you can get," said the Captain. "Now there's Europe."

"And here were the battles,"—said Daisy, touching the little spot of wet sand which stood for the Crimea.

"*The* battles!" said Gary. "What battles?"

"Why, where the English and French fought the Russians."

"*The* battles! Shades of all the heroes! Why Daisy, Europe has done nothing but fight for a hundred thousand years. There isn't a half inch of it that hasn't had a battle. See, *there* was one,—and there was another—tremendous;—and there,—and there,—and there,—and there,—and all over! This little strip here that is getting swallowed up in the Mediterranean—there has been blood enough shed on it to make it red from one end to the other, a foot deep. That's because it has had so many great men belonging to it."

Daisy looked at Capt. Drummond.

"It's pretty much so, Daisy," he said; "all over the south of Europe, at any rate."

"Why over the south and not the north?"

"People in the north haven't anything to fight for," said Gary. "Nobody wants a possession of ice and snow—more than will cool his butter."

"A good deal so, Daisy," said Capt. Drummond, taking the silent appeal of her eyes.

"Besides," continued Gary, "great men don't grow in the north. Daisy, I want to know which is the battle-field *you* are going to die on."

Daisy sat back from the map of Europe and looked at Gary with unqualified amazement.

"Well?" said Gary. "I mean it."

"I don't know what you mean."

"I hear you are going to die on the field of battle—and I want to be there that I may throw myself after you, as Douglas did after the Bruce's locket; saying 'Go thou first, brave heart, as thou art wont, and I will follow thee!"

"Daisy," said the Captain, "you were singing a battle-song as we came down the hill—that is what he means."

"Oh!—" said Daisy, her face changing from its amazed look. But her colour rose too a little.

"What was it?"

"That?" said Daisy. "O that was a hymn."

"A hymn!" shouted Gary. "Good! A hymn! That's glorious! Where did you get it, Daisy? Have you got a collection of Swedish war-songs? *They* used to sing and fight together, I am told. They are the only people I ever heard of that did—except North American Indians. Where did you get it?"

"I got it from June."

"June! what, by inspiration? June is a fine month, I know—for strawberries—but I had no idea——"

"No, no," said Daisy, half laughing,—"I mean my June—there she is; I got it from her."

"Hollo!" cried Gary. "Come here, my good woman—Powers of Darkness! Is your name June?"

"Yes sir, if you please," the woman said, in her low voice, dropping a courtesy.

"Well, nobody offers more attractions—in a name," said Gary;—"I'll say that for you. Where did you get that song your little mistress was singing when we came down the hill? Can you sing it?"

June's reply was unintelligible.

"Speak louder, my friend. *What* did you say?"

June made an effort. "If you please, sir, I can't sing," she was understood to say. "They sings it in camp meeting."

"In camp meeting!" said Gary. "I should think so! What's that! You see I have never been there, and don't understand."

"If you please, sir—the gentleman knows"—June said, retreating backwards as she spoke, and so fast that she soon got out of their neighbourhood. The shrinking, gliding action accorded perfectly with the smothered tones and subdued face of the woman.

"Don't *she* know!" said Gary. "Isn't that a character now? But, Daisy, are you turning Puritan?"

"I don't know what that is," said Daisy.

"Upon my word you look like it! It's a dreadful disease, Daisy;—generally takes the form of—I declare I don't know!—fever, I believe, and delirium; and singing is one of the symptoms."

"You don't want to stop her singing?" said Capt. Drummond.

"That sort? yes I do. It wouldn't be healthy, up at the house. Daisy, sing that gipsy song from 'The Camp in Silesia,' that I heard you singing a day or two ago."

"'The Camp in Silesia?'" said Capt. Drummond. "Daisy, can you sing *that?*"

"Whistles it off like a gipsy herself," said Gary. "Daisy, sing it."

"I like the other best," said Daisy.

But neither teasing nor coaxing could make her sing again, either the one or the other.

CHAPTER IX.

It was bright morning, the pony chaise at the door, and Daisy in it; standing to arrange matters.

"Now, Daisy, have you got all in there? I don't believe it."

"Why don't you believe it?"

"How much will that concern hold?"

"A great deal more than you want. There's a big box under all the seat."

"What have you got in it?"

Daisy went off into a laugh, such a laugh of glee as did her father's heart good. Mr. Randolph was standing in the doorway to see the expedition set forward.

"What's the matter, Daisy?" he said.

"Papa, he don't think anybody is a person of forethought but himself."

It was Preston's turn to laugh, and Mr. Randolph joined him.

"Shews he don't know you, Daisy, as well as I do. When do you expect to be home again?"

Mr. Randolph had come down to the side of the chaise and was looking with a very pleased face at what was in it. Daisy said she supposed they would stay till Preston had caught as many fish as he wanted.

"And won't you be tired before that?"

"O no, papa! I am going to fish too."

"I'll have all you catch, Daisy,—for my own eating!"

He bent his head down as he spoke, to kiss the little fisherwoman; but Daisy, answering some unusual tenderness of face or manner, sprung up and threw her arms round his neck, and only released him after a very close pressure.

"She is in a fair way to be cured of her morbid seriousness"—Mr. Randolph thought as he saw the cavalcade set forth; and well pleased he went in to breakfast. Daisy and Preston had breakfasted already, before the family; and now were off to the hills just as other people were stirring sugar into cups of coffee.

Preston led the way on a fine bay of his uncle's; taking good gallops now and then to ease his own and his horse's spirits, and returning to go quietly for a space by the side of the pony-chaise. Loupe never went into anything more exciting than his waddling trot; though Daisy made him keep that up briskly.

"What a thing it is, to have such short legs!" said Preston, watching the movements of the pony.

"*You* go over the road without seeing it," said Daisy.

"I don't want to see it. What I want to see is Hillsdale."

"So do I; but I want to see *everything*."

Preston smiled, he could not help it, at the very happy and busy little face and spirit down in the pony chaise.

"What do you see, Daisy, that you have not seen a hundred times before?"

"That makes no difference," said Daisy. "I have seen *you* a hundred times before."

Preston laughed, set spurs to his horse, and went off for another gallop.

Daisy enjoyed her morning's drive. The light was clear and the air was fresh; Preston gallopping before and Sam jogging on behind; everything was fine! Then it was quite true that she liked to see everything; those grey eyes of hers were extremely busy. All the work going on in the fields had interest for her, and all the passers-by on the road. A strange interest, often, for Daisy was very apt to be wondering whether any of them knew and loved the name she loved best; wondering who among all those rough-looking, unknown people, might be her fellow-servants. And with that a thought which, if Mr. Randolph had known it, would have checked his self-congratulations. He had not guessed what made the clasp of Daisy's arms round his neck so close that morning.

Till they passed through Crum Elbow everything had been, as Preston said, seen a hundred times before. A little way beyond that everything became new. Mrs. Randolph's carriage never came that road. The country grew more rough and broken, and the hills in their woody dress shewed more and more near.

"Do you see that break in the woods?" said Preston, pointing with his whip; "that is where the brook comes out,—that is where we are going."

"What time is it, Preston?"

"Time?—it is half past nine. What about it?"

"I'm hungry—that's all. I wanted to know what time it was."

"Hungry! O what a fisher you will make, Daisy! Can't stand fasting for two hours and a half."

"No, but Preston, I didn't eat much breakfast. And I've had all this ride since. I am going to stand fasting; but I am going to be hungry too."

"No you aren't," said Preston. "Just let Loupe take you up to that little gate, will you? I'll see if we can leave the horses here. Sam!—take this fellow!"

Preston jumped down from the saddle and went into the house, to the front yard of which the little gate opened. Daisy looked after him. It was a yard full of grass and weeds, among which a few poppies and hollyhocks and balsams grew straggling up where they could. Nothing kept them out of the path but the foot-tread of the people that went over it; hoe and rake were never known there since the walk was first made. The house was a little.

low, red-front house, with one small window on each side the door.

"All right!" said Preston, coming back. "Sam, take the horses round to the barn; and bring the baskets out of the chaise-box and wait at this gate for us."

"Why is he to wait? where are we going?"

"Going in to get some breakfast."

"*Here*, Preston?—O I can't."

"What's the matter?"

"I can't eat anything in there. I can wait."

"Why it looks clean," said Preston; "room and table and woman and all."—But Daisy still shook her head and was not to be persuaded; and Preston laughing went back to the house. But presently he came out again bearing a tray in his hand, and brought it to Daisy. On the tray was very nice looking brown and white bread, and milk and cheese and a platter of strawberries. Preston got into the chaise and set the tray on his knees. After him had come from the house a woman in a fly-away cap and short-gown. She stood just inside the gate leaning her arms on it. If she had not been there, perhaps Daisy would still have refused to touch the food; but she was afraid of offending or hurting the woman's feelings; so first she tried a strawberry, and found it of rare flavour; for it was a wild one; then she broke a morsel of bread, and that was excellent. Daisy discovered that breakfast in a pony chaise, out in the air, was a very fine thing. So did Preston.

"So you're agoin' afishin'?" said the woman at the gate.

"Yes, ma'am," Preston said.

"And that little one too?"

"Certainly."

"I declare! I never see nobody so little and gauzy as was willin' to do such indelicate work! But I shouldn't wonder, now, if she was to catch some. Fishes—and all things—is curious creeturs, and goes by contrairies."

"Hope they won't to-day!" said Preston, who was eating strawberries and bread and milk at a great rate.

"Where's the rest of your party?" the woman went on.

"We're all here, ma'am," said Preston.

"Well, I see a horse there that haint nobody on top of him?"

"I was on top of him a little while ago," said Preston.

"Well, I expect that little creetur haint druv herself?"

"Drove the pony, anyhow," said Preston. "Now, ma'am, what do we owe you, besides thanks, for your excellent hospitality?"

"I reckon you don't owe me much," said the woman, as Preston got out of the chaise. "You can set the tray in there on the table, if you're a mind to. We always calculate to set a good meal, and we're allowed to; but we don't never calculate to live by it and we've no dispensary. There's only my husband and me, and there's a plenty for more than us."

Preston had handed the tray to Sam to carry in, and as soon as he could get a chance bade good morning, and went forward with Daisy. On foot now they took their way to the woods, and presently plunged into them. It was very pleasant under the deep shade, for the sun had grown warm, and there was hardly air enough to flutter the leaves in the high branches. But Daisy and Preston pushed on briskly, and soon the gurgle of the brook gave its sweet sound to their ears. They followed up the stream then, over stones and rocks, and crossing from side to side on trunks of trees that had fallen across the water; till a part of the brook was reached far enough back among the hills to be wild and lonely; where the trout might be supposed to be having a good time.

"Now, Daisy," said Preston, "I think this will do. Can't have a better place. I'll try and get you to work here."

"And now, how must I manage, Preston?" said Daisy anxiously.

"I'll shew you."

Daisy watched while Preston took out and put together the light rod which she was to use, and fixed a fly for the bait.

"Do you see that little waterfall, Daisy?"

"Yes."

"And you see where the water curls round just under the fall?"

"Yes."

"That is where you must cast your fly. I should think there must be some speckled fellows there. What glory, Daisy, if you should catch one!"

"Well, what must I do, Preston?"

"Throw your fly over, so that it may light just there, and then watch; and if a fish jumps up and catches it, you pull your line away and catch the fish."

"But I can't throw it from here? I must go nearer."

"No, you mustn't—you're near enough; stand just here. Try if you can't throw your fly there. If you went nearer, you would frighten the fish. They are just about as shy as if they were Daisies. Now I will go a little further off and see what I can do. You'll catch the first fish!"

"No, I shall not," said Daisy, gravely.

She tried with a beating heart to throw her line; she tried very hard. The first time it landed on the opposite side of the brook. The next time it landed on a big stone this side of the waterfall. The third trial fastened the hook firmly in Daisy's hat. In vain Daisy gently sought to release it; she was obliged at last to ask help of Sam.

"That ar's no good, Miss Daisy," said Sam, as he got the fly out of its difficulty.

"If I could only throw it in——" said Daisy. And this time with a very great effort she did succeed in swinging the bait by a gentle motion to the very spot. No statue was more motionless than Daisy then. She had eyes and ears for nothing but the trout in the brook.

Minutes went by. The brook leaped and sang on its way the air brought the sweet odours of mosses and ferns; the leaves flapped idly overhead; you could hear every little sound. For there sat Daisy and there stood Sam, as still as the stones. Time went by. At last a sigh came from Daisy's weary little body, which she had not dared to move an inch for half an hour.

HILLSDALE.

"Tain't no good, Miss Daisy," whispered Sam.

"I can't keep it still," said Daisy under her breath, as if the fishes would hear and understand her.

"Suppos'n you try t'other bait, Miss Daisy."

"What bait?"

"O t'other kind, Miss Daisy. Will I put it on for you to try?"

Daisy sat awhile longer however, in silence and watching, until every joint was weary and her patience too. Then she left the rod in Sam's hands and went up to see what Preston was doing. He was some distance higher up the stream. Slowly and carefully Daisy crept near, till she could see his basket, and find out how much he had in it. That view loosed her tongue.

"Not one yet, Preston!" she exclaimed.

"Not a bite," said Preston.

"I hadn't either."

"I don't believe that there are any fish," said Preston.

"O but Sam said he saw lots of them."

"Lots of them! It's the flies then. Sam!—Hollo, Sam!—Sam!—"

"Here, sir," said Sam, coming up the brook.

"Just find me some worms, will you?—and be spry. I can't get a bite."

Daisy sat down to look about her, while Preston drew in his line and threw the fly away. It was a pretty place! The brook spread just there into a round pool several feet across, deep and still; and above it the great trees towered up as if they would hide the sun. Sam came presently with the bait. Preston dressed his hook, and gave his line a swing, to cast the bait into the pool; rather incautiously, seeing that the trees stood so thick and so near. Accordingly the line lodged in the high branches of an oak on the opposite side of the pool. Neither was there any coaxing it down.

"What a pity!" said Daisy.

"Not at all," said Preston. "Here, Sam—just go up that tree and clear the line—will you?"

Sam looked at the straight high stem of the oak, which had shot up high before it put forth a single branch, and he did not like the job. His slow motions said so.

"Come!" said Preston,—"be alive and do it quick, will you?"

"He can't—" said Daisy.

"Yes he can," said Preston. "If he can't he isn't worth his bread and salt. That's it, Sam—hand over hand, and you'll be there directly."

Sam shewed what he *could* do, if he did not like it; for he worked himself up the tall tree like a monkey. It was not so large but he could clasp it; so after a little rough work on his part and anxious watching on Daisy's, he got to the branches. But now the line was caught in the small forks at the leafy end of the branch. Sam lay out upon it as far as he dared; he could not reach the line.

"O he'll fall!" cried Daisy softly. "O Preston, let him come down!—he can't get it."

"He'll come to no harm," said Preston coolly. "A little further, Sam—it's oak wood, it will hold you; a little further, and you will have it—a little further!—"

And Daisy saw that Sam had gone too far. The bough swayed,—Sam made a lunge after the line, lost his hold, and the next minute his dark body was falling through the air and splashed into the pool. The water flew all over the two fishers who stood by its side; Preston awe-struck for the moment, Daisy white as death. But before either of them could speak or move, Sam's head reappeared above water.

"O get him out! get him out, Preston!" was Daisy's distressed cry. Preston spoke nothing, but he snatched a long stick that lay near and held it out to Sam; and so in a few minutes drew him to the shore and helped him out. Sam went to a little distance and stood dripping with water from head to foot; he did not shake himself as a Newfoundland dog would have done.

"Are you hurt, Sam?" said Preston.

"No, sir—" Sam answered, in a tone as if he felt very wet.

"Well, you've cleared the line for me at last," said Preston. "All's well that ends well. Hollo!—here's my hook gone,—broken off, float and all. Where's that basket, Sam?"

"It's below, sir."

"Below? where? just fetch it here, will you? *This* misfortune can be mended."

Sam moved off, dripping from every inch of him. "O Preston," said Daisy, "he's all wet as he can be—do let him go right down to that house and dry himself! We can get the basket."

"Do him good to move about," said Preston. "Nonsense, Daisy!—a ducking like that won't do anybody any harm in a summer's day."

"I don't think *you'd* like it," said Daisy; "and all his clothes are full of water, and the sun don't come down here. Tell him to go and get dry!

"I will, as soon as I've done with him. Here, Sam—just bend on this hook for me, while I see how the brook is further up. I've no time to lose,—and then you can go sun yourself somewhere."

Preston bounded off; Sam stood with the tackle in hand, silently at work. Daisy sat still on a stone near by, looking at him.

"Were you hurt, Sam?" she asked tenderly.

"No, Miss Daisy." This answer was not discontented but stoical.

"As soon as you have done that, Sam, run down to Mrs. Dipper's, and maybe she can give you something dry to put on while your clothes can be hung out."

Silence on Sam's part.

"Have you almost finished that?"

"Yes, ma'am."

"Then run off, Sam! Make haste to Mrs. Dipper's and get yourself dry—and don't come back till you are quite dry, Sam."

Sam finished his piece of work, flung down the line, and with a grateful "Thank you, Miss Daisy!" set off at a bound. Daisy watched him running at full speed down the brook till he was out of sight.

"Has he done it?" said Preston returning. "The rascal hasn't put any bait on. However, Daisy, it's no use coaxing the trout in *this* place at present—and I haven't found any other good spots for some distance up;—suppose we have our lunch and try again?"

"O yes!" said Daisy. "The other basket is down by my fishing-place—it's just as pleasant there, Preston."

They went back to the basket, and a very convenient huge rock was found on the edge of the brook, which would serve for table and seats too, it was so large and smooth. Preston took his place upon it, and Daisy at the other end with the basket began to unpack.

"Napkins?" said Preston—"you have no right to be so luxurious on a fishing party."

"Why not?"

"Why because a fisher is a kind of a Spartan animal, while he is about his business."

'What kind of an animal is that?" said Daisy, looking up from her arrangements. She had set out a plate of delicate rolls, and another with bread and butter folded in a napkin; and still she paused with her hand in the basket.

"Go on, Daisy. I want to see what comes next."

"I don't know," said Daisy. "Why, Joanna has made us a lemon pie!"

"Capital!" said Preston. "And what have you got in that dish?"

"I know," said Daisy. "Joanna has put in some jelly for me. "What sort of an animal is that, Preston?"

"It is a sort I shall not be to-day—with jelly and lemon pie. But what has Joanna put in for me? nothing but bread?"

"Why there are sandwiches."

"Where?"

"Why there! Those rolls are stuffed with meat, Preston."

"Splendid!" said Preston, falling foul of the rolls immediately. "What sort of an animal is a Spartan? My dear little Daisy, don't you know?"

"I don't believe I know anything," said Daisy humbly.

"Don't you want to?"

"O yes, Preston! if I had anybody to help me,—I do."

"Well—we'll see. How perfect these sandwiches are! when one's hungry."

"I am hungry too," said Daisy. "I think the sound of the water makes me hungry. O I wish I had given Sam some!—I never thought of it. How hungry he must be!"

"He'll get along," said Preston, helping himself to another roll.

"But how could I forget!" said Daisy. "And *he* did not have a second breakfast either. I am so sorry!" Daisy's hands fell from her own dainties.

"There is nothing here fit for him," said Preston. "I dare say he has his own pockets full."

"They were full of water, the last thing," said Daisy, quaintly.

Preston could not help laughing. "My dear Daisy," he said, "I hope you are not getting soft-hearted on the subject of servants?"

"How, Preston?"

"Don't;—because it is foolish."

"But Preston," said Daisy, looking earnestly at his handsome pleasant face which she liked very much,—"don't you know what the Bible says?"

"No."

It says, "The rich and the poor meet together; the Lord is the maker of them all."

"Well," said Preston, "that dor't mean that he made them all alike."

"Then if they are not made alike, what is the difference?"

"Good gracious!" said Preston; "do you often ask such questions, Daisy? I hope you are not going to turn out a Mrs. Child, or a philanthropist, or anything of that sort?"

"I am not going to be a Mrs. Anybody," said Daisy; "but why don't you answer me?"

"Where did you get hold of those words?"

"What words?"

"Those words that you quoted to me about rich and poor."

"I was reading them this morning."

"In what?"

"Why, in the Bible of course," said Daisy, with a little check upon her manner.

"This morning! Before we started! How came you to be reading the Bible so early in the morning?"

"I like to read it."

"Well, I'd take proper times for reading it," said Preston. "Who set you to reading it at five o'clock in the morning?"

"Nobody. O Preston, it was a great deal after five o'clock. What are proper times for reading it?"

"Are you going to cut that lemon pie?—or shall I? Daisy, I thought you were hungry. What is the use of jelly, if you don't eat it? You'll never catch fish at that rate. Fishers must eat."

"But Preston, what do you mean by proper times for reading the Bible?"

"Daisy, eat some lemon pie. It's capital. It melts in your mouth. Joanna Underwood is an excellent woman!"

"But Preston, what do you mean?"

"I don't mean you shall be religious, Daisy, if I can help it."

"What do you mean by being religious?"

"I declare!" said Preston, laughing at her grave little face, "I believe you've begun already. I am come in good time. I won't let you be anything but just what you ought to be, Daisy. Come—eat some jelly, or some pie, or something."

"But tell me then, Preston!" Daisy persisted.

"It is something ridiculous,—and you would not wish to be ridiculous."

"I do not think I have ever seen ridiculous religious people," said Daisy steadily; "and they couldn't be ridiculous *because* they were religious."

"Couldn't they?" said Preston. "Look out well, Daisy—I shall watch you. But they won't like it much down at Melbourne House, Daisy. If I were you, I would stop before you begin."

Daisy was silent. One thing was clear, she and Preston were at issue; and the value she set upon his favour was very high. She would not risk it by contending. Another thing was as clear, that Preston's last words were truth. Among her opposers Daisy must reckon her father and mother, if she laid herself open at all to the charge of being "religious." And what opposition that would be, Daisy did not let herself think. She shrunk from it. The lunch was finished, and she set her attention to pack the remainder of the things back into the basket. Suddenly she stopped.

"Preston, I wish you to consider my words confidential."

"Perfectly!" said Preston.

"You are honourable"—said Daisy.

"O Daisy, Daisy! you ought to have lived hundreds of years ago! You have me under command. Come," said he, kissing her grave little face, "are all these things to go in here? Let me help—and then we will go up stream."

He helped her with a delicate kind of observance which was not like most boys of sixteen, and which Daisy fully relished. It met her notions. Then she went to get her fishing-rod which lay fallen into the water.

"O Preston!" she exclaimed, "there is something on it!—it's heavy!—it's a fish!"

"It *is* a fish!" repeated Preston, as a jerk of Daisy's line threw it out high and dry on the shore—"and what's more, it's a splendid one. Daisy, you've done it now!"

"And papa will have it for breakfast! Preston, put it in a pail of water till we come back. There's that tin pail—we don't want it for anything—won't you? O I have caught one!"

It was done; and Daisy and Preston set off on a charming walk up the brook; but though they tried the virtue of their bait in various places, however it was, that trout was the only one caught. Daisy thought it was a fine day's fishing.

They found Sam, sound and dry, mounting guard over the tin pail when they came back to it. And I think Daisy held to her own understanding of the text that had been in debate; for there was a fine portion of lemon pie, jelly and sandwiches, laid by for him in the basket, and by Sam devoured with great appreciation.

CHAPTER X.

June came the next morning to dress her young mistress as usual. Daisy was not soon done with that business on this particular day; she would break off, half dressed, and go to lean out of her window. There was a honey-suckle below the window; its dewy sweet smell came up to her, and the breath of the morning was sweet beside in all the trees and leaves around; the sun shone on the short turf by glimpses, where the trees would let it. Daisy leaned out of her window. June stood as often before, with comb and brush in hand.

"Miss Daisy—it's late."

"June," said Daisy,—"it's Sunday."

"Yes, ma'am."

"It'll be hot too," Daisy went on. "June, are you glad when Sunday comes?"

"Yes ma'am," said June, shifting her position a little.

"I am," said Daisy. "Jesus is King to-day. To be sure, he is King always; but to-day *everything* is his."

"Miss Daisy, you won't be dressed."

Daisy drew her head in from the window and sat down to submit it to June's brush; but she went on talking.

"What part of the Bible do you like best to read, June?"

"Miss Daisy, will you wear your white muslin to-day —or the one with blue spots?"

"White. But tell me, June—which part of the Bible do you like best?"

"I like where it tells about all they had to go through" —June answered, rather unwillingly.

"They?—who?"

"The people, Miss Daisy—Christians, I s'pose."

"What did they have to go through?"

"Things, ma'am," said June very confusedly. "Miss Daisy, please don't turn your head round."

"But what things? and what for? Where is it, June?"

"I can't tell—I can find it for you, Miss Daisy. But you won't be ready."

June however had to risk that and find the chapter; and then Daisy read perseveringly all through the rest of her dressing, till it was finished. All the while June was fastening her frock, and tying her sash, and lacing her boots, Daisy stood or sat with the Bible in her hands and her eyes on the eleventh of Hebrews.

"June, I wonder when all this happened?"

"A great while ago, it's likely, Miss Daisy—but it's good to read now"—June added but half distinctly, as it was her manner often to speak. Daisy was accustomed to her, and heard it. She did not answer except by breaking out into the chorus she had learnt from June—

"'Die in the field of battle,
Die in the field of battle,
Die in the field of battle,
Glory in your view!'"

"Miss Daisy—I wouldn't sing that in the house," June ventured. For the child's voice, clear and full, raised the sweet notes to a pitch that might have been heard at least through several of the large rooms. Daisy hushed her song.

The trout was to be for breakfast, and Daisy when she was quite ready went gaily down to see if it would be approved. Her father was engaged to eat it all, and he held to his promise; only allowing Daisy herself to share with him; and on the whole Daisy and he had a very gay breakfast.

"It is too hot to do anything," said Mrs. Randolph, as the trout was very nearly reduced to a skeleton. "I shall not go to church this morning."

A shade passed over Daisy's face, but she did not look towards her mother.

"If you do not, I can't see why I should," said Mr. Randolph. "The burden of setting a good example lies upon you."

"Why?" said his wife quickly.

"Nobody will know whether I am there or not."

"Nobody will know that *I* am there at any rate," the lady rejoined. "The heat will be insufferable." Mrs. Gary declared herself of the same opinion.

An hour after Daisy came into her mother's room.

"Mamma, may I go to church with Joanna?"

"It's too hot, Daisy."

"No, mamma—I don't mind it. I would like to go."

"Children don't mind anything! Please yourself. But how are you going?"

"On foot, mamma; under the shade of the trees. It is nice and shady, all the way."

"It is enough to kill you! But go."

So Daisy's great flat set off alongside of Miss Underwood's Sunday gown to walk to church. They set out all right, on the way to the church by the evergreens. Preston Gary was a good deal surprised to find them some time later in another part of the grounds and going in a different direction.

"Where are you bound, Daisy?" he asked.

"To church, Preston."

"Church is the other way."

"Yes, but Mr. Pyne is sick and the church is closed, and we are going over to that little church on the other side of the road."

"Why that is a dissenting chapel, isn't it?"

"There's no more dissent amongst 'em than there is among other folks!" broke in Miss Underwood with a good deal of expression. "I wish all other folks and churches was as peaceable and kept as close to their business! Anyhow, it's a church, and the other one won't let us in."

Preston smiled and stepped back, and to Daisy's satisfaction they met with no further stay. They got to the little church and took their places in the very front; that place was empty, and Joanna said it was the only one that she could see. The house was full. It was a plain little church, very neat, but very plain compared with what Daisy was accustomed to. So were the people. These were not rich people, not any of them, she thought. At least there were no costly bonnets nor exquisite lace shawls nor embroidered muslin dresses among them; and many persons that she saw looked absolutely poor. Daisy however did not see this at first; for the service began almost as soon as they entered.

Daisy was very fond of the prayers always in church, but she seldom could make much of the sermon. It was not so to-day. In the first place, when the prayers and hymns were over, and what Daisy called "the good part" of the service was done, her astonishment and delight were about equal to see Mr. Dinwiddie come forward to speak. It is impossible to tell how glad Daisy was; even a sermon she thought she could relish from his lips; but when he began, she forgot all about it's being a sermon. Mr. Dinwiddie was talking to her and to the rest of the people; that was all she knew; he was not looking down at his book, he was looking at them; his eyes were going right through hers. And he did not speak as if he was preaching; his voice sounded exactly as it did every day out of church. It was delightful. Daisy forgot all about it's being a sermon, and only drank in the words with her ears and her heart, and never took her eyes from those bright ones that every now and then looked down at her. For Mr. Dinwiddie was telling of Him "who though he was rich yet for our sakes became poor." He told how rich he was, in the glories and happiness of heaven, where everything is perfect and all is his. And then he told how Jesus made himself poor; how he left all that glory and everything that pleased him; came where everything displeased him; lived among sin and sinners; was poor, and despised, and rejected, and treated with every shame, and at last shamefully put to death and his dead body laid in the grave. All this because he loved us; all this because he wanted to make us rich, and without his death to buy our forgiveness there was no other way. "Herein is love, not that we loved God, but that he loved us, and sent his Son to be the propitiation for our sins."

Daisy forgot even Mr. Dinwiddie in thinking of that wonderful One. She thought she had never seen before how good he is, or how beautiful; she had never felt how loving and tender Jesus is in his mercy to those that seek him, and whom *he* came to seek first; she never saw "the kindness and love of God our Saviour" before. As the story went on, again and again Daisy would see a cloud or mist of tears come over the brightness of those brilliant eyes; and saw the lips tremble; and Daisy's own eyes filled and ran over and her cheeks were wet with tears, and she never knew it!

But when Mr. Dinwiddie stopped she was so full of gladness in her little heart,—gladness that this beautiful Saviour loved her and that she loved him, that although if she *could* have been sorry, she would have been very sorry that the sermon was over, she was not; she could be nothing but glad.

She thought they were going home then, after the hymn was sung; but in her thoughts she had missed some words not spoken by Mr. Dinwiddie. And now she perceived that not only it was sacrament day, which she had seen before; but further, that the people who would not share in that service were going, and that Miss Underwood was staying, and by consequence she must stay too. Daisy was pleased. She had never in her life, as it happened, seen the observance of this ordinance; and she had, besides a child's curiosity, a deep, deep interest in all that Christians are accustomed to do. Was she not one?

Mr. Dinwiddie had spoken about the service and the purpose of it; he explained how the servants of Christ at his command take the bread and wine in remembrance of him and what he has done for them; and as a sign to all the world that they believe in him and love him, and wait for him to come again. Now some prayers were made, and there were spoken some grave words of counsel and warning, which sounded sweet and awful in Daisy's ears; and then the people came forward, a part of them, and knelt around a low railing which was before the pulpit. As they did this, some voices began to sing a hymn, in a wonderfully sweet and touching music. Daisy was exceedingly fond of every melody and harmony that was worthy the name; and this—plaintive, slow, simple—seemed to go not only through her ears, but down to the very bottom of her heart. They sang but a verse and a chorus; and then after an interval, when those around the railings rose and gave place to others, they sang a verse and a chorus again; and this is the chorus that they sang. It dwelt in Daisy's heart for many a day; but I can never tell you the sweetness of it.

"O the Lamb! the loving Lamb!
The Lamb on Calvary;
The Lamb that was slain, but lives again,
To intercede for me."

It seemed to Daisy a sort of paradise while they were singing. Again and again after a pause the notes measuredly rose and fell; and little Daisy who could take no other open part in what was going on, responded to them with her tears. Nobody was looking, she thought; nobody would see.

At last it was all done; the last verses were sung; the last prayers spoken; the little crowd turned to go. Daisy standing behind Joanna in the front place was obliged to wait till the aisle was clear. She had turned too when everybody else did, and so was standing with her back to the pulpit, when a hand was laid on her shoulder. The next minute Daisy's little fingers were in Mr. Dinwiddie's clasp, and her face was looking joyfully into his.

"Daisy—I am glad to see you."

Another look, and a slight clasp of her little fingers, answered him.

"I wish you had been with us just now."

"I am too little—" was Daisy's humble and regretful reply.

"Nobody is too little, who is old enough to know what Jesus has done and to love him for it, and to be his servant. Do you love him, Daisy?"

"Yes, Mr. Dinwiddie."

A very soft but a very clear answer; and so was the answer of the eyes raised to his. To Daisy's great joy, he did not let go her hand when they got out of the church. Instead of that, keeping it fast, he allowed Miss Underwood to go on a little before them, and then he lingered with Daisy along the shady, overarched walks of Melbourne grounds, into which they presently turned. Mr. Dinwiddie lingered purposely, and let Joanna get out of hearing. Then he spoke again.

"If you love Jesus, you want to obey him, Daisy."

"Yes, Mr. Dinwiddie!"

He felt the breathless manner of her answer.

"What will you do, little one, when you find that to obey him, you may have a great deal of hard fighting to go through?"

"I'll die on the field of battle, Mr. Dinwiddie."

He looked at her a little curiously. It was no child's boast. Her face was quiet, her eye steady; so had her tone been. It was most unlike Daisy to make protestations of feeling; just now she was speaking to the one person in the world who could help her, whom in this matter she trusted; speaking to him maybe for the last time, she knew; and moreover Daisy's heart was full. She spoke as she might live years and not do again, when she said, "I'll die on the field of battle."

"That is as the Lord pleases," returned Mr. Dinwiddie; "but how will you *fight*, Daisy? you are a weak little child. The fight must be won, in the first place."

"Please tell me, Mr. Dinwiddie."

He sat down on a bank and drew Daisy down beside him.

"In the first place, you must remember that you are the Lord's and that everything you have belongs to him; so that his will is the only thing to be considered in every case. Is it so, Daisy?"

"Yes, Mr. Dinwiddie! But tell me what you mean by 'everything I have.' That is what I wanted to know."

"I will tell you presently. In the next place—whenever you know the Lord's will, don't be afraid, but trust him to help you to do it. He always will,—he always can. Only trust him, and don't be afraid."

"Yes, Mr. Dinwiddie!" Daisy said; but with a gleam on her face which even then reflected the light of those words.

"That's all, Daisy."

"Then Mr. Dinwiddie, please tell me what you mean by 'everything?'"

"If you love the Lord, Daisy, you will find out."

"But I am afraid I don't know, Mr. Dinwiddie, what all my talents are."

"He is a wise man that does. But if you love the Lord Jesus with all your heart, you will find that in everything you do you can somehow please him, and that he is first to be pleased."

They looked into each other again, those two faces, with perfect understanding; grateful content in the child's eyes, watchful tenderness in those of Mr. Dinwiddie, through all their keenness and brightness. Then he rose up and offered his hand to Daisy; just said "good bye," and was gone. He turned off another way, Daisy followed Miss Underwood's steps. But Joanna had got to the house long before she reached it; and Daisy thought herself very happy that nobody saw her come home alone. She got to her own room in safety.

Daisy's heart was full of content. That day was the King's, to be sure; the very air seemed to speak of the love of Jesus, and the birds and the sunshine and the honeysuckle repeated the song of "The Lamb on Calvary." There was no going to church a second time; after luncheon, which was Daisy's dinner, she had the time all to herself. She sat by her own window, or sometimes she lay down—for Daisy was not very strong yet—but sitting or lying and whatever she was doing, the thought that that King was hers, and that Jesus loved her, made her happy; and the hours of the day rolled away as bright as its own sunshine.

"Well, mouse," said her mother when Daisy came down to tea,—"where have you been? What a mouse you are!"

"Intelligent—for a lower order of quadrupeds," said Mr. McFarlane.

"The day has been insufferable!" said Mrs. Randolph. "Have you been asleep, Daisy?"

"No, mamma."

"You were lying down?"

"Yes, mamma."

Daisy had drawn up close to her mother who had thrown an arm round her. The family were gathered in the library; the windows open, the fresh air coming faintly in; the light fading, but no lamps needed yet.

"I am glad the day is over!" said Mrs. Gary. "This morning I did not know how I was going to live through it. There is a little freshness now. Why is it always so much hotter on Sundays than on any other day?"

"Because you think about it," said Mr. Randolph, who was moving from window to window setting the glass doors wider open.

"There is nothing else to think about," said Mrs. Randolph with a yawn. "Gary, do bring me a cup of tea."

"You ought to think about your evil deeds," said Mr. McFarlane obeying the command. "Then you would have enough."

"*You* would, you mean."

"I know it. I speak from experience. I tried it once, for a whole afternoon; and you've no idea how good tea-time was when it came!"

"What *could* set you about such a piece of work, Gary?" said his hostess laughing.

"Conscience, my dear," said her sister. "I am not at all surprised. I wonder if anybody has been to church to-day?"

"I am sorry for the clergyman, if anybody has," remarked Gary.

Mrs. Randolph's arm had slipped from Daisy, and Daisy slipped away from her mother's sofa to the table; where she dipped sponge biscuits in milk and wondered at other people's Sundays. A weight seemed settling down on her heart. She could not bear to hear the talk; she eat her supper and then sat down on the threshold of one of the glass doors that looked towards the west, and watched the beautiful colours on the clouds over the mountains; and softly sung to herself the tune she had heard in church in the morning. So the colours faded away, and the light, and the dusk grew on, and still Daisy sat in the window door humming to herself. She did not know that Gary McFarlane had stolen up close behind her and gone away again.

He went away just as company came in; some gay neighbours who found the evening tempting, and came for a little diversion. Lamps were lit and talking and laughing went round, till Mrs. Randolph asked where Daisy was.

"In the window, singing to the stars," Gary McFarlane whispered. "Do you know, Mrs. Randolph, how she can sing?"

"No,—how? She has a child's voice."

"But not a child's taste or ear," said Gary. "I heard her the other day warbling the gypsy song in 'The Camp in Silesia,' and she did it to captivation. Do, Mrs. Randolph, ask her to sing it. I was astonished."

"Do!" said Capt. Drummond; and the request spread and became general.

"Daisy—" said Mrs. Randolph. Daisy did not hear; but the call being repeated she came from her window, and after speaking to the strangers, whom she knew, she turned to her mother. The room was all light and bright and full of gay talkers.

"Daisy," said her mother, "I want you to sing that gypsy song from the 'Camp in Silesia.' Gary says you know it—so he is responsible. *Can* you sing it?"

"Yes, ma'am."

"Then sing it. Never mind whether you succeed or not; that is of no consequence."

"Mamma——," began Daisy.

"Well, what?"

Daisy was in great confusion. What to say to her mother she did not know.

"No matter how you get along with it," repeated Mrs. Randolph. "That is nothing."

"It isn't that, mamma,—but—"

"Then sing. No more words, Daisy; sing."

"Mamma, please don't ask me!"

"I *have* asked you. Come Daisy—don't be silly."

"Mamma," whispered Daisy trembling, "I will sing it any other night but to night!"

"To-night? what's to-night?"

"To-night is Sunday."

"And is that the reason?"

Daisy stood silent, very much agitated.

"I'll have no nonsense of the kind, Daisy. Sing immediately!" But Daisy stood still.

"Do you refuse me?"

"Mamma—" said Daisy pleadingly.

"Go and fetch me a card from the table."

Daisy obeyed. Mrs. Randolph rapidly wrote a word or two on it with a pencil.

"But where is the gypsy?" cried Gary McFarlane.

"She has not found her voice yet. Take that to your father, Daisy."

Daisy's knees literally shook under her as she moved across the room to obey this order. Mr. Randolph was sitting at some distance talking with one of the gentlemen. He broke off when Daisy came up with the card.

"What is it your mother wishes you to sing?" he inquired, looking from the writing to the little bearer. Daisy answered very low.

"A gypsy song from an opera.

"Can you sing it?"

"Yes, sir."

"Then do so at once, Daisy."

The tone was quiet but imperative. Daisy stood with eyes cast down, the blood all leaving her face to reinforce some attacked region. She grew white from second to second.

"It is the charge of the Light Brigade," said Capt. Drummond to himself. He had heard and watched the whole proceeding and had the key to it. He thought good-naturedly to suggest to Daisy an escape from her difficulty, by substituting for the opera song something else that she *could* sing. Rising and walking slowly up and down the room, he hummed near enough for her to hear and catch it, the air of "Die in the field of battle." Daisy heard and caught it, but not his suggestion. It was the thought of the *words* that went to her heart,—not the thought of the tune. She stood as before, only clasped her little hands close upon her breast. Capt. Drummond watched her. So did her father, who could make nothing of her.

"Do you understand me, Daisy ?"

"Papa—"

"Obey me first, and then talk about it."

Daisy was in no condition to talk; she could hardly breathe that one word. She knew the tone of great displeasure in her father's voice. He saw her condition.

"You are not able to sing at this minute," said he. "Go to your room—I will give you ten minutes to recover yourself. Then, Daisy, come here and sing—if you like to be at peace with me."

But Daisy did not move; she stood there with her two hands clasped on her breast.

"Do you mean that you will not ?" said Mr. Randolph.

"If it wasn't Sunday, papa—" came from Daisy's parted lips.

"Sunday ?" said Mr. Randolph—"is that it ? Now we know where we are. Daisy—do you hear me ?—turn about and sing your song. Do not give me another refusal !"

But Daisy stood, growing paler and paler, till the whiteness reached her lips, and her father saw that in another minute she would fall. He snatched her from the floor and placed her upon his knee with his arm round her; but though conscious that she was held against his breast,

Daisy was conscious too that there was no relenting in it; she knew her father; and her deadly paleness continued. Mr. Randolph saw that there would be no singing that night, and that the conflict between Daisy and him must be put off to another day. Making excuse to those near, that she was not well, he took his little daughter in his arms and carried her up stairs to her own room. There he laid her on the bed and rang for June, and staid by her till he saw her colour returning. Then without a word he left her.

Meanwhile Capt. Drummond, down stairs, had taken a quiet seat in a corner; his talking mood having deserted him.

"Did I ever walk up to the cannon's mouth like that?" he said to himself.

CHAPTER XI.

Daisy kept herself quite still while her father and June were present. When Mr. Randolph had gone down stairs, and June seeing her charge better, ventured to leave her to get some brandy and water, then Daisy seized that minute of being alone to allow herself a few secret tears. Once opened, the fountain of tears gushed out a river; and when June came back Daisy was in an agony which prevented her knowing that anybody was with her. In amaze June set down the brandy and water and looked on. She had never in her life seen Daisy so. It distressed her; but though June might be called dull, her poor wits were quick to read some signs; and troubled as she was, she called neither Daisy's father nor her mother. The child's state would have warranted such an appeal. She never heard June's tremulous "Don't, Miss Daisy!" She was shaken with the sense of the terrible contest she had brought on herself; and grieved to the very depths of her tender little heart that she must bear the displeasure of her father and her mother. She struggled with tears and agitation until she was exhausted, and then lay quiet, panting and pale, because she had no strength to weep longer.

"Miss Daisy," said June, "drink this."

"What is it?"

"It is brandy and water. It is good for you."

"I am not faint. I don't like it."

"Miss Daisy, please! You want something. It will make you feel better and put you to sleep."

Disregarding the tumbler which June offered, Daisy

slowly crawled off the bed and went and kneeled down before her open window, crossing her arms on the sill. June followed her, with a sort of submissive pertinacity.

"Miss Daisy, you want to take some of this, and lie down and go to sleep."

"I don't want to go to sleep."

"Miss Daisy, you're weak—won't you take a little of this, to strengthen you a bit?"

"I don't want it, June."

"You'll be sick to-morrow."

"June," said Daisy, "I wish a chariot of fire would come for me!"

"Why, Miss Daisy?"

"To take me right up. But I shall not be sick. You needn't be afraid. You needn't stay."

June was too much awed to speak, and dared not disobey. She withdrew; and in her own premises stood as Daisy was doing, looking at the moonlight; much wondering that storms should pass over her little white mistress such as had often shaken her own black breast. It was mysterious.

Daisy did not wish to go to sleep; and it was for fear she should, that she had crawled off the bed, trembling in every limb. For the same reason she would not touch the brandy and water. Once asleep, the next thing would be morning and waking up; she was not ready for that. So she knelt by the window and felt the calm glitter of the moonlight, and tried to pray. It was long, long since Daisy had withstood her father or mother in anything. She remembered the last time; she knew now they *would* have her submit to them, and now she thought she must not. Daisy dared not face the coming day. She would have liked to sit up all night; but her power of keeping even upon her knees was giving way when June stole in behind her, too uneasy to wait for Daisy's ring.

"Miss Daisy, you'll be surely sick to-morrow, and Mis' Randolph will think I ought to be killed."

"June, didn't the minister say this morning—"

"What minister?"

"O it wasn't you,—it was Joanna. Where is Joanna? I want to see her."

"Most likely she's going to bed, Miss Daisy."

"No matter—I want to see her. Go and tell her, June—no matter if she is in her night-gown,—tell her I want to speak to her one minute."

June went, and Daisy once more burst into tears. But she brushed them aside when Joanna came back with June a few minutes after.

"Joanna—didn't the minister say this morning, that when we are doing what Jesus tells us, he will help us through?"

"It's true," said Joanna, looking startled and troubled at the pale little tear-stained face lifted to her;—"but I don't just know as that minister said it this morning."

"Didn't he?"

"Why it's true, Miss Daisy; for I've heard other ministers say it; but that one this morning was preaching about something else—don't you know?"

"Was he? Didn't he say that?"

"Why no, Miss Daisy; he was preaching about how rich——"

"O I know!" said Daisy—"I remember; yes, it wasn't then—it was afterwards. Yes, he said it—I knew it—but it wasn't in his sermon. Thank you, Joanna—that's all; I don't want you any more."

"What ails her?" whispered Joanna, when June followed her out with a light.

But June knew her business better than to tell her little mistress's secrets; and her face shewed no more of them than it shewed of her own. When she returned, Daisy was on her knees, with her face hidden in her hands, at the foot of the bed.

June stopped; and the little white figure there looked so slight, the attitude of the bended head was so childlike and pitiful, that the mulatto woman's face twinkled and twitched in a way most unwonted to its usual stony lines. She never stirred till Daisy rose up and submissively allowed herself to be put to bed; and then waited on her with most reverent gentleness.

So she did next morning. But Daisy was very pale, and trembled frequently, June noticed; and when she was dressed sat down patiently by the window. She was not going down to breakfast, she told June; and June went away to her own breakfast, very ill satisfied.

Breakfast was brought up to Daisy, as she expected; and then she waited for her summons. She could not eat much. The tears were very ready to start, but Daisy kept them back. It did not suit her to go weeping into her father and mother's presence, and she had self-command enough to prevent it. She could not read; yet she turned over the pages of her Bible to find some comfort. She did not know or could not remember just where to look for it; and at last turned to the eleventh of Hebrews, and with her eye running over the record there of what had been done and borne for Christ's sake, felt her own little heart beating hard in its own trial.

June came at length to call her to her mother's room.

Mrs. Randolph was half lying on a couch, a favourite position; and her eye was full on Daisy as she came in. Daisy stopped at a little distance; and June took care to leave the door ajar.

"Daisy," said Mrs. Randolph, "I want in the first place an explanation of last night's behaviour."

"Mamma, I am very sorry to have offended you!" said Daisy, pressing both hands together upon her breast to keep herself quiet.

"Looks like it," said Mrs. Randolph; and yet she did see and feel the effect of the night's work upon the child. "Go on;—tell me why you disobeyed me last night."

"It was Sunday—" said Daisy softly.

"Sunday!—well, what of that? what of Sunday?"

"That song—wasn't a Sunday song."

"What do you mean by a Sunday song?"

"I mean"—Daisy was on dangerous ground, and she knew it,—"I mean, one of those songs that God likes to hear people sing on his day."

"Who is to be judge?" said Mrs. Randolph,—"you or I?"

"Mamma," said Daisy, "I will do everything else in the world you tell me!"

"You will have to do everything else and this too. Isn't there a commandment about children obeying their mothers?"

"Yes, ma'am."

"That is the very first commandment I mean you shall obey," said Mrs. Randolph, rousing herself enough to bring one foot to the floor. "You have no business to think whether a thing is right or wrong, that I order you to do; if I order it, that makes it right; and anybody but a fool would tell you so. You will sing that song from the 'Camp in Silesia' for me next Sunday evening, or I will whip you, Daisy—you may depend upon it. I have done it before, and I will again; and you know I do not make believe. Now go to your father."

"Where is he, mamma?" said Daisy, with a perceptible added paleness in her cheek.

"I don't know. In the library, I suppose."

To the library Daisy went, with trembling steps, in great uncertainty what she was to expect from her father. It was likely enough that he would say the same as her mother, and insist on the act of submission to be gone through next Sunday ; but Daisy had an inward consciousness that her father was likely to come to a point with her sooner than that. It came even sooner than she expected.

Mr. Randolph was pacing up and down the library when Daisy slowly opened the door. No one else was there. He stopped when she came in, and stood looking at her as she advanced towards him.

"Daisy, you disobeyed me last night."

"Yes, papa,—but—"

"I have but one answer for that sort of thing," said Mr. Randolph, taking a narrow ruler from the library table. "Give me your hand !"

Daisy gave it, with a very vague apprehension of what he was about to do. The sharp, stinging stroke of the ruler the next moment upon her open palm, made her understand very thoroughly. It drew from her one cry of mixed pain and terror ; but after that first forced exclamation Daisy covered her face with her other hand and did not speak again. Tears, that she could not help, came plentifully ; for the punishment was sufficiently severe, and it broke her heart that her father should inflict it ; but she stood perfectly still, only for the involuntary wincing that was beyond her control, till her hand was released and the ruler was thrown down. Heart and head bowed together then, and Daisy crouched down on the floor where she stood, unable either to stand or to move a step away.

"There ! that account's settled !" said Mr. Randolph as he flung down his ruler. And the next moment his hands came softly about Daisy and lifted her from the floor and placed her on his knee ; and his arms were wrapped tenderly round her. Daisy almost wished he had let her alone ; it seemed to her that her sorrow was more than she could bear.

"Is your heart almost broken ?" said Mr. Randolph softly, as he felt rather than heard the heavy sobs so close to him. But to speak was an impossibility, and so he knew, and did not repeat his question; only he held Daisy fast, and it was in his arms that she wept out the first over-charged fulness of her heart. It was a long time before she could quiet those heavy sobs; and Mr. Randolph sat quite still holding her.

"Is your heart quite broken?" he whispered again, when he judged that she could speak. Daisy did not speak, however. She turned, and rising upon her knees, threw her arms round her father's neck and hid her soft little head there. If tears came Mr. Randolph could not tell; he thought his neck was wet with them. He let her alone for a little while.

"Daisy——"

"Papa——"

"Can you talk to me?"

Daisy sank back into her former position. Her father put his lips down to hers for a long kiss.

"That account is settled," said he; "do you understand? Now Daisy, tell me what was the matter last night."

"Papa, it was Sunday night."

"Yes. Well?"

"And that song—that mamma wanted me to sing"—Daisy spoke very low,—"was out of an opera; and it was good for any other day, but not for Sunday."

"Why not?"

Daisy hesitated, and at last said, "It had nothing to do with Sunday, papa."

"But obedience is not out of place on Sunday, is it?"

"No, papa,—except——"

"Well, except what?"

"Papa, if God tells me to do one thing, and you tell me another, what shall I do?" Daisy had hid her face in her father's breast.

"What counter command have you to plead in this case?"

"Papa, may I shew it to you?"

"Certainly."

She got down off his lap, twinkling away a tear hastily, and went to the bookcase for the big Bible aforesaid. Mr. Randolph seeing what she was after and that she could not lift it, went to her help and brought it to the library table. Daisy turned over the leaves with fingers that trembled yet, hastily, flurriedly; and paused and pointed to the words that her father read.

"Remember that thou keep holy the Sabbath day."

Mr. Randolph read them and the words following and the words that went before; then he turned from them and drew Daisy to her place in his arms again.

"Daisy, there is another commandment there, 'Honour thy father and thy mother.' Is there not?"

"Yes, papa."

"Is not one command as good as the other?"

"Papa, I think not," said Daisy. "One command tells me to obey you,—the other tells me to obey God."

Childish as the answer was, there was truth in it; and Mr. Randolph shifted his ground.

"Your mother will not be satisfied without your obeying the lesser command—nor shall I!'

Silence.

"She will expect you to do next Sunday evening what you refused to do last evening."

Still silence, but a shiver ran over Daisy's frame.

"Do you know it?" said Mr. Randolph, noticing also that Daisy's cheek had grown a shade paler than it was.

"Papa—I wish I could die!" was the answer of the child's agony.

"Do you mean that you will not obey her, Daisy?"

"How can I, papa? how can I!" exclaimed Daisy.

"Do you think that song is so very bad, Daisy?"

"No, papa, it is very good for other days; but it is not *holy*." Her accent struck strangely upon Mr. Randolph's ear; and sudden contrasts rushed together oddly in his mind.

"Daisy, do you know that you are making yourself a judge of right and wrong? over your mother and over me?"

Daisy hid her face again in his breast; what could she answer? Mr. Randolph unfolded the little palm swollen and blistered from the marks of his ruler.

"Why did you offend me, Daisy?" he said gravely.

"Oh papa!" said Daisy beside herself,—"I didn't—I couldn't—I wouldn't, for anything in the world! but I couldn't offend the Lord Jesus!"——

She was weeping again bitterly.

"That will not do," said Mr. Randolph. "You must find a way to reconcile both duties. I shall not take an alternative." But after that he said no more and only applied himself to soothing Daisy; till she sat drooping in his arms, but still and calm. She started when the sound of steps and voices came upon the verandah.

"Papa, may I go?"

He let her go, and watched her measured steps through the long room to the door, and heard the bound they made as soon as she was outside of it. He rang the bell and ordered June to be called.

She came.

"June," said Mr. Randolph, "I think Daisy wants to be taken care of to-day—I wish you would not lose sight of her."

June courtesied her obedience.

A few minutes afterwards her noiseless steps entered Daisy's room. June's footfall was never heard about the house. As noiseless as a shadow she came into a room; as stealthily as a dark shadow she went out. Her movements were always slow; and whether from policy or caution originally, her tread would not waken a sleeping mouse. So she came into her little mistress's chamber now. Daisy was there, at her bureau, before an open drawer; as June advanced, she saw that a great stock of little pairs of gloves was displayed there, of all sorts, new and old; and Daisy was trying to find among them one that would do for her purpose. One after another was tried on the fingers of her right hand, and thrown aside; and tears were running over the child's cheeks and dropping into the drawer all the time. June came near, with a sort of anxious look on her yellow face. It was strangely full of wrinkles and lines, that generally never stirred to express or reveal anything. Suddenly she exclaimed, but June's very exclamations were in a smothered tone.

"O Miss Daisy! what have you done to your hand?"

"I haven't done anything to it," said Daisy, trying furtively to get rid of her tears,—"but I want a glove to put on, June, and they are all too small. Is Cecilia at work here to-day?"

"Yes, Miss Daisy; but let me look at your hand!—let me put some liniment on."

"No, I don't want it," said Daisy; and June saw the suppressed sob that was not allowed to come out into open hearing;—"but June, just rip that glove, will you, here in the side seam; and then ask Cecilia to make a strip of lace-work there—so that I can get it on." Daisy drew a fur glove over the wounded hand as she spoke; it was the only one large enough; and put on her flat hat.

"Miss Daisy, Mr. Randolph said I was to go with you anywhere you went—to take care of you."

"Then come down to the beach, June; I'll be there."

Daisy stole down stairs and slipped out of the first door she came to. What she wanted was to get away from seeing anybody; she did not wish to see her mother, or Preston, or Capt. Drummond, or Ransom; and she meant even if possible to wander off and not be at home for dinner. She could not bear the thought of the dinner-table with all the faces round it. She stole out under the shrubbery, which soon hid her from view of the house.

It was a very warm day, the sun beating hot wherever it could touch at all. Daisy went languidly along under cover of the trees, wishing to go faster, but not able, till she reached the bank. There she waited for June to join her, and together they went down to the river shore. Safe there from pursuit, on such a day, Daisy curled herself down in the shade with her back against a stone, and then began to think. She felt very miserable; not merely for what had passed, but for a long stretch of trouble that she saw lying before her. Indeed where or how it was to end, Daisy had no idea. Her father indeed, she felt pretty sure would not willingly allow his orders to come in conflict with what she thought her duty; though if he happened to do it unconsciously,—— Daisy would not follow that train of thought. But here she was now, at this moment, engaged in a trial of strength with her mother; very unequal, for Daisy felt no power at all for the struggle,—and yet she could not yield! Where was it to end? and how many other like occasions of difference might arise, even after this one should somehow have been settled? Had the joy of being a servant of Jesus so soon brought trouble with it? Daisy had put the trunk of a large tree between her and June; but the mulatto woman where she sat heard the stifled sobs of the child. June's items of intelligence picked up by eye and ear, had given her by this time an almost reverent feeling towards Daisy; she regarded her as hardly earthly; nevertheless this sort of distress must not be suffered to go on, and she was appointed to prevent it.

"Miss Daisy—it is luncheon time," she said without moving. Daisy gave no response. June waited and then came before her and repeated her words.

"I am not going in."

"But you want your dinner, Miss Daisy."

"No, I don't, June. I don't want to go in."

June looked at her a minute. "I'll get you your luncheon out here, Miss Daisy. You'll be faint for want of something to eat. Will you have it out here?"

"You needn't say where I am, June."

June went off, and Daisy was left alone. Very weary and exhausted, she sat leaning her head against the stone at her side, in a sort of despairing quiet. The little ripple of the water on the pebbly shore struck her ear; it was the first thing eye or ear had perceived to be pleasaat that day. Daisy's thoughts went to the hand that had made the glittering river, with all its beauties and wonders; then they went to what Mr. Dinwiddie had said, that God will help his people when they are trying to do any difficult work for him; he will take care of them; he will not forsake them. Suddenly it filled Daisy's soul like a flood, the thought that Jesus *loves* his people; that she was his little child and that he loved her; and all his wisdom and power and tenderness were round her and would keep her. Her trouble seemed to be gone, or it was like a cloud with sunlight shining all over it. The very air was full of music, to Daisy's feeling, not her sense. There never was such sunlight, or such music either, as this feeling of the love of Jesus. Daisy kneeled down by the rock and rested her forehead against it, to pray for joy.

She was there still, when June came back and stopped and looked at her, a vague expression of care sitting in her black eyes, into which now an unwonted moisture stole. June had a basket, and as soon as Daisy sat down again, she came up and began to take things out of it. She had brought everything for Daisy's dinner. There was a nice piece of beefsteak, just off the gridiron; and rice and potatoes; and a fine bowl of strawberries for dessert. June had left nothing; there was the roll and the salt, and a tumbler and a carafe of water. She set the other things about Daisy, on the ground and on the rock, and gave the plate of beefsteak into her hand.

"Miss Daisy, what will you do for a table?"

"It's nicer here than a table. How good you are, June. I didn't know I wanted it."

"I know you do, Miss Daisy."

And she went to her sewing, and sewed perseveringly, while Daisy eat her dinner.

"June, what o'clock is it?"

"It's after one, ma'am."

"You haven't had your own dinner?"

June mumbled something, of which nothing could be understood except that it was a general abnegation of all desire or necessity for dinner on her own part.

"But you have not had it?" said Daisy.

"No, ma'am. They've done dinner by this time."

"June, I have eaten up all the beefsteak—there is nothing left but some potato and rice and strawberries; but you shall have some strawberries."

June in vain protested. Daisy divided the strawberries into two parts, sugared them both, broke the remaining roll in two, and obliged June to take her share. When this was over, Daisy seated herself near June and laid her head against her knee. She could hardly hold it up.

"June,"—she said presently, "I think those people in the eleventh chapter of Hebrews—you know?"

"Yes, Miss Daisy."

"I think they were very happy, because they knew that Jesus loved them."

June made no audible answer; she mumbled something; and Daisy sat still. Presently her soft breathing made June look over at her; Daisy was asleep. In her hand, in her lap, lay a book. June looked yet further, to see what book it was. It was Mr. Dinwiddie's Bible. June sat up and went on with her work, but her face twitched.

CHAPTER XII.

Daisy was at the dinner-table. After having a good sleep on June's knee, she had come home and dressed as usual, and she was in her place when the dessert was brought on. Mr. Randolph from his distant end of the table watched her a little; he saw that she behaved just as usual; she did not shun anybody, though her mother shunned her. A glove covered her right hand, yet Daisy persisted in using that hand rather than attract notice, though from the slowness of her movements it was plain it cost her some trouble. Gary McFarlane asked why she had a glove on, and Mr. Randolph heard Daisy's perfectly quiet and true answer, that "her hand was wounded, and had to wear a glove,"—given without any confusion or evasion. He called his little daughter to him, and giving her a chair by his side, spent the rest of *his* time in cracking nuts and preparing a banana for her; doing it carelessly, not as if she needed but as if it pleased him to give her his attention.

After dinner Daisy sought Preston, who was out on the lawn, as he said, to cool himself; in the brightness of the setting sun to be sure, but also in a sweet light air which was stirring.

"Phew! it's hot. And you, Daisy, don't look as if the sun and you had been on the same side of the earth to-day. What do you want now?"

"I want a good talk with you, Preston."

"I was going to say 'fire up,'" said Preston, "but no,

don't do anything of that sort! If there is any sort of talking that has a chilly effect, I wish you'd use it."

"I have read of such talk, but I don't think I know how to do it," said Daisy. "I read the other day of somebody's being 'frozen with a look.'"

Preston went off into a fit of laughter and rolled himself over on the grass, declaring that it was a splendid idea; then he sat up and asked Daisy again what she wanted? Daisy cast a glance of her eye to see that nobody was too near.

"Preston, you know you were going to teach me."

"O, ay!—about the Spartans."

"I want to learn everything," said Daisy. "I don't know much."

Preston looked at the pale, delicate child, whose doubtful health he knew had kept her parents from letting her "know much"; and it was no wonder that when he spoke again, he used a look and manner that were caressing, and even tender.

"What do you want to know, Daisy?"

"I want to know everything," whispered Daisy; "but I don't know what to begin at."

"No!" said Preston,—"'everything' seems as big as the world, and as hard to get hold of."

"I want to know geography," said Daisy.

"Yes. Well—you shall. And you shall not study for it neither; which you can't."

"Yes I can."

"No you can't. You are no more fit for it, little Daisy—but look here! I wish you would be a red daisy."

"Then what else, Preston?"

"Nothing else. Geography is enough at once."

"O no, it isn't. Preston, I can't do the least little bit of a sum in the world."

"Can't you? Well—I don't see that that is of any very great consequence. What sums do *you* want to do?"

"But I want to know how."

"Why?"

"Why Preston, you know I *ought* to know how. It might be very useful, and I ought to know."

"I hope it will never be of any use to you," said Preston; "but you can learn the multiplication table if you like."

"Then will you shew it to me?"

"Yes; but what has put you in such a fever of study, little Daisy? It excites me, this hot weather."

"Then won't you come in and shew me the multiplication table now, Preston?"

In came Preston laughing, and found an arithmetic for Daisy; and Daisy, not laughing, but with a steady seriousness, sat down on the verandah in the last beams of the setting sun to learn that "twice two is four."

The same sort of sweet seriousness hung about all her movements this week. To those who knew what it meant, there was something extremely touching in the gentle gravity with which she did everything, and the grace of tenderness which she had for everybody. Daisy was going through great trouble. Not only the trouble of what was past, but the ordeal of what was to come. It hung over her like a black cloud, and her fears were like muttering thunder. But the sense of right, the love of the Master in whose service she was suffering, the trust in his guiding hand, made Daisy walk with that strange, quiet dignity between the one Sunday and the other. Mr. Randolph fancied sometimes when she was looking down, that he saw the signs of sadness about her mouth; but whenever she looked up again, he met such quiet, steady eyes, that he wondered. He was puzzled; but it was no puzzle that Daisy's cheeks grew every day paler, and her appetite less.

"I do not wish to flatter you"—said Mrs. Gary one evening—"but that child has very elegant manners! Really, I think they are very nearly perfect. I don't believe there is an English court beauty who could shew better."

"The English beauty would like to be a little more robust in her graces," remarked Gary McFarlane.

"That is all Daisy wants," her aunt went on; "but that will come, I trust, in time."

"Daisy would do well enough," said Mrs. Randolph, "if she could get some notions out of her head."

"What, you mean her religious notions? How came she by them, pray?"

"Why there was a person here—a connexion of Mrs. Sandford's—that set up a Sunday school in the woods; and Daisy went to it for a month or two, before I thought anything about it, or about him. Then I found she was beginning to ask questions, and I took her away."

"Is asking questions generally considered a sign of danger?" said Gary McFarlane.

"What was that about her singing the other night?" said Mrs. Gary—"that had something to do with the same thing, hadn't it?"

"Refused to sing an opera song because it was Sunday."

"Ridiculous!" said Mrs. Gary. "I'll try to make her see it so herself—if I get a chance. She is a sensible child."

Mr. Randolph was walking up and down the room, and had not spoken a word. A little time after he found himself nearly alone with Mrs. Randolph, the others having scattered away. He paused near his wife's sofa.

"Daisy is failing," he said. "She has lost more this week than she had gained in the two months before."

Mrs. Randolph made no answer, and did not even move her handsome head, or her delicate hands.

"Can't you get out of this business, Felicia?"

"In the way that I said I would. You expect your words to be obeyed, Mr. Randolph; and I expect it for mine."

Mr. Randolph resumed his walk.

"Daisy has got some things in her head that must get out of it. I would as lieve not have a child, as not to have her mind me."

Mr. Randolph passed out upon the verandah, and continuing his walk there, presently came opposite the windows of the library. There he saw Daisy seated at the table, reading. Her hand was over her brow, and Mr. Randolph did not feel satisfied with the sober lines of the little mouth upon which the lamplight shone. Once too, Daisy's head went down upon her book and lay there a little while. Mr. Randolph did not feel like talking to her just then, or he would have liked to go in and see what she was studying. But while he stood opposite the window, Capt. Drummond came into the library.

"You here, Daisy! What are you busy about?" he said kindly. "What are you studying now?"

"I am reading the History of England, Capt. Drummond."

"How do you like it?"

"I have not got very far. I do not like it very much."

"Where are you?"

"I have just got to where it tells about Alfred."

"Why do you read it, Daisy? Is it a lesson?"

"No, Capt. Drummond,—but—I think proper to read it."

"It is proper," said the Captain. "Come, Daisy,—suppose we go down on the sand-beach to-morrow, and we will play out the Saxon Heptarchy there as we played out the Crimea. Shall we?"

Daisy's face changed. "O thank you, Capt. Drummond!—that will be nice! Shall we?"

"If you will, I will," said the Captain.

Mr. Randolph moved away.

The next day after luncheon, Daisy followed her father when he left the table. She followed till they were got quite away from other ears.

"Papa, I would like to go to Mrs. Harbonner's again. You said I must not go without leave."

"Who is Mrs. Harbonner?"

"Papa, it is the place where I took the ham,—do you remember? Joanna has enquired about her, and found that she is respectable."

"What do you want to go there again for, Daisy?"

"Joanna has found some work for her, papa. She would not have the ham unless she could work to pay for it. I want to see her to tell her about it."

Mr. Randolph had it on his tongue to say that somebody else might do that; but looking down at Daisy, the sight of the pale face and hollow eyes stopped him. He sat down and drew Daisy up to his side.

"I will let you go."

"Thank you, papa!"

"Do you know," said Mr. Randolph, "that your mother is going to ask you to sing that song again when Sunday evening comes?"

The smile vanished from Daisy's face; it grew suddenly dark; and a shuddering motion was both seen and felt by Mr. Randolph, whose arm was round her.

"Daisy," said he, not unkindly, "do you know that I think you a little fool?"

She lifted her eyes quickly, and in their meeting with her father's there was much; much that Mr. Randolph felt without stopping to analyze, and that made his own face as suddenly sober as her own. There was no folly in that quick grave look of question or appeal; it seemed to carry the charge in another direction.

"You think it is not right to sing such a song on a Sunday?" he asked.

"No, papa."

"But suppose, by singing it, you could do a great deal of good, instead of harm?"

"How, papa?"

"I will give you a hundred dollars for singing it,—which you may spend as you please for all the poor people about Melbourne or Crum Elbow."

It was very singular to him to see the changes in Daisy's face. Light and shadow came and went with struggling quickness. He expected her to speak, but she waited for several minutes; then she said in a troubled voice,—"Papa, I will think of it."

"Is that all, Daisy?" said Mr. Randolph, disappointed.

"I am going to Mrs. Harbonner's, papa, and I will think, and tell you."

Mr. Randolph was inclined to frown and suspect obstinacy; but the meek little lips which offered themselves for a kiss disarmed him of any such thought. He clasped Daisy in his arms and gave her kisses, many a one, close and tender. If he had known it, he could have done nothing better for the success of his plan; under the pressure of conscience Daisy could bear trouble in doing right, but the argument of affection went near to trouble her conscience. Daisy was obliged to compound for a good many tears, before she could get away and begin her drive. And when she did, her mind was in a flutter. A hundred dollars! how much good could be done with a hundred dollars. Why would it not be right to do something, even sing such a song on Sunday, when it was sung for such a purpose and with such results? But Daisy could not feel quite sure about it; while at the same time the prospect of getting quit of her difficulties by this means—escaping her mother's anger and the punishment with which it was sure to be accompanied, and also pleasing her father—shook Daisy's very soul. What should she do? She had not made up her mind when she got to the little brown house where Mrs. Harbonner lived.

She found mother and daughter both in the little bare room; the child sitting on the floor and cutting pieces of calico and cloth into strips, which her mother was sewing together with coarse thread. Both looked just as when Daisy had seen them before—slim and poor and uncombed; but the room was clean.

"I thought you warn't coming again," said Mrs. Harbonner.

"I couldn't come till to-day," said Daisy, taking a chair. "I came as soon as I could." Partly from policy, partly because she felt very sober, she left it to Mrs. Harbonner to do most of the talking.

"I never see more'n a few folks that thought much of doing what they said they'd do—without they found their own account in it. If I was living in a great house, now, I'd have folks enough come to see me."

Daisy did not know what answer to make to this, so she made none.

"I used to live in a better house once," went on Mrs. Harbonner; "I didn't always use to eat over a bare floor. I was well enough, if I could ha' let well alone; but I made a mistake, and paid for it; and what's more, I'm paying for it yet. 'Taint *my* fault, that Hephzibah sits there cuttin' rags, instead of going to school."

Again Daisy did not feel herself called upon to decide on the mistakes of Mrs. Harbonner's past life; and she sat patiently waiting for something else that she could understand.

"What are you come to see me for now?" said the lady. "I suppose you're going to tell me you haven't got no work for me to do, and I must owe you for that ham?"

"I have got something for you to do," said Daisy. "The boy has got it at the gate. The housekeeper found some clothes to make—and you said that was your work.'

"Tailoring," said Mrs. Harbonner. "I don't know nothing about women's fixtures,—except what'll keep me and Hephzibah above the savages. I don't suppose I could dress a doll so's it would sell."

"This is tailoring work," said Daisy. "It is a boy's

suit—and there will be more to do if you like to have it."

"Where is it? at the gate, did you say? Hephzibah, go and fetch it in. Who's got it?"

"The boy who is taking care of the horses."

"I declare, have you got that little covered shay there again?—it's complete! I never see a thing so pretty! And Hephzibah says you drive that little critter yourself. Aint you afraid?"

"Not at all," said Daisy. "The pony won't do any harm."

"He looks skeery," said Mrs. Harbonner. "I wouldn't trust him. What a tremenjious thick mane he's got! Well, I s'pect you have everything you want, don't you?"

"Of such things—" said Daisy.

"That's what I meant. Gracious! I s'pose every one of us has wishes—whether they are in the air or on the earth. Wishes is the butter to most folks' bread. Here, child."

She took the bundle from Hephzibah, unrolled it, and examined its contents with a satisfied face.

"What did *you* come along with this for?" she said suddenly to Daisy. "Why didn't you send it?"

"I wanted to come and see you," said Daisy pleasantly.

"What ails you? You ain't so well as when you was here before," said Mrs. Harbonner, looking at her narrowly.

"I am well," said Daisy.

"You aint fur from bein' something else then. I suppose you're dyin' with learning—while my Hephzibah can't get schooling enough to read her own name. That's the way the world's made up!"

"Isn't there a school at Crum Elbow?" said Daisy.

"Isn't there! And isn't there a bench for the rags? No, my Hephzibah don't go to shew none."

Mrs. Harbonner was so sharp and queer, though not unkindly towards herself, that Daisy was at a loss how to go on; and moreover, a big thought began to turn about in her head.

"Poverty ain't no shame, but it's an inconvenience," said Mrs. Harbonner. "Hephzibah may stay to home and be stupid, when she's as much right to be smart as anybody. That's what I look at; it ain't having a little to eat now and then."

"Melbourne is too far off for her to get there, isn't it?" said Daisy.

"What should she go there for?"

"If she could get there," said Daisy, "and would like it,—I would teach her."

"*You* would?" said Mrs. Harbonner. "What would you learn her?"

"I would teach her to read," said Daisy, colouring a little; "and anything else I could."

"La, she can read," said Mrs. Harbonner, "but she don't know nothing, for all that. Readin' don't tell a person much, without he has books. I wonder how long it would hold out, if you begun? 'Taint no use to begin a thing and then not go on."

"But could she get to Melbourne?" said Daisy.

"I don't know. Maybe she can. Who'd she see at your house?"

"Nobody, but the man at the lodge, or his mother."

"Who's that?"

"He's the man that lives in the lodge, to open the gate."

"Open the gate, hey? Who pays him for it?"

"Papa pays him, and he lives in the lodge."

"I shouldn't think it would take a man to open a gate. Why Hephzibah could do it as well as anybody."

Daisy did not see the point of this remark, and went on. "Hephzibah wouldn't see anybody else, but me."

"Well, I believe you mean what you say," said Mrs. Harbonner, "and I hope you will when you're twenty years older—but I don't believe it. I'll let Hephzibah come over to you on Sundays—I know she's jumpin' out of her skin to go—she shall go on Sundays, but I can't let her go other days, 'cause she's got work to do; and anyhow it would be too fur. What time would you like to see her?"

"As soon as it can be after afternoon church, if you please. I couldn't before."

"You're a kind little soul!" said the woman. "Do you like flowers?"

Daisy said yes. The woman went to a back door of the room, and opening it, plucked a branch from a great rose-bush that grew there.

"We haint but one pretty thing about this house," said she presenting it to Daisy,—"but that's kind o' pretty."

It was a very rich and delicious white rose, and the branch was an elegant one, clustered with flowers and buds. Daisy gave her thanks and took leave.

"As we have opportunity, let us do good unto all men." There was a little warm drop of comfort in Daisy's heart as she drove away. If she could not go to Sunday-school herself, she might teach somebody else yet more needy; that would be the next best thing. Sunday afternoon—it looked bright to Daisy; but then her heart sank; Sunday evening would be near. What should she do? She could not settle it in her mind what was right; between her mother's anger and her father's love, Daisy could not see what was just the plumb line of duty. Singing would gain a hundred dollars' worth of good; and not singing would disobey her mother and displease her father; but then came the words of one that Daisy honoured more than father and mother—"Remember that thou keep holy the Sabbath day;" and she could not tell what to do.

CHAPTER XIII.

Daisy had gone but a little way out of the village, when she suddenly pulled up. Sam was at the side of the chaise immediately.

"Sam, I want a glass of water; where can I get it?"

"Guess at Mrs. Benoit's, Miss Daisy. There's a fine spring of cold water."

"Who is Mrs. Benoit?"

"It's Juanita—Miss Daisy has heard of Mrs. St. Leonard's Juanita. Mr. St. Leonard built a house for her,—just the other side o' them trees."

Daisy knew who Juanita was. She had been brought from the West Indies by the mother of one of the gentlemen who lived in the neighbourhood; and upon the death of her mistress had been established in a little house of her own. Daisy judged that she would be quite safe in going there for water.

"If I turn into that road, can I go home round that way, Sam?"

"You can, Miss Daisy; but it's a ways longer."

"I like that," said Daisy.

She turned up the road that led behind the trees, and presently saw Juanita's cottage. A little grey stone house, low-roofed, standing at the very edge of a piece of woodland, and some little distance back from the road. Daisy saw the old woman sitting on her doorstep. A grassy slope stretched down from the house to the road. The sun shone up against the grey cottage.

"You take care of Loupe, Sam, and I'll go in," said Daisy. A plan which probably disappointed Sam, but Daisy did not know that. She went through a little wicket and up the path.

Juanita did not look like the blacks she had been accustomed to see. *Black* she was not, but of a fine olive dark skin; and though certainly old, she was still straight and tall and very fine in her appearance and bearing. Daisy could see this but partially while Juanita was sitting at her door; she was more struck by the very grave look her face wore just then. It was not turned towards her little visiter, and Daisy got the impression that she must be feeling unhappy.

Juanita rose however with great willingness to get the water, and asked Daisy into her house. Daisy dared not, after her father's prohibition, go in, and she stood at the door till the water was brought. Then with a strong feeling of kindness towards the lonely and perhaps sorrowful old woman, and remembering to "do good as she had opportunity," Daisy suddenly offered her the beautiful rose-branch.

"Does the lady think I want pay for a glass of water?" said the woman, with a smile that was extremely winning.

"No," said Daisy,—"but I thought, perhaps, you liked flowers."

"There's another sort of flowers that the Lord likes," —said the woman looking at her; "they be his little children."

Daisy's heart was tender, and there was something in Juanita's face that won her confidence. Instead of turning away, she folded her hands unconsciously and said, more wistfully than she knew, "I want to be one!"

"Does my little lady know the Lord Jesus?" said the woman, with a bright light coming into her eye.

Daisy's heart was sore as well as tender; the question

touched two things,—the joy that she did know him, and the trouble that following him had cost her; she burst into tears. Then turning away and with a great effort throwing off the tears, she went back to the chaise. There stood Sam with the pony's foot in his hand.

"Miss Daisy, this fellow has kicked one of his shoes half off; he can't go home so; it's hanging. Could Miss Daisy stop a little while at Mrs. Benoit's, I could take the pony to the blacksmith's—it ain't but a very little ways off—and get it put on, in a few minutes."

"Well, do, Sam,"—said Daisy after she had looked at the matter; and while he took Loupe out of harness she turned back to Juanita.

"What is gone wrong?" said the old woman.

"Nothing is wrong," said Daisy; "only the pony has got his shoe off, and the boy is taking him to the blacksmith's."

"Will my lady come into my house?"

"No, thank you. I'll stay here."

The woman brought out a low chair for her and set it on the grass; and took herself her former place on the sill of the door. She looked earnestly at Daisy; and Daisy on her part had noticed the fine carriage of the woman, her pleasant features, and the bright handkerchief which made her turban. Through the open door she could see the neat order of the room within, and her eye caught some shells arranged on shelves; but Daisy did not like to look, and she turned away. She met Juanita's eye; she felt she must speak.

"This is a pleasant place."

"Why does my lady think so?"

"It looks pleasant," said Daisy. "It is nice. The grass is pretty, and the trees; and it is a pretty little house, I think." The woman smiled.

"I think it be a palace of beauty," she said,—"for Jesus is here."

Daisy looked, a little wondering but entirely respectful; the whole aspect of Juanita commanded that.

"Does my little lady know, that the presence of the King makes a poor house fine?"

"I don't quite know what you mean," said Daisy humbly.

"Does my little lady know that the Lord Jesus loves his people?"

"Yes," said Daisy,—"I know it."

"But she know not much. When a poor heart say any time, 'Lord, I am all thine!'—then the Lord comes to that heart and he makes it the house of a King—for he comes there *himself*. And where Jesus is,—all is glory! Do not my little lady read that in the Bible?"

"I don't remember"—said Daisy.

The woman got up, went into the cottage, and brought out a large print Testament which she put into Daisy's hands, open at the fourteenth chapter of John. Daisy read with curious interest the words to which she was directed.

"Jesus answered and said unto him, If a man love me, he will keep my words: and my Father will love him, and we will come unto him and make our abode with him."

Daisy looked at the promise, with her heart beating under troublesome doubts; when the voice of Juanita broke in upon them by saying, tenderly,

"Does my little lady keep the Lord's words?"

Down went the book, and the tears rushed into Daisy's eyes.

"Don't call me so," she cried,—"I am Daisy Randolph; —and I do want to keep his words!—and—I don't know how."

"What troubles my love?" said the woman, in low tones of a voice that was always sweet. "Do not she know what the words of the Lord be?"

"Yes,"—said Daisy, hardly able to make herself understood,—"but—"

"Then do 'em," said Juanita. "The way is straight. What he say, do."

"But suppose ——" said Daisy.

"Suppose what? What do my love suppose?"

"Wouldn't it make it right, if it would do a great deal of good?"

This confused sentence Juanita pondered over.

"What does my love mean?"

"If it would do a great deal of good—wouldn't that make it right to do something?"

"Right to do something that the Lord say *not* do?"

"Yes."

"If you love Jesus, you not talk so," said Juanita sorrowfully. But that made Daisy give way altogether.

"O I do love him!—I do love him!" she cried;—"but I don't know what to do." And tears came in a torrent. Juanita was watchful and thoughtful. When Daisy had very soon checked herself, she said in the same low, gentle way in which she had before spoken, "What do the Lord say—to do that some good thing,—or to keep his words?"

"To keep his words."

"Then keep 'em—and the Lord will do the good thing himself; that same or another. He can do what he please; and he tell you, only keep his words. He want you to shew you love him—and he tell you how."

Daisy sat quite still to let the tears pass away and the struggle in her heart grow calm; then when she could safely she looked up. She met Juanita's eye. It was fixed on her.

"Is the way straight now?" she asked. Daisy nodded, with a little bit of a smile on her poor little lips.

"But there is trouble in the way?" said Juanita.

"Yes," said Daisy, and the old woman saw the eyes redden again.

"Has the little one a good friend at home to help?"

Daisy shook her head.

"Then let Jesus help. My little lady keep the Lord's words, and the sweet Lord Jesus will keep her." And rising to her feet and clasping her hands, where she stood, Juanita poured forth a prayer. It was for her little visiter. It was full of love. It was full of confidence too; and of such clear simplicity as if, like Stephen, she had *seen* the heavens open. But the loving strength of it won Daisy's heart; and when the prayer was finished she came close to the old woman and threw her arms round her as she stood, and wept with her face hid in Juanita's dress. Yet the prayer had comforted her too, greatly. And though Daisy was very shy of intimacies with strangers, she liked to feel Juanita's hand on her shoulder; and after the paroxysm of tears was past, she still stood quietly by her, without attempting to increase the distance between them; till she saw Sam coming down the lane with the pony.

"Good bye," said Daisy, "there's the boy."

"My lady will come to see old Juanita again?"

"I am Daisy Randolph. I'll come,"—said the child, looking lovingly up. Then she went down the slope to Sam.

"The blacksmith couldn't shoe him, Miss Daisy—he hadn't a shoe to fit. He took off the old shoe—so Miss Daisy please not drive him hard home."

Daisy wanted nothing of the kind. To get home soon was no pleasure; so she let Loupe take his own pace, anything short of walking; and it was getting dusk when they reached Melbourne. Daisy was not glad to be there. It was Friday night; the next day would be Saturday.

Mrs. Randolph came out into the hall to see that nothing was the matter, and then went back into the drawing-room. Daisy got her dress changed, and came there too, where the family were waiting for tea. She came in softly and sat down by herself at a table somewhat removed from the others, who were all busily talking and laughing. But presently Capt. Drummond drew near and sat down at her side.

"Have you had a good drive, Daisy?"

"Yes, Capt. Drummond."

"We missed our history to-day, but I have been making preparations. Shall we go into the Saxon Heptarchy to-morrow—you and I—and see if we can get the kingdom settled?"

"If you please. I should like it very much."

"What is the matter with you, Daisy?"

Daisy lifted her wise little face, which indeed looked as if it were heavy with something beside wisdom, towards her friend; she was not ready with an answer.

"You aren't going to die on the field of battle yet, Daisy?" he said half lightly, and half he knew not why. It brought a rush of colour to the child's face; the self-possession must have been great which kept her from giving way to further expression of feeling. She answered with curious calmness,

"I don't think I shall, Capt. Drummond."

The Captain saw it was a bad time to get anything from her, and he moved away. Preston came the next minute.

"Why Daisy," he whispered, drawing his chair close, "where have you been all day? No getting a sight of you. What have you been about?"

"I have been to Crum Elbow this afternoon."

"Yes, and how late you stayed. Why did you?"

"Loupe lost a shoe. I had to wait for Sam to go to the blacksmith's with him."

"Really. Did you wait in the road?"

"No. I had a place to wait."

"I dare say you are as hungry as a bear," said Preston. "Now here comes tea—and waffles, Daisy; you shall have some waffles and cream. That will make you feel better."

"Cream isn't good with waffles," said Daisy.

"Yes it is. Cream is good with everything. You shall try. I know! I am always cross myself when I am hungry."

"I am not hungry, Preston; and I don't think I am cross."

"What are you, then? Come, Daisy,—here is a cup of tea, and here is a waffle. First the sugar—there,—then the cream. So."

"You have spoiled it, Preston."

"Eat it—and confess you are hungry and cross too."

Daisy could have laughed, only she was too sore-hearted, and would surely have cried. She fell to eating the creamed waffle.

"Is it good?"

"Very good!"

"Confess you are hungry and cross, Daisy."

"I am not cross. And Preston, please!—don't!" Daisy's fork fell; but she took it up again.

"What is the matter, then, Daisy?"

Daisy did not answer; she went on eating as diligently as she could.

"Is it that foolish business of the song?" whispered Preston. "Is *that* the trouble, Daisy?"

"Please don't, Preston!"—

"Well I won't, till you have had another waffle. Sugar and cream, Daisy?"

"Yes."

"That's brave! Now eat it up—and tell me, Daisy, is *that* the trouble with you?"

He spoke affectionately, as he almost always did to her; and Daisy did not throw him off.

"You don't understand it, Preston," she said.

"Daisy, I told you my uncle and aunt would not like that sort of thing."

Daisy was silent, and Preston wondered at her. Mrs.

Gary drew near at this moment, and placed herself opposite Daisy's tea-cup, using her eyes in the first place.

"What are you talking about?" said she.

"About Daisy's singing, ma'am."

"That's the very thing," said Mrs. Gary, "that I wanted to speak about. Daisy, my dear, I hope you are going to sing it properly to your mother the next time she bids you?"

Daisy was silent.

"I wanted to tell you, my dear," said Mrs. Gary impressively, "what a poor appearance your refusal made, the other evening. You could not see it for yourself; but it made you seem awkward, and foolish, and ill-bred. I am sure everybody would have laughed, if it had not been for politeness towards your mother; for the spectacle was ludicrous, thoroughly. You like to make a graceful appearance, don't you?"

Daisy answered in a low voice,—"Yes, ma'am; when I can."

"Well you *can*, my dear, for your behaviour is generally graceful, and unexceptionable; only the other night it was very rough and uncouth. I expected you to put your finger in your mouth the next thing, and stand as if you had never seen anybody. And Daisy Randolph!—the heiress of Melbourne and Cranford!"—

The heiress of Melbourne and Cranford lifted to her aunt's face a look strangely in contrast with the look bent on her; so much worldly wisdom was in the one, so much want of it in the other. Yet those steady grey eyes were not without a wisdom of their own; and Mrs. Gary met them with a puzzled feeling of it.

"Do you understand me, Daisy, my dear?"

"Yes, ma'am."

"Do you see that it is desirable never to look ridiculous, and well-bred persons never do?"

"Yes, aunt Gary."

"Then I am sure you won't do it again. It would mortify me for your father and mother."

Mrs. Gary walked away. Daisy looked thoughtful.

"Will you do it, Daisy?" whispered Preston.

"What?"

"Will you sing the song for them next time? You will, won't you?"

"I'll do what I can"—said Daisy. But it was said so soberly, that Preston was doubtful of her. However he, like Capt. Drummond, had got to the end of his resources for that time; and seeing his uncle approach, Preston left his seat.

Mr. Randolph took it and drew Daisy from her own to a place in his arms. He sat then silent a good while, or talking to other people; only holding her close and tenderly. Truth to tell, Mr. Randolph was a little troubled about the course things were taking; and Daisy and her father were a grave pair that evening.

Daisy felt his arms were a pleasant shield between her and all the world; if they might only *keep* round her! And then she thought of Juanita's prayer, and of the invisible shield, of a stronger and more loving arm, that the Lord Jesus puts between his children and all real harm.

At last Mr. Randolph bent down his head and brought his lips to Daisy's, asking her if she had had a nice time that afternoon.

"Very, papa!" said Daisy gratefully; and then added after a little hesitation, "Papa, do you know old Juanita? —Mrs. St. Leonard's woman, that Mr. St. Leonard built a little house for?"

"I do not know her. I believe I have heard of her."

"Papa, would you let me go into *her* house? She has some beautiful shells that I should like to see."

"How do you know?"

"I saw them, papa, through the doorway of her house,

I waited there while Sam went with Loupe to the blacksmith's."

"And you did not go in?"

"No, sir—you said I must not, you know."

"I believe Juanita is a safe person, Daisy. You may go in, if ever you have another opportunity."

"Thank you, papa."

"What are you going to do with the hundred dollars?" said Mr. Randolph, putting his head down and speaking softly.

Daisy waited a minute, checked the swelling of her heart, forbade her tears, steadied her voice to speak; and then said, "I sha'n't have them, papa."

"Why not?"

"I can't fulfil the conditions." Daisy spoke again after waiting a minute.

"Don't you mean to sing?"

Every time Daisy waited.—"I can't, papa."

"Your mother will require it."

Silence, only Mr. Randolph saw that the child's breath went and came under excitement.

"Daisy, she will require it."

"Yes, papa"—was said rather faintly.

"And I think you must do it."

No response from Daisy; and no sign of yielding.

"How do you expect to get over it?"

"Papa, won't you help me?" was the child's agonized cry. She hid her face in her father's breast.

"I have tried to help you. I will give you what will turn your fancied wrong deed into a good one. It is certainly right to do charitable things on Sunday."

There was silence, and it promised to last some time. Mr. Randolph would not hurry her: and Daisy was thinking, "If ye love me, keep my commandments." "*If ye love me.*"—

"Papa,"—said she at last, very slowly, and pausing between her words,—" would you be satisfied,—if I should disobey you—for a hundred dollars?"

This time it was Mr. Randolph that did not answer, and the longer he waited the more the answer did not come. He put Daisy gently off his knee and rose at last without speaking. Daisy went out upon the verandah and sat down on the step; and there the stars seemed to say to her—"If a man love me, he will keep my words." They were shining very bright; so was that saying to Daisy. She sat looking at them, forgetting all the people in the drawing-room; and though troubled enough, she was not utterly unhappy. The reason was, she loved her King.

Somebody came behind her and took hold of her shoulders. "My dear little Daisy!" said the voice of Preston, "I wish you were an India-rubber ball, that I might chuck you up to the sky and down again a few times!"

"Why? I don't think it would be nice."

"Why?—why because you want shaking; you are growing dull,—yes, absolutely you are getting heavy! you, little Daisy! of all people in the world. It won't do."

"I don't think such an exercise would benefit me," said Daisy.

"I'd find something else then. Daisy, Daisy," said he, shaking her shoulders gently, "this religious foolery is spoiling you. Don't *you* go and make yourself stupid. Why I don't know you. What is all this ridiculous stuff? You aren't yourself."

"What do you want me to do, Preston?" said Daisy standing before him, not without a certain childish dignity. It was lost on him.

"I want you to be my own little Daisy," said he coaxingly. "Come!—say you will, and give up these outlandish notions you have got from some old woman or other. What is it they want you to do?—sing?—Come, promise you will. Promise me!"

"I will sing any day but Sunday."

"Sunday? Now Daisy! I'm ashamed of you. Why I never heard such nonsense. Nobody has such notions but low people. It isn't sensible. Give it up, Daisy, or I shall not know how to love you."

"Good night, Preston"——

"Daisy, Daisy! come and kiss me and be good."

"Good night"—repeated Daisy without turning; and she walked off.

It half broke June's heart that night to see that the child's eyes were quietly dropping tears all the while she was getting undressed. Preston's last threat had cut very close. But Daisy said not a word; and when, long after June had left her, she got into bed and lay down, it was not Preston's words but the reminder of the stars that was with her and making harmony among all her troubled thoughts—"If a man love me, he will keep my words."

CHAPTER XIV.

In spite of the burden that lay on Daisy's heart, she and Capt. Drummond had a good time the next morning over the Saxon Heptarchy. They went down to the shore for it, at Daisy's desire, where they would be undisturbed; and the morning was hardly long enough. The Captain had provided himself with a shallow tray filled with modelling clay; which he had got from an artist friend living a few miles further up the river. On this the plan of England was nicely marked out, and by the help of one or two maps which he cut up for the occasion, the Captain divided off the seven kingdoms greatly to Daisy's satisfaction and enlightenment. Then, how they went on with the history! introduced Christianity, enthroned Egbert, and defeated the Danes under Alfred. They read from the book, and fought it all out on the clay plan as they went along. At Alfred they stopped a good while, to consider the state of the world in the little island of Britain at that time. The good king's care for his people, his love for study and encouragement of learning; his writing fables for the people; his wax candles to mark time; his building with brick and stone; his founding the English navy, and victories with the same; no less than his valour and endurance in every time of trial; all these things Capt. Drummond whose father had been an Englishman, duly enlarged upon, and Daisy heard them with greedy ears. Truth to tell, the Captain had read up a little for the occasion, being a good deal moved with sympathy for his little friend, who he saw was going through a time of some trial. Nothing was to be seen of that just now, indeed, other than the peculiarly soft and grave expression which Daisy's face had worn all this week; and which kept reminding the Captain to be sorry for her.

They got through with Alfred at last—by the way, the Captain had effaced the dividing lines of the seven kingdoms and brought all to one in Egbert's time—and now they went on with Alfred's successors. A place was found on the sand for Denmark and Norway to shew themselves; and Sweyn and Canute came over; and there was no bating to the interest with which the game of human life went on. In short, Daisy and the Captain having tucked themselves away in a nook of the beach and the tenth and eleventh centuries, were lost to all the rest of the world and to the present time; till a servant at last found them with the information that the luncheon bell had rung, and Mrs. Randolph was ready to go out with the Captain. And William the Conqueror had just landed at Hastings!

"Never mind, Daisy," said the Captain; "we'll go on with it, the next chance we get."

Daisy thanked him earnestly, but the thought that Sunday must come and go first, threw a shadow over her thanks. The Captain saw it; and walked home thinking curiously about the "field of battle"—not Hastings.

Daisy did not go in to luncheon. She did not like meeting all the people who felt so gay, while she felt so much trouble. Nor did she like being with her mother, whose manner all the week had constantly reminded Daisy of what Daisy never forgot. The rest of Saturday passed soberly away. There was a cloud in the air.

And the cloud was high and dark Sunday morning, though it was as fair a summer day as might be seen. Some tears escaped stealthily from Daisy's eyes, as she knelt in the little church beside her mother; but the prayers were deep and sweet and strong to her, very much.

Sadly sorry was Daisy when they were ended. The rest of the service was little to her. Mr. Pyne did not preach like Mr. Dinwiddie; and she left the church with a downcast heart, thinking that so much of the morning was past.

The rest of the day Daisy kept by herself, in her own room; trying to get some comfort in reading and praying. For the dread of the evening was strong upon her; every movement of her mother spoke displeasure and determination. Daisy felt her heart beating gradually quicker and quicker, as the hours of the day wore on.

"Ye ain't well, Miss Daisy,"—said June, who had come in as usual without being heard.

"Yes I am, June," said Daisy. But she had started when the woman spoke, and June saw that now a tear sprang.

"Did you eat a good lunch, Miss Daisy?"

"I don't know, June. I guess I didn't eat much."

"Let me bring you something!"—said the woman coaxingly—"some strawberries, with some good cream to 'em."

"No—I can't, June—I don't want them. What o'clock is it?"

"It is just on to five, Miss Daisy."

Five! Daisy suddenly recollected her scholar, whom she had directed to come to her at this hour. Jumping up she seized her hat and rushed off down stairs and through the shrubbery, leaving June lost in wonder and concern.

At a Belvidere, some distance from the house and nearer the gate, Daisy had chosen to meet her pupil; and she had given orders at the Lodge to have her guided thither when she should come. And there she was; Daisy could see the red head of hair before she got to the place herself. Hephzibah looked very much as she did on week days; her dress partially covered with a little shawl; her bonnet she had thrown off; and if the hair had been coaxed into any state of smoothness before leaving home, it was all gone now.

THE BELVIDERE.

"How do you do, Hephzibah?" said Daisy. "I am glad to see you."

Hephzibah smiled, but unless that meant a civil answer, she gave none. Daisy sat down beside her.

"Do you know how to read, Hephzibah?"

The child first shook her shaggy head—then nodded it. What that meant, Daisy was somewhat at a loss.

"Do you know your letters?"

Hephzibah nodded.

"What is that letter?"

Daisy had not forgotten to bring a reading book, and now put Hephzibah through the alphabet, which she seemed to know perfectly, calling each letter by its right name. Daisy then asked if she could read words; and getting an assenting nod again, she tried her in that. But here Hephzibah's education was defective; she could read indeed, after a fashion; but it was a slow and stumbling fashion; and Daisy and she were a good while getting through a page. Daisy shut the book up.

"Now Hephzibah," said she, "do you know anything about what is in the Bible?"

Hephzibah shook her head in a manner the reverse of encouraging.

"Did you never read the Bible, nor have any one read it to you?"

Another shake.

Daisy thereupon began to tell her little neighbour the grand story which concerned them both so nearly, making it as clear and simple as she could. Hephzibah's eyes were fixed on her intently all the while; and Daisy, greatly interested herself, wondered if any of the interest had reached Hephzibah's heart, and made the gaze of her eyes so unwavering. They expressed nothing. Daisy hoped, and went on, till at a pause Hephzibah gave utterance to the first words (of her own) that she had spoken during the interview. They came out very suddenly, like an unexpected jet of water from an unused fountain.

"Mother says, you're the fus'ratest little girl she ever see!"

Daisy was extremely confounded. The thread of her discourse was so thoroughly broken indeed, that she could not directly begin it again; and in the minute of waiting she saw how low the sun was. She dismissed Hephzibah, telling her to be at the Belvidere the same hour next Sunday.

As the shaggy little red head moved away through the bushes, Daisy watched it, wondering whether she had done the least bit of good. Then another thought made her heart beat, and she turned again to see how low the sun was. Instead of the sun she saw Gary McFarlane.

"Who is that, Daisy?" said he, looking after the disappearing red head.

"A poor little girl—" said Daisy.

"So I should think,—very poor!—looks so indeed! How came she here?"

"She came by my orders, Mr. McFarlane."

"By your orders! What have you got there, Daisy? Let's see! As sure as I'm alive!—a spelling book. Keeping school, Daisy? Don't say no!"

Daisy did not say no, nor anything. She had taken care not to let Gary get hold of her Bible; the rest she must manage as she could.

"This *is* benevolence!" went on the young man. "Teaching a spelling lesson in a Belvidere with the thermometer at 90° in the shade? What sinners all the rest of us are! I declare, Daisy, you make me feel bad."

"I should not think it, Mr. McFarlane."

"Daisy, you have *à plomb* enough for a princess, and gravity enough for a Puritan! I should like to see you when you are grown up,—only then I shall be an old man, and it will be of no consequence. What *do* you expect to do with that little red head?—now do tell me."

"She don't know anything, Mr. McFarlane."

"No more don't I! Come Daisy—have pity on me. You never saw anybody more ignorant than I am. There are half a dozen things at this moment which I don't know—and which you can tell me. Come, will you?"

"I must go in, Mr. McFarlane."

"But tell me first. Come, Daisy! I want to know why

is it so much more wicked to sing a song than to make somebody else singsong?—for that's the way they all do the spelling book, *I* know. Hey, Daisy?"

"How did you know anything about it, Mr. McFarlane?"

"Come, Daisy,—explain. I am all in a fog—or else you are. This spelling book seems to me a very wicked thing on Sunday."

"I will take it, if you please, Mr. McFarlane."

"Not if I know it! I want my ignorance instructed, Daisy. I am persuaded you are the best person to enlighten me—but if not, I shall try this spelling book on Mrs. Randolph. I regard it as a great curiosity, and an important question in metaphysics."

Poor Daisy! She did not know what to do; conscious that Gary was laughing at her all the while, and most unwilling that the story of the spelling book should get to Mrs. Randolph's ears. She stood hesitating and troubled, when her eye caught sight of Preston near. Springing to him she cried, "O Preston, get my little book from Mr. McFarlane—he won't give it to me."

There began then a race of the most uproarious sort between the two young men—springing, turning, darting round among the trees and bushes, shouting to and laughing at each other. Daisy another time would have been amused; now she was almost frightened, lest all this boisterous work should draw attention. At last, however, Preston got the spelling book, or Gary let himself be overtaken and gave it up.

"It's mischief, Preston!" he said;—"deep mischief—occult mischief. I give you warning."

"What is it, Daisy?" said Preston. "What is it all about?"

"Never mind. Oh Preston! don't ask anything, but let me have it!"

"There it is then; but Daisy," he said affectionately,

catching her in his arms,—" you are going to sing to-night, aren't you?"

"Don't Preston—don't! let me go," cried Daisy struggling to escape from him; and she ran away as soon as he let her, hardly able to keep back her tears. She felt it very hard. Preston and Gary, and her mother and her father,—all against her in different ways. Daisy kneeled down by her window-sill in her own room, to try to get comfort and strength; though she was in too great tumult to pray connectedly. Her little heart was beating sadly. But there was no doubt at all in Daisy's mind as to what she should do.—"If a man love me, he will keep my words." She never questioned now about doing that.

The dreaded tea bell rang, and she went down; but utterly unable to eat or drink through agitation. Nobody seemed to notice her particularly, and she wandered out upon the verandah; and waited there. There presently her father's arms came round her before she was aware.

"What are you going to do, Daisy?"

"Nothing, papa," she whispered.

"Are you not going to sing?"

"Papa, I can't!" cried Daisy dropping her face against his arm. Her father raised it again and drawing her opposite one of the windows, looked into the dark-ringed eyes and white face.

"You are not well," said he. "You are not fit to be up; and my orders to you, Daisy, are to go immediately to bed. I'll send you some medicine by and by. Good night!"

He kissed her, and Daisy needed no second bidding. She sprang away, getting into the house by another door; and lost no time. Her fear was that her mother might send for her before she could get undressed. But no summons came; June was speedy, thinking and saying it was a very good thing for Daisy to do; and then she went off and left her alone with the moonlight. Daisy was in no hurry then. She knelt by her beloved window, where the scent of the honeysuckle was strong in the dewy air; and with a less throbbing heart prayed her prayer. But she was not at ease yet; it was very uncertain in her mind how her mother would take this order of her father's; and what would come after, if she was willing to let it pass. So Daisy could not go to sleep, but lay wide awake and fearing in the moonlight, and listening to every sound in the house that came to her ears.

The moonlight shone in peacefully, and Daisy lying there and growing gradually calmer, began to wonder in herself that there should be so much difficulty made about anybody's doing right. If she had been set on some wrong thing, it would have made but a very little disturbance—if any; but now, when she was only trying to do right, the whole house was roused to prevent her. Was it so in those strange old times that the eleventh chapter of Hebrews told of?—when men, and women, were stoned, and sawn asunder, and slain with the sword, and wandered like wild animals in sheepskins and goatskins and in dens and caves of the earth? all for the name of Jesus. But if they suffered once, they were happy now. Better anything, at all events, than to deny that name!

The evening seemed excessively long to Daisy, lying there on her bed awake, and listening with strained ears for any sound near her room. She heard none; the hours passed, though so very slowly, as they do when all the minutes are watched; and Daisy heard nothing but dim distant noises, and grew pretty quiet. She had heard nothing else, when turning her head from the moonlight window she caught the sight of a white figure at her bedside; and by the noble form and stately proportions Daisy knew instantly whose figure it was. Those soft flowing draperies had been before her eyes all day. A pang shot through the child, that seemed to go from the crown of her head to the soles of her feet

"Are you awake, Daisy?"

"Yes, mamma," she said feebly.

"Get up. I want to speak to you."

Daisy got off the bed, and the white figure in the little night dress stood opposite the other white figure, robed in muslin and laces that fell around it like a cloud.

"Why did you come to bed?"

"Papa—papa ordered me."

"It's all the same. If you had not come to bed, Daisy if you had been well,—would you have sung when I ordered you to-night?"

"Daisy hesitated, and then said in a whisper:

"No, mamma—not that."

"Think before you answer me, for I shall not ask twice. Will you promise to sing the gypsy song, because I command you, next Sunday in the evening? Answer, Daisy."

Very low it was, for Daisy trembled so that she did not know how she could speak at all, but the answer came,—

"I can't, mamma."

Mrs. Randolph stepped to the bell and rang it. Almost at the same instant June entered, bearing a cup in her hand.

"What is that?" said Mrs. Randolph.

"Master sent Miss Daisy some medicine."

"Set it down. I have got some here better for her. June, take Daisy's hands."

"Oh mamma, no!" exclaimed Daisy. "Oh please send June away!"

The slight gesture of command to June which answered this, was as imperious as it was slight. It was characteristically like Mrs. Randolph; graceful and absolute. June obeyed it, as old instinct told her to do; though sorely against her will. She had held hands before, though not Daisy's; and she knew very well the look of the little whip with which her mistress stepped back into the room, having gone to her own for it. In a Southern home that whip had been wont to live in Mrs Randolph's pocket. June's heart groaned within her.

The whip was small but it had been made for use, not for play; and there was no play in Mrs. Randolph's use of it. This was not like her father's ferule, which Daisy could bear in silence, if tears would come; her mother's handling forced cries from her; though smothered and kept under in a way that shewed the child's self-command.

"What have you to say to me?" Mrs. Randolph responded, without waiting for the answer. But Daisy had none to give. At length her mother paused.

"Will you do what I bid you?"

Daisy was unable to speak for tears—and perhaps for fear. The wrinkles on June's brow were strangely folded together with agitation; but nobody saw them.

"Will you sing for me next Sunday?" repeated Mrs. Randolph.

There was a struggle in the child's heart, as great almost as a child's heart can bear. The answer came, when it came, tremblingly—

"I can't, mamma."

"You cannot?" said Mrs. Randolph.

"I can't, mamma."

The chastisement which followed was so severe, that June was moved out of all the habits of her life, to interfere in another's cause. The white-skinned race were no mark for trouble in June's mind; least of them all, her little charge. And if white skin was no more delicate in reality than dark skin, it answered to the lash much more speakingly.

"Missus, you'll kill her!" June said, using in her agitation a carefully disused form of speech; for June was a freedwoman. A slight turn of the whip brought the lash sharply across her wrist, with the equally sharp words, "Mind your own business!"

A thrill went through the woman, like an electric spark

firing a whole life-train of feeling and memory; but the lines of her face never moved, and not the stirring of a muscle told what the touch had reached, besides a few nerves. She had done her charge no good by her officiousness, as June presently saw with grief. It was not till Mrs. Randolph had thoroughly satisfied her displeasure at being thwarted, and not until Daisy was utterly exhausted, that Mrs. Randolph stayed her hand.

"I will see what you will say to me next Sunday!" she remarked calmly. And she left the room.

It was not that Mrs. Randolph did not love her daughter, in her way; for in her way she was fond of Daisy; but the habit of bearing no opposition to her authority was life-strong, and probably intensified in the present instance by perceiving that her husband was disposed to shield the offender. The only person in whose favour the rule ever relaxed, was Ransom.

June was left with a divided mind, between the dumb indignation which had never known speech, and an almost equally speechless concern. Daisy as soon as she was free had made her way to the window; there the child was, on her knees, her head on her window sill, and weeping as if her very heart were melting and flowing away drop by drop. And June stood like a dark statue, looking at her; the wrinkles in her forehead scarce testifying to the work going on under it. She wanted first of all to see Daisy in bed; but it seemed hopeless to speak to her; and there the little round head lay on the window-sill, and the moonbeams poured in lovingly over it. June stood still and never stirred.

It was a long while before Daisy's sobs began to grow fainter, and June ventured to put in her word and got Daisy to lay herself on the bed again. Then June went off after another sort of medicine of her own devising, despising the drops which Mr. Randolph had given her. Without making a confidant of the housekeeper, she contrived to get from her the materials to make Daisy a cup of arrowroot with wine and spices. June knew well how to be a cook when she pleased; and what she brought to Daisy was, she knew, as good as a cook could make it. She found the child lying white and still on the bed, and not asleep, nor dead, which June had almost feared at first sight of her. She didn't want the arrowroot, she said.

"Miss Daisy, s'pose you take it?" said June. "It won't do you no hurt—maybe it'll put you to sleep."

Daisy was perhaps too weak to resist. She rose half up and eat the arrowroot, slowly, and without a word. It did put a little strength into her, as June had said. But when she gave back the cup and let herself fall again upon her pillow, Daisy said,

"June, I'd like to die."

"O why, Miss Daisy?" said June.

"Jesus knows that I love him now; and I'd like—" said the child steadying her voice—"I'd like—to be in heaven!"

"O no, Miss Daisy—not yet; you've got a great deal to do in the world first."

"Jesus knows I love him—" repeated the child.

"Miss Daisy, he knowed it before—he's the Lord."

"Yes, but—he wants people to *shew* they love him, June."

"Do, don't! Miss Daisy," said June half crying. "Can't ye go to sleep? Do, now!"

It was but three minutes more, and Daisy had complied with her request. June watched and saw that the sleep was real; went about the room on her noiseless feet; came back to Daisy's bed, and finally went off for her own pillow, with which she lay down on the matting at the foot of the bed, and there passed the remainder of the night.

CHAPTER XV.

The sun was shining bright the next morning, and Daisy sat on one of the seats under the trees, half in sunshine, half in shadow. It was after breakfast, and she had been scarcely seen or heard that morning before. Ransom came up.

"Daisy, do you want to go fishing?"

"No, I think not."

"You don't! What are you going to do?"

"I am not going to do anything."

"I don't believe it. What ails you? Mother said I was to ask you—and there you sit like a wet feather. I am glad I am not a girl, however!"

Ransom went off, and a very faint colour rose in Daisy's cheek.

"Are you not well, Daisy?" said Mr. Randolph, who had also drawn near.

"I am well, papa."

"You don't look so. What's the matter, that you don't go a fishing, when Ransom has the consideration to ask you?"

Daisy's tranquillity was very nearly overset. But she maintained it, and only answered without the change of a muscle, "I have not the inclination, papa." Indeed her face was *too* quiet; and Mr. Randolph putting that with its colourless hue, and the very sweet upward look her eyes had first given him, was not satisfied. He went away to the breakfast room.

"Felicia," said he low, bending down by his wife,—"did you have any words with Daisy last night?"

"Has she told you about it?" said Mrs. Randolph.

"Told me what? What is there to tell?"

"Nothing, on my part," answered the lady nonchalantly. "Daisy may tell you what she pleases."

"Felicia," said Mr. Randolph looking much vexed, "that child has borne too much already. She is ill."

"It is her own fault. I told you, Mr. Randolph, I would as lief not have a child as not have her mind me. She shall do what I bid her, if she dies for it."

"It won't come to that," said Mrs. Gary. Mr. Randolph turned on his heel.

Meantime, another person who had seen with sorrow Daisy's pale face, and had half a guess as to the cause of it, came up to her side and sat down.

"Daisy, what is to be done to-day?"

"I don't know, Capt. Drummond."

"You don't feel like storming the heights, this morning?"

Again, to him also, the glance of Daisy's eye was so very sweet and so very wistful, that the captain was determined in a purpose he had half had in his mind.

"What do you say to a long expedition, Daisy?"

"I don't feel like driving, Capt. Drummond."

"No, but suppose I drive,—and we will leave Loupe at home for to-day. I want to go as far as Schroeder's Hill, to look after trilobites; and I do not want anybody with me but you. Shall we go?"

"What are those things, Capt. Drummond?"

"Trilobites?"

"Yes. What are they?"

"Curious things, Daisy! They are a kind of fish that are found on land."

"Fish on land! But then they can't be fish, Capt. Drummond?"

"Suppose we go and see," said the captain; "and then

if we find any, we shall know more about them than we do now."

"But how do you catch them?"

"With my hands, I suppose."

"With your *hands*, Capt. Drummond?"

"Really I don't know any other way,—unless your hands will help. Come! shall we go and try?"

Daisy slowly rose up, very mystified, but with a little light of interest and curiosity breaking on her face. The Captain moved off on his part to get ready, well satisfied that he was doing a good thing.

It went to the Captain's heart nevertheless, for he had a kind one, to see all the way how pale and quiet Daisy's face was. She asked him no more about trilobites, she did not talk about anything; the subjects the Captain started were soon let drop. And not because she was too ill to talk, for Daisy's eye was thoughtfully clear and steady, and the Captain had no doubt but she was busy enough in her own mind with things she did not bring out. What sort of things? he was very curious to know. For he had never seen Daisy's face so exceeding sweet in its expression as he saw it now; though the cheeks were pale and worn, there was in her eye whenever it was lifted to his a light of something hidden that the Captain could not read. It was true. Daisy had sat stunned and dull all the morning until he came with his proposal for the drive; and with the first stir of excitement in getting ready, a returning tide of love had filled the dry places in Daisy's heart; and it was full now of feelings that only wanted a chance to come out. Meanwhile she sat as still as a mouse and as grave as a judge.

The hill for which they were bound was some dozen or more miles away. It was a wild rough place. Arrived at the foot of it, they could go no further by the road; the Captain tied his horse to a tree, and he and Daisy scrambled up the long winding ascent, thick with briars and bushes, or strewn with pieces of rock and shaded with a forest of old trees. This was hard walking for Daisy today; she did not feel like struggling with any difficulties, and her poor little feet almost refused to carry her through the roughnesses of the last part of the way. She was very glad when they reached the ground where the Captain wanted to explore, and she could sit down and be still. It was quite on the other side of the mountain; a strange looking place. The face of the hill was all bare of trees, and seemed to be nothing but rock; and jagged and broken as if quarriers had been there cutting and blasting. Nothing but a steep surface of broken rock; bare enough; but it was from the sun, and Daisy chose the first smooth fragment to sit down upon. Then what a beautiful place! For from that rocky seat, her eye had a range over acres and acres of waving slopes of tree tops; down in the valley at the mountain foot, and up and down so many slopes and ranges of swelling and falling hillsides and dells, that the eye wandered from one to another and another, softer and softer as the distance grew, or brighter and more varied as the view came nearer home. A wilderness all, no roof of a house nor smoke from a chimney even; but those sunny ranges of hills, over which now and then a cloud shadow was softly moving, and which finished in a dim blue horizon.

"Well, are you going to sit here?" said the Captain, "or will you help me to hunt up my fishes?"

"O I'll sit here," said Daisy. She did not believe much in the success of the Captain's hunt.

"Won't you be afraid, while I am going all over creation?"

"Of what?" said Daisy.

The Captain laughed a little and went off; thinking however not so much of his trilobites as of the sweet fearless look the little face had given him. Uneasy about the child too, for Daisy's face looked not as he liked to see it look. But where got she that steady calm, and curious fearlessness. "She is a timid child," thought the Captain as he climbed over the rocks; "or she was, the other night."

But the Captain and Daisy were looking with different eyes; no wonder they did not find the same things. In all that sunlit glow over hill and valley, which warmed every tree-top, Daisy had seen only another light,—the love of the Lord Jesus Christ. With that love round her, over her, how could she fear anything. She sat a little while resting and thinking; then being weary and feeling weak, she slipped down on the ground, and like Jacob taking a stone for her pillow, she went to sleep.

So the Captain found her, every time he came back from his hunt to look after his charge; he let her sleep, and went off again. He had a troublesome hunt. At last he found some traces of what he sought; then he forgot Daisy in his eagerness, and it was after a good long interval the last time that he came to Daisy's side again. She was awake.

"What have you got?" she said as he came up with his hands full.

"I have got my fish."

"Have you! O where is it?"

"How do you do?" said the Captain sitting down beside her.

"I do very well. Where is the fish? You have got nothing but stones there, Capt. Drummond?"

The Captain without speaking displayed one of the stones he had in his hand. It looked very curious. Upon a smooth flat surface, where the stone had been split, there was a raised part which had the appearance of some sort of animal; but this too seemed to be stone, and was black and shining, though its parts were distinct.

"What is that, Capt. Drummond? It is a stone."

"It is a fish."

"*That?*"

"That."

"But you are laughing."

"Am I?" said the Captain, as grave as a senator. "It's a fish for all that."

"This curious black thing?"

"Precisely."

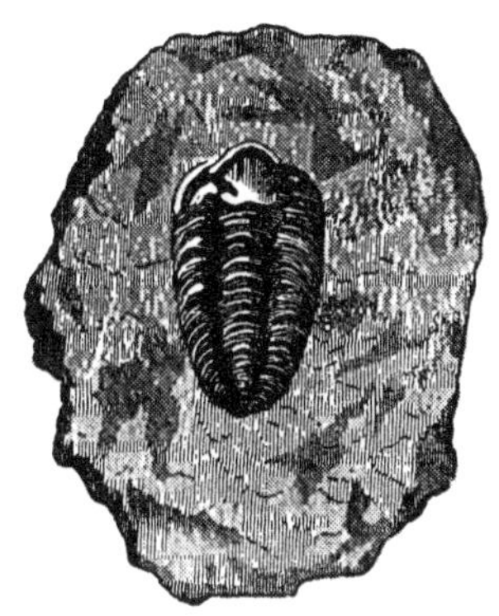

"What sort of a fish?"

"Daisy, have you had any luncheon?"

"No, sir."

"Then you had better discuss that subject first. Soldiers cannot get along without their rations, you'll find."

"What is that?" said Daisy.

"Rations?"

"Yes, sir."

"Daily bread, Daisy. Of one sort or another as the case may be. Where is that basket?"

Daisy had charge of it and would not let him take it out of her hands. She unfolded napkins, and permitted the Captain to help himself when she had all things ready. Then bread and butter and salad were found to be very refreshing. But while Daisy eat, she looked at the trilobite.

"Please tell me what it is, Capt. Drummond."

"It is a Crustacean."

"But you know I don't know what a Crustacean is."

"A Crustacean, is a fellow who wears his bones on the outside."

"Capt. Drummond! What do you mean?"

"Well I mean that, Daisy. Did you never hear of the way soldiers used to arm themselves for the fight in old times? in plates of jointed armour?"

"Yes, I know they did."

"Well these fellows are armed just so—only they do not put on steel or brass, but hard plates of bone or horn that do exactly as well, and are jointed just as nicely."

"And those are Crustaceans?"

"Those are Crustaceans."

"And was this thing armed so?"

"Splendidly. Don't you see those marks?—those shew the rings of his armour. Those rings fitted so nicely, and played so easily upon one another, that he could curl himself all up into a ball if he liked, and bring his armour all round him; for it was only on his back, so to speak."

"And how came he into this rock, Capt. Drummond?"

"Ah! how did he?" said the Captain, looking contentedly at the trilobite. "That's more than I can tell you, Daisy. Only he lived before the rock was made, and when it was made, it wrapped him up in it, somehow; and now we have got him!"

"But, Capt. Drummond!——"

"What is it?"

"When do you suppose this rock was made?"

"Can't just say, Daisy. Some rocks are young, and some are old, you know. This is one of the old rocks."

"But how do you know, Capt. Drummond?"

"I know by the signs," said the Captain.

"What is an old rock? how old?"

"I am sure I can't say, Daisy. Only that a *young* rock is apt to be a good deal older than Adam and Eve."

"How can you tell that?"

"When you see a man's hair grey, can't you tell that he is old?"

"But there are no grey hairs in rocks?" said Daisy.

"Yes, there are. Trilobites do just as well."

"But I *say*," said Daisy laughing, "how can you tell that the rock is old? You wouldn't know that grey hairs were a sign, if you saw them on young people."

"Pretty well, Daisy!" said the Captain, delighted to see her interested in something again;—"pretty well! But you will have to study something better than me, to find out about all that. Only it is true."

"And you were not laughing?"

"Not a bit of it. That little fellow, I suppose, lived a thousand million years ago; may as well say a thousand as anything."

"I can't see how you can tell," said Daisy, looking puzzled.

"That was a strange old time, when he was swimming about—or when most of them were. There were no trees, to speak of; and no grass or anything but sea-weed and mosses; and no living things but fishes and oysters and such creatures?"

"Where were the beasts then, and the birds?"

"They were not made yet. That's the reason, I suppose, there was no grass for them to eat."

Daisy looked down at the trilobite; and looked profoundly thoughtful. That little, shiny, black, stony thing, *that* had lived and flourished so many ages ago! Once more she looked up into the Captain's face to see if he were trifling with her. He shook his head.

"True as a book, Daisy."

"But Capt. Drummond, please, how do you know it?"

"Just think, Daisy,—this little fellow frolicked away in the mud at the bottom of the sea, with his half moons of eyes—and round him swam all sorts of fishes that do not live now-a-days; fishes with plate armour like himself; everybody was in armour."

"Half moons of eyes, Capt. Drummond?"

"Yes. He had, or some of them had, two semi-circular walls of eyes—one looked before and behind and all round to the right, and the other looked before and behind and all round at the left; and in each wall were two hundred eyes."

The Captain smiled to himself to see Daisy's face at this statement, though outwardly he kept perfectly grave. Daisy's own simple orbs were so full and intent. She looked from him to the fossil.

"But Capt. Drummond——" she began slowly.

"Well, Daisy? After you have done, I shall begin."

"Did you say that this thing lived at the bottom of the sea?"

"Precisely."

"But then how could he get up here?"

"Seems difficult, don't it?" said the Captain. "Well, Daisy, the people that know, tell us that all the land we have was once at the bottom of the sea; so these rocks had their turn."

"All the land?" said Daisy. "O that is what the Bible says!"

"The Bible!" said the Captain in his turn. "Pray where, if you please?"

"Why don't you know, Capt. Drummond?—when God said, 'Let the waters be gathered together into one place, and let the dry land appear.'"

The Captain whistled softly, with an amused face, and stealthily watched Daisy, whose countenance was full of the most beautiful interest. Almost lovingly she bent over the trilobite, thinking her own thoughts; while her friend presently from observing the expression of her face began to take notice anew of the thin and pale condition of the cheeks, that had been much healthier a week ago.

"You like to look at armour, Daisy," he said.

She made no answer.

"Are you still in the mind to 'die on the field of battle?'"

He guessed the question would touch her, but curiosity got the better of sympathy with him. He was not prepared for the wistful, searching look that Daisy gave him instantly, nor for the indescribable tenderness and sorrow that mingled in it. As before, she did not answer.

"Forgive me, Daisy," said the Captain involuntarily "You know you told me you were a soldier."

Daisy's heart was very tender, and she had been living all the morning in that peculiar nearness to Christ which those know who suffer for him. She looked at the Captain, and burst into tears.

"You told me you were a soldier—" he repeated, not quite knowing what to say.

"O Capt. Drummond!" said Daisy weeping,—"I wish you were!"

It stung the Captain. He knew what she meant. But he quietly asked her why?

"Because then," said Daisy, "you would know Jesus; and I want you to be happy."

"Why Daisy," said Capt. Drummond, though his conscience smote him,—"you don't seem to me very happy lately."

"Don't I?" she said. "But I *am* happy. I only wish everybody else was happy too."

She presently wiped her eyes and stood up. "Capt. Drummond," said she, "don't you think we can find another of these things?"

Anything to change the course matters had taken, the

Captain thought, so he gave ready assent; and he and Daisy entered upon a most lively renewed quest among the rocks that covered all that mountain side. Daisy was more eager than he; she wanted very much to have a trilobite for her own keeping; the difficulty was, she did not know how to look for it. All she could do was to follow her friend and watch all his doings and direct him to new spots in the mountain that he had not tried. In the course of this business the Captain did some adventurous climbing; it would have distressed Daisy if she had not been so intent upon his object; but as it was she strained her little head back to look at him, where he picked his way along at a precipitous height above her, sometimes holding to a bramble or sapling, and sometimes depending on his own good footing and muscular agility. In this way of progress, while making good his passage from one place to another, the Captain's foot in leaping struck upon a loosely poised stone or fragment of rock. It rolled from under him. A spring saved the Captain, but the huge stone once set a going continued its way down the hill.

"Daisy—look out!" he shouted.

"Have you got one?" said Daisy, springing forward. She misunderstood his warning; and her bound brought her exactly under the rolling stone. She never saw it till it had reached her and knocked her down.

"Hollo, Daisy!" shouted Capt. Drummond,—"is all right?"

He got no answer, listened, shouted again, and then made two jumps from where he stood to the bottom. Daisy lay on the ground, her little foot under the stone; her eyes closed, her face paler than ever. Without stopping to think how heavy the stone was, with a tremendous exertion of strength the young man pushed it from where it lay and released the foot; but he was very much afraid damage was done. "It couldn't help it"—said the Captain to himself as he looked at the great piece of rock; but the first thing was to get Daisy's eyes open. There was no spring near that he knew of; he went back to their lunch basket and brought from it a bottle of claret—all he could find—and with it wetted Daisy's lips and brow. The claret did perhaps as well as cold water; for Daisy revived; but as soon as she sat up and began to move, her words were broken off by a scream of pain.

"What is it, Daisy?" said the Captain. "Your foot?—that confounded stone!—can't you move it?"

"No,"—said Daisy with a short breath, "I can't move it. Please excuse me, Capt. Drummond—I couldn't help crying out that minute; it hurt me so. It doesn't hurt me so much now when I keep still."

The Captain kept still too, wishing very much that he and Daisy and the trilobites were all back in their places again. How long could they sit still up there on the mountain? He looked at the sun; he looked at his watch. It was three o'clock. He looked at Daisy.

"Let me see," said he, "if anything is the matter. Hard to find out, through this thick boot! How does it feel now?"

"It pains me very much, these two or three minutes."

The Captain looked at Daisy's face again, and then without more ado took his knife and cut the lacings of the boot. "How is that?" he asked.

"That is a *great* deal better."

"If it hadn't been, you would have fainted again directly. Let us see—Daisy, I think I had better cut the boot off. You have sprained the ancle, or something, and it is swollen."

Daisy said nothing, and the Captain went on very carefully and tenderly to cut the boot off. It was a very necessary proceeding. The foot was terribly swollen already. Again the Captain mused, looking from the child's foot to her face.

"How is the pain now?"

"It aches a good deal."

He saw it was vastly worse than her words made it.

"My little soldier," said he, "how do you suppose I am going to get you down the hill, to where we left our carriage?"

"I don't know," said Daisy. "You can't carry me."

"What makes you think so?"

"I don't *know*," said Daisy,—"but I don't think you can." And she was a little afraid, he saw.

"I will be as careful as I can, and you must be as brave as you can, for I don't see any other way, Daisy. And I think, the sooner we go the better; so that this foot may have some cold or hot lotion or something."

"Wait a minute," said Daisy hastily.

And raising herself up to a sitting position, she bent over her little head and covered her eyes with her hand. The Captain felt very strangely. He guessed in a minute what she was about; that in pain and fear, Daisy was seeking an unseen help, and trusting in it; and in awed silence the young officer was as still as she, till the little head was raised.

"Now," she said, "you may take me."

The Captain always had a good respect for Daisy; but he certainly felt now as if he had the dignity of twenty-five years in his arms. He raised her as gently as possible from the ground; he knew the changed position of the foot gave her new pain, for a flush rose to Daisy's brow, but she said not one word either of suffering or expostulation. Her friend stepped with her as gently as he could over the rough way; Daisy supported herself partly by an arm round his neck, and was utterly mute, till they were passing the place of luncheon; then she broke out,—

"Oh! the trilobite!"

"Never mind the trilobite."

"But are you going to lose it, Capt. Drummond?"

"Not if you want it. I'll come back for it another day —if I break my furlough."

"I could hold it in my other hand—if I had it."

The Captain thought the bottle of claret might chance to be the most wanted thing; nevertheless he stopped, stooped, and picked up the fossil. Daisy grasped it; and they went on their way down the mountain. It was a very trying way to both of them. The Captain was painfully anxious to step easily, which among rocks and bushes he could not always do, especially with a weight in his arms; and Daisy's foot hanging down, gave her dreadful pain because of the increased rush of blood into it. Her little lips were firmly set together many a time, to avoid giving her friend the distress of knowing how much she suffered; and once the Captain heard a low whisper not meant for his ear but uttered very close to it,—"O Lord Jesus, help me." It went through and through the Captain's mind and heart. But he only set his teeth too, and plunged on, as fast as he could softly, down the rough mountain side. And if ever anybody was glad, that was he when they reached the wagon.

There was a new difficulty now, for the little vehicle had no place in which Daisy could remain lying down. The seat was fast; the Captain could not remove it. He did the best he could. He put Daisy sideways on the seat, so that the hurt foot could be stretched out and kept in one position upon it; and he himself stood behind her, holding the reins. In that way he served as a sort of support for the little head which he sometimes feared would sink in a swoon; for while she lay on the ground and he was trying measures with the wagon, the closed eyes and pale cheeks had given the Captain a good many desperately uneasy thoughts. Now Daisy sat still, leaning against him, with her eyes open; and he drove as tenderly as he could. He had a frisky horse to manage, and the Captain congratulated himself for this occasion at least that he was a skilled whip. Still the motion of the wagon was very trying to Daisy, and every jar went through the Captain's foot up to his heart.

"How is it, Daisy?" he asked after they had gone some distance.

"It isn't good, Capt. Drummond," she said softly.

"Bad, isn't it?"

"Rather."

"I have to make this fellow go slowly, you see, or he would shake you too much. Could you bear to go faster?"

"I'll try."

The Captain tried cautiously. But his question, and possibly Daisy's answer, were stimulated by the view of the western horizon, over which clouds were gathering thick and fast. Could they get home in time? that was the doubt in both minds.

"Capt. Drummond," said Daisy presently, "I can't bear this shaking."

"Must I go slower?"

"If you please."

"Daisy, do you see how the sky bodes yonder? What do you suppose we shall do if those clouds come up?"

"I don't know," she answered. But she said it with such a quiet tone of voice, that the Captain wondered anew. He had hoped that her fears might induce her to bear the pain.

"Daisy, do you think it will come up a storm?"

"I think it will."

"How soon? you know the signs better than I do. How soon will it be here?"

"It will come soon, I think."

Yet there was no anxiety in Daisy's voice. It was perfectly calm, though feeble. The Captain held his peace, looked at the clouds, and drove on; but not as fast as he would have liked. He knew it was a ride of great suffering to his little charge, for she became exceedingly pale;

still she said nothing, except her soft replies to his questions. The western clouds rolled up in great volumes of black and grey, rolling and gathering and spreading at a magnificent rate. The sun was presently hid behind the fringe of this curtain of blackness; by and by the mountains were hid beneath a further fringe of rain; a very thick fringe. Between, the masses of vapour in the sky seemed charging for a tremendous outburst. It had not come yet when the slow going little wagon passed through Crum Elbow; but by this time the Captain had seen distant darts of lightning, and even heard the far-off warning growl of the thunder. A new idea started up in the Captain's mind; his frisky horse might not like lightning.

"Daisy," said he, "my poor little Daisy—we cannot get to Melbourne—we must stop and wait a little somewhere. Is there any house you like better than another? I had best turn back to the village."

"No, don't,—stop!" cried Daisy, "don't go back, Capt. Drummond; there is a place nearer. Turn up that road—right round there. It is very near."

The Captain obeyed, but pulled in the reins presently as he heard a nearer growl of the coming thunder. "Daisy, where is it? I don't see anything."

"There it is, Capt. Drummond—that little house."

"*That?*" said the Captain; but there was no more time now for retreat or question. He sprang out, threw the reins two or three times over the gate-post; then executed the very difficult operation of taking Daisy out of the wagon. He could not do it without hurting her; she fainted on his shoulder; and it was in this state, white and senseless, that he carried her into Mrs. Benoit's cottage. The old woman had seen them and met him at the door. Seeing the state of the case, she immediately and with great quickness spread a clean covering over a comfortable chintz couch which stood under the window, and Daisy was laid there from her friend's arms. Juanita applied water and salts too, deftly; and then asked the Captain, "What is it, sir?"

"There's a foot hurt here," said the Captain, giving more attention to the hurt than he had had chance to do before. "Pray heaven it is not broken! I am afraid it is,—the ancle,—or dislocated."

"Then Heaven knows *why* it is broken," said the old woman quietly. "The gentleman will go for a doctor, sir?"

"Yes, that must be the first thing," said Capt. Drummond gravely. "Where shall I find him?"

"Dr. Sandford—the gentleman knows the road to Mr. St. Leonard's?"

"Yes—the Craigs—I know."

"Dr. Sandford is half way there—where the gentleman remembers a great brown house in the middle of the cedar trees."

The Captain beat his brain to remember, thought he did, and was starting away, but turned back to see Daisy's eyes open first; fearing lest she might be alarmed if he were not by her when she came to herself. There was a bright flash and near peal of thunder at the moment. Juanita looked up.

"The gentleman will not fear the storm? There is work *here*"—touching the foot.

The Captain remembered that Daisy herself had directed him to the house, and dashed away again. The clouds were growing blacker every moment. In the darkening light Juanita bent over Daisy and saw her eyes open.

"Does my little lady know Juanita?"

Daisy sighed, looked round the room, and then seemed to recollect herself.

"O I am here!" she said. "Where is Capt. Drummond?"

"The gentleman is gone for the doctor, to see to the hurt foot. How is it now, dear?"

"It hurts me a good deal."

Juanita's first business was to take off the stocking; this could only be done by cutting it down. When it was removed, a very sorrowful-looking little foot was seen. Juanita covered it up lightly, and then turned her attention again to Daisy's pale face.

"What can I give my little lady?"

"I am Daisy Randolph."

"What may I do for Miss Daisy? to give her some comfort."

"Juanita,—I wish you would pray for me again."

"What does Miss Daisy want of the Lord?"

"My foot hurts me very much, and I want to be patient. And, Juanita, I want to thank him too."

"What for, Miss Daisy?"

"Because—I love him; and he has made me so happy.'

"Praise the Lord!" came with a most glad outburst from Juanita's lips; but then she knelt down, and so uttered her warm petitions for help needed and so her deep thanksgiving for help rendered, that Daisy was greatly overcome and poured out her tears as the prayer went on. When it was ended, Juanita went about her room for a little while, making certain arrangements that she foresaw would be necessary; then came and sat down. All this while the storm had been furious; the lightning hardly ceased, or the thunder, and both were near; but the two inmates of the little cottage seemed hardly to be conscious what was going on outside its walls. There was a slight lessening now of the storm's fury.

"Has it gone well with my little lady then, since she gave Juanita the rose branch?"

This was the new opening of conversation. Daisy hesitated a little what to answer; not for want of confidence, for there was something about the fine old woman that had won her completely.

"I don't know"—she said at length, slowly. "It has been very hard to do right, Juanita."

"But has my little lady kept her Lord's words?"

"Yes, Juanita, I did; but I don't know whether I should, if it hadn't been for what you said."

"And did she meet the trouble too?"

Juanita saw that she had, for a flush rose on Daisy's poor pale cheeks, and her face was strangely grave. She did not answer the question either; only as the flush passed away she looked placidly up and said,

"I am not in trouble now, Juanita."

"Bless the Lord!" was the utterance of Juanita's heart. "The Lord knows how to deliver out of trouble, Miss Daisy."

"Yes," said Daisy. "O!"—she exclaimed suddenly, with a new light breaking all over her face—but then she stopped.

"What is it, my love?"

"Nothing—only I am so glad now that my foot is hurt."

Juanita's thanksgiving rose to her lips again, but this time she only whispered it; turning away, perhaps to hide the moisture which had sprung to her eyes. For she understood more of the case than Daisy's few words would have told most people.

Meantime Capt. Drummond and his frisky horse had a ride which was likely to make both of them remember that thunderstorm. They reached Dr. Sandford's house; but then the Captain found that the doctor was not at home; where he was, the servant could not say. The only other thing to do seemed to be to go on to Melbourne and at least let Daisy have the counsel of her father and mother. To Melbourne the Captain drove as fast as his horse's state of mind would permit.

The drawing room was blazing with lights as usual, and full of talkers.

"Hollo!" cried Gary McFarlane, as the Captain entered,—"here he is. We had given you up for a fossil, Drummond—and no idea of your turning up again for another thousand years. Shouldn't have known where to look for you either, after this storm—among the aqueous or the igneous rocks. Glad to see you! Let me make you acquainted with Dr. Sandford."

"I am glad to see you, sir," said the Captain involuntarily, as he shook hands with this latter.

"You haven't left Daisy somewhere, changed into a stone lily?" pursued McFarlane.

"Yes," said the Captain. "Dr. Sandford, I am going to ask you to get ready to ride with me. Mr. Randolph, I have left Daisy by the way. She has hurt her foot—I threw down a stone upon it—and the storm obliged her to defer getting home. I left her at a cottage near Crum Elbow. I am going to take Dr. Sandford to see what the foot wants."

Mr. Randolph ordered the carriage, and then told his wife.

"Does it storm yet?" she asked.

"The thunder and lightning are ceasing, but it rains hard."

The lady stepped out of the room to get ready, and in a few minutes she and her husband, Capt. Drummond and the doctor, were seated in the carriage and on their way to Mrs. Benoit's cottage. Capt. Drummond told how the accident happened; after that he was silent; and so were the rest of the party, till the carriage stopped.

Mrs. Benoit's cottage looked oddly, when all these grand people poured into it. But the mistress of the cottage never looked more like herself, and her reception of the grand people was as simple as that she had given to Daisy. Little Daisy herself lay just where her friend the Captain had left her, but looked with curious expression at the others who entered with him now. The father and mother advanced to the head of the couch; the Captain and Juanita stood at the foot. The doctor kept himself a little back.

"Are you suffering, Daisy?" Mr. Randolph asked.

The child's eyes went up to him. "Papa—*yes!*"

She had begun quietly, but the last word was given with more than quiet expression, and the muscles about her lips quivered. Mr. Randolph stooped and pressed his own lips upon them.

"I have brought Dr. Sandford to look at your foot, Daisy. He will see what it wants."

"Will he hurt me, papa?" said the child apprehensively.

"I hope not. No more than is necessary."

"It hurts to have anybody touch it, papa."

"He must touch it, Daisy. Can't you bear it bravely?"

"Wait, papa!"——

And again the child clasped her two hands over her face and was still. Mr. Randolph had no idea what for, though he humoured her and waited. The Captain knew, for he had seen more of Daisy that day, and he looked very grave indeed. The black woman knew, for as Daisy's hands fell from her face, she uttered a deep, soft "Amen!" which no one understood but one little heart.

"Papa—I am ready. He may look now."

Juanita removed the covering from the foot, and the doctor stepped forward. Daisy's eyes rested on him, and she saw gratefully a remarkably fine and pleasant countenance. Mrs. Randolph's eyes rested on the foot, and she uttered an exclamation. It was the first word she had uttered. Everybody else was still, while the doctor passed his hands over and round the distressed ankle and foot, but tenderly, and in a way that gave Daisy very little pain. Then he stepped back and beckoned Juanita to a consultation. Juanita disappeared, and Dr. Sandford came up to Mr. Randolph and spoke in a low tone. Then Mr. Randolph turned again to Daisy.

"What is it, papa?" asked the child.

"Daisy, to make your foot well, Dr. Sandford will be

obliged to do something that will hurt you a little—will you try and bear it? He will not be long about it."

"What is the matter with my foot, papa?"

"Something that the doctor can set right in a few minutes—if you will try and bear a little pain."

A little pain! And Daisy was suffering so much all the while! Again her lip trembled.

"Must he touch me, papa?"

"He must touch you."

Daisy's hands were clasped to her face again for a minute; after that she lay quite still and quiet. Mr. Randolph kept his post, hardly taking his eye off her; Mrs. Randolph sat down where she had stood; behind the head of Daisy's couch, where her little daughter could not see her; and all the party indulged in silence. At length the doctor was ready and came to the foot, attended by Juanita; and Mr. Randolph took one of Daisy's hands in his own. With the other the child covered her eyes, and so lay, perfectly still, while the doctor set the ankle bone which had been broken. As the foot also itself had been very much hurt, the handling of necessity gave a great deal of pain, more than the mere setting of the broken bone would have caused. Mr. Randolph could feel every now and then the convulsive closing of Daisy's hand upon his; other than that she gave no sign of what she was suffering. One sign of what another person was feeling, was given as Dr. Sandford bound up the foot and finished his work. It was given in Juanita's deep breathed "Thank the Lord!" The doctor glanced up at her with a slight smile of curiosity. Capt. Drummond would have said "Amen," if the word had not been so unaccustomed to his mouth.

Mrs. Randolph rose then, and inquired of the doctor what would be the best means of removing Daisy?

"She must not be moved," the doctor said.

"Not to-night?"

"No, madam; nor to-morrow, nor for many days."

"Must she be left *here?*"

"If she were out in the weather, I would move her," said the doctor; "not if she were under a barn that would shed the rain."

"What harm would it do?"

The doctor could not take it upon him to say.

"But I cannot be with her here," said Mrs. Randolph; "nor anybody else, that I can see."

"Juanita will take care of her," said the doctor. "Juanita is worth an army of nurses. Miss Daisy cannot be better cared for than she will be."

"Will you undertake the charge?" said Mrs. Randolph, facing round upon Daisy's hostess.

"The Lord has given it to me, madam,—and I love to do my Lord's work," was Juanita's answer. She could not have given a better one, if it had been meant to act as a shot, to drive Mrs. Randolph out of the house. The lady waited but till the doctor had finished his directions which he was giving to the black woman.

"I don't see," then she said to her husband, "that there is anything to be gained by my remaining here any longer; and if we are to go, the sooner we go the better, so that Daisy may be quiet. Dr. Sandford says that is the best thing for her."

"Capt. Drummond will see you home," said her husband. "I shall stay."

"You can't do anything, in this box of a place."

"Unless the child herself desires it, there is no occasion for your remaining here over night," said the doctor. "She will be best in quiet, and sleep, if she can. You might hinder, if your presence did not help her to this."

"What do you say, Daisy?" said her father tenderly, bending over her;—"shall I stay or go? Which do you wish?"

"Papa, you would not be comfortable here. I am not afraid."

"Do you want me to go?" said her father, putting his face down to hers. Daisy clasped her two arms round his neck and kissed him and held him while she whispered,

"No, papa, but maybe you had better. There is no place for you, and I am not afraid."

He kissed her silently and repeatedly, and then rose up and went to look at the storm. It had ceased; the moon was struggling out between great masses of cloud driving over the face of the sky. Mrs. Randolph stood ready to go, putting on her "capuche" which she had thrown off, and Juanita laying her shawl round her shoulders. The doctor stood waiting to hand her to the carriage. The Captain watched Daisy, whose eye was wistfully fixed on her mother. He watched, and wondered at its very grave, soft expression. There was very little affection in the Captain's mind at that moment towards Mrs. Randolph.

The carriage was ready, and the lady turned round to give a parting look at the child. A cold look it was, but Daisy's soft eye never changed.

"Mamma," said she whisperingly, "won't you kiss me?"

Mrs. Randolph stooped instantly and gave the kiss; it could not be refused, and was fully given; but then she immediately took Doctor Sandford's arm and went out of the house. The Captain reverently bent over Daisy's little hand, and followed her.

The drive was a very silent one till Dr. Sandford was left at his own door. So soon as the carriage turned again, Mrs. Randolph broke out.

"How long did he say, Mr. Randolph, the child must be left at that woman's cottage?"

"He said she must not be moved for weeks."

"She might as well stay forever," said Mrs. Randolph,—"for the effect it will have. It will take a year to get

Daisy back to where she was! I wish fanatics would confine their efforts to children that have no one else to care for them."

"What sort of fanaticism has been at work here, Mrs. Randolph?" the Captain enquired.

"The usual kind, of course; religious fanaticism. It seems to be catching."

"I have been in dangerous circumstances to day, then," said the Captain. "I am afraid I have caught it. I feel as if something was the matter with me."

"It will not improve you," said Mrs. Randolph drily.

"How has it wrought with Daisy?"

"Changed the child so that I do not recognize her. She never set up her own will before; and now she is as difficult to deal with as possible. She is an impersonation of obstinacy."

"Perhaps, after all, she is only following orders," said the Captain with daring coolness. "A soldier's duty makes him terribly obstinate sometimes. You must excuse me,—but you see I cannot help appreciating military qualities."

"Will you be good enough to say what you mean?" the lady asked with sufficient displeasure of manner.

"Only, that I believe in my soul Daisy takes her orders from higher authority than we do. And I have seen to-day—I declare! I have seen a style of obedience and soldierly following, that would win any sort of a field—ay, and die in it!" added the Captain musingly. "It is the sort of thing that gets promotion from the ranks."

"How did all this happen to-day?" asked Mr. Randolph, as the lady was now silent. "I have heard only a bit of it."

In answer to which, Capt. Drummond went into the details of the whole day's experience; told it point by point, and bit by bit; having a benevolent willingness that Daisy's father and mother should know, if they would, with what sort of a spirit they were dealing. He told the whole story; and nobody interrupted him.

"It is one thing," said the Captain thoughtfully as he concluded,—"it is one thing to kneel very devoutly and say after the minister, "Lord, have mercy upon us, and write all these laws in our hearts;"—I have done that myself; but it gives one an entirely different feeling to see some one in whose heart they are written!"

"There is only one thing left for you, Capt. Drummond," said Mrs. Randolph slightly; "to quit the army and take orders."

"I am afraid, if I did, you would never want to see me settled in Mr. Pyne's little church over here," the Captain answered, as he helped the lady to alight at her own door.

"Not till Daisy is safely married," said Mrs. Randolph laughing.

CHAPTER XVI.

TILL the sound of the carriage wheels had died away in the distance, Juanita stood at the door looking after them; although the trees and the darkness prevented her seeing anything along the road further than a few yards. When the rustle of the breeze among the branches was the only thing left to hear, beside the dripping of the rain drops shaken from the leaves, Juanita shut the door and came to Daisy. The child was lying white and still, with her eyes closed. Very white and thin the little face looked, indeed; and under each eyelid lay a tear glistening, that had forced its way so far into notice. Juanita said not a word just then; she bustled about and made herself busy. Not that Juanita's busy ways were ever bustling in reality; she was too good a nurse for that; but she had several things to do. The first was to put up a screen at the foot of Daisy's couch. She lay just a few feet from the door, and everybody coming to the door and having it opened, could look in if he pleased; and so Daisy would have no privacy at all. That would not do; Juanita's wits went to work to mend the matter. Her little house had been never intended for more than one person. There was another room in it, to be sure, where Mrs. Benoit's own bed was; so that Daisy could have the use and possession of this outer room all to herself.

Juanita went about her business too noiselessly to induce even those closed eyelids to open. She fetched a tolerably large clothes-horse from somewhere—some shed or out-building; this she set at the foot of the couch, and hung an old large green moreen curtain over it. Where the curtain came from, one of Mrs. Benoit's great locked chests knew; there were two or three such chests in the inner room, with more treasures than a green moreen curtain stowed away in them. The curtain was too large for the clothes-horse to hold up; it lay over the floor. Junita got screws and cords; fixed one screw in the wall, another in the ceiling, and at last succeeded in stretching the curtain neatly on the cords and the clothes-horse, where she wanted it to hang. That was done; and Daisy's couch was quite sheltered from any eyes coming to the door that had no business to come further. When it was finished, and the screws and cords put away, Juanita came to Daisy's side. The eyes were open now.

"That is nice," said Daisy.

"It'll keep you by yourself, my little lady. Now what will she have?"

"Nothing—only I am thirsty," said Daisy.

Juanita went to the well for some cold water, and mixed with it a spoonful of currant jelly. It was refreshing to the poor little dry lips.

"What will my love have next?"

"I don't know," said Daisy—"my foot aches a good deal, and all my leg. I think—Juanita—I would like it if you would read to me."

Juanita took a somewhat careful survey of her, felt her hands, and finally got the book.

"Is there too much air for my love from that window?"

"No, it is nice," said Daisy. "I can see the stars so beautifully, with the clouds driving over the sky. Every now and then they get between me and the stars—and then the stars look out again so bright. They seem almost right over me. Please read, Juanita."

Mrs. Benoit did not consider that it made much difference to Daisy where she read; so she took the chapter that came next in the course of her own going through the New Testament. It was the eighth chapter of Mark. She read very pleasantly; not like a common person; and with a slight French accent. Her voice was always sweet, and the words came through it as loved words. It was very pleasant to Daisy to hear her; the long chapter was not interrupted by any remark. But when Mrs. Benoit paused at the end of it, Daisy said,

"How can anybody be ashamed of him, Juanita?"

The last verse of the chapter has these words—

"Whosoever therefore shall be ashamed of me, and of my words, in this adulterous and sinful generation; of him also shall the Son of man be ashamed, when he cometh in the glory of his Father with the holy angels."

"How *can* anybody be ashamed of him, Juanita?"

"They not see the glory of the Lord, my lady."

"But *we* do not see it yet."

"My love will see it. Juanita has seen it. This little house be all full of glory sometimes, when Jesus is here."

"But that is because you love him, Juanita."

"Praise the Lord!" echoed the black woman. "He do shew his glory to his people, before he come with the holy angels."

"I don't see how anybody can be *ashamed* of him," Daisy repeated, uttering the words as if they contained a simple impossibility.

"My little lady not know the big world yet. There be ways, that the Lord know and that the people not know."

"What do you mean, Juanita?"

"My lady will find it," said the black woman folding her arms. "When all the world go one way, then folks not like to go another way and be looked at; they be ashamed of Christ's words then, and they only think they do not want to be looked at."

A colour came all over Daisy's face—a suffusion of colour; and tears swam in her eyes.

"I didn't like to be looked at, the other night!" she said, in a self-accusing tone.

"Did my love turn and go with the world?"

"No, I didn't do that."

"Then Jesus won't turn away neither," said the black woman.

"But I ought not to have felt so, Juanita."

"Maybe. My love is a little child. The good Lord shall 'stablish her and keep her from evil. Now she must not talk no more, but trust the Lord, and go to sleep."

"I can't sleep, Juanita—my leg aches so."

"That will be better. Is my love thirsty again?"

"Very thirsty! I wish I had some oranges."

"They would be good," said Juanita, bringing another glass of jelly and water for Daisy. And then she sat down and sang softly; hymns in French and English; sweet and low, and soothing in their simple and sometimes wild melody. They soothed Daisy. After a time, wearied and exhausted by all her long day of trial, she did forget pain in slumber. The eyelids closed, and Juanita's stealthy examination found that quiet soft breathing was really proving her fast asleep. The singing ceased; and for a while nothing was to be heard in the cottage but the low rush and rustle of the wind which had driven away the storm clouds, and the patter of a dislodged rain drop or two that were shaken from the leaves. Daisy's breathing was too soft to be heard, and Juanita almost held her own lest it should be too soon disturbed. But the pain of the hurt foot and ankle would not suffer a long sleep. Daisy waked up with a sigh.

"Are you there, Juanita?"

"I am here."

"What o'clock is it?"

Juanita drew back the curtain of the window by Daisy's couch, that the moonlight might fall in and shew the face of the little clock. It was midnight.

"It won't be morning in a great while, will it?" said Daisy.

"Does my lady want morning?"

"My foot hurts me dreadfully, Juanita—the pain shoots and jumps all up my leg. Couldn't you do something to it?"

"My dear love, it will be better by and by—there is no help now for it, unless the Lord sends sleep. I s'pose it must ache. Can't Miss Daisy remember who sends the pain?"

The child answered her with a curious smile. It was not strange to the black woman; she read it and knew it and had seen such before; to anybody that had not, how strange would have seemed the lovingness that spread over all Daisy's features and brightened on her brow as much as on her lips. It was not patient submission; it was the light of joyful affection shining out over all Daisy's little pale face.

"Ay, it isn't hard with Jesus," said the black woman with a satisfied face. "And the Lord is here now,—praise his name!"

"Juanita—I have been very happy to-day," said Daisy.

"Ay? how has that been, my love?"

"Because I knew he was taking care of me. It seemed that Jesus was so near me all the time. Even all that dreadful ride."

"The Lord is good!" said the black woman with strong expression. "But my love must not talk."

She began to sing again.

"O what shall I do, my Saviour to praise!
So faithful and true, so plenteous in grace.
So good to deliver, so strong to redeem
The weakest believer that hangs upon him."

O that's good, Juanita!" said Daisy. "Hush!—Juanita, it is very late for anybody to be out riding!"

"Who is out riding, Miss Daisy?"

"I don t know—I hear a horse's feet. Don't you hear? —there!"

"It's some young gentleman, maybe, going home from a dinner-party."

"Don't draw the curtain, Juanita, please! I like it so, I can look out. The moonlight is nice. Somebody is very late, going home from a dinner party."

"They often be. Miss Daisy, the moonlight will hinder you sleeping, I am afraid."

"I can't sleep. It's so good to look out! Juanita—there's that horse's feet, stopping just here."

Juanita went to her door, and perceived that Daisy spoke truth. Somebody down at her little wicket had dismounted and was fastening his horse to the fence. Then a figure came up the walk in the moonlight.

"Juanita!" cried Daisy with an accent of joy, though she could not see the figure from where she lay,—"it's papa!"

"Is she asleep?" said the voice of Mr. Randolph the next minute softly.

"No, sir. She knows it's you, sir. Will his honour walk in?"

Mr. Randolph with a gentle footfall came in and stood by the side of the couch.

"Daisy—my poor little Daisy!"—he said.

"Papa!——"

This one word was rich in expression; joy and love so filled it. Daisy added nothing more. She put her arms round her father's neck as he stooped his lips to her face, held him fast and returned his kisses.

"Cannot you sleep?" The question was very tenderly put.

"I did sleep, papa."

"I did not wake you?"

"No, papa. I was awake, looking at the moonlight."

"Pain would not let you sleep, my poor darling?"

The sympathy was a little too trying. Tears started to the child's eyes. She said with a most gentle, loving accent, "I don't mind, papa. It will be better by and by. I am very happy."

An indignant question as to the happiness which had been so rudely shaken, was on Mr. Randolph's lips. He remembered Daisy must not be excited; nevertheless he wondered, for he saw the child's eyes full, and knew that the brow was drawn with pain; and the poor little thin face was as white as a sheet. What did she mean by talking about being happy?

"Daisy, I have brought you some oranges."

"Thank you, papa!—May I have one now?"

Silently and almost sternly Mr. Randolph stood and pared the orange with a fruit knife—he had thought to bring that too—and fed Daisy with it, bit by bit. It was pleasant and novel to Daisy to have her father serve her so; generally others had done it when there had been occasion. Mr. Randolph did it nicely, while his thoughts worked.

"What are you going to do to-night, papa?" she said when the orange was finished and he stood looking at her.

"Stay here with you."

"But papa, how can you sleep?"

"I can do without sleeping, if it is necessary. I will take a chair here in the doorway, and be near if you want anything."

"O I shall not want anything, papa, except what Juanita can give me."

He stood still watching her. Daisy looked up at him with a loving face; a wise little face it always was; it was gravely considerate now.

"Papa, I am afraid you will be uncomfortable."

"Can nobody bear that but you?" said Mr. Randolph, stooping down to kiss her.

"I am very happy, papa," said the child placidly; while a slight tension of her forehead witnessed to the shooting pains with which the whole wounded limb seemed to be filled.

"If Mr. Randolph pleases——" said the voice of Juanita,—"the doctor recommended quiet, sir."

Off went Mr. Randolph at that, as if he knew it very well and had forgotten himself. He took a chair and set it in the open doorway, using the door-post as a rest for his head; and then the cottage was silent. The wind breathed more gently; the stars shone out; the air was soft after the storm; the moonlight made a bright flicker of light and shade over all the outer world. Now and then a grasshopper chirruped, or a little bird murmured a few twittering notes at being disturbed in its sleep; and then came a soft sigh from Daisy.

On noiseless foot the black woman stole to the couch. Daisy was weeping; her tears were pouring out and making a great wet spot on her pillow.

"Is my love in pain?" whispered the black woman.

"It's nothing—I can't help it," said Daisy.

"Where is it—in the foot?"

"It's all over, I think; in my head and everywhere. Hush, Juanita; never mind."

Mrs. Benoit, however, tried the soothing effect of a long gentle brushing of Daisy's head. This lasted till Daisy said she could bear it no longer. She was restless.

"Will my love hear a hymn?"

"It will wake papa."

Mrs. Benoit cared nothing for that. Her care was her poor little charge. She began immediately one of the hymns that were always ready on her tongue, and which were wonderfully soothing to Daisy. Juanita was old, but her voice was sweet yet and clear; and she sang with a deal of quiet spirit.

"'A few more days or years at most,
My troubles will be o'er;
I hope to join the heavenly host
On Canaan's happy shore.
My raptured soul shall drink and feast
In love's unbounded sea;
The glorious hope of endless rest
Is ravishing to me.'"

Mr. Randolph raised his head from leaning against the door-post, and turned it to listen; with a look of lowering impatience. The screen of the hanging curtain was between him and the couch, and the look did nobody any harm.

"'O come, my Saviour, come away,
And bear me to the sky!
Nor let thy chariot wheels delay—
Make haste and bring it nigh:
I long to see thy glorious face,
And in thy image shine;
To triumph in victorious grace,
And be forever thine.'"

Mr. Randolph's chair here grated inharmoniously on the floor, as if he were moving; but Juanita went on without heeding it.

"'Then will I tune my harp of gold
To my eternal King.
Through ages that can ne'er be told
I'll make thy praises ring.
All hail, eternal Son of God,
Who died on Calvary!
Who bought me with his precious blood,
From endless misery.'"

Mr. Randolph stood by Mrs. Benoit's chair.

"My good woman," he said in suppressed tones, "this is a strange way to put a patient to sleep."

"As your honour sees!" replied the black woman placidly. Mr. Randolph looked. Daisy's eyes were closed; the knitted brow had smoothed itself out in slumber; the deep breath told how profound was the need that weakness and weariness had made. He stood still. The black woman's hand softly drew the curtain between Daisy's face and the moonlight, and then she noiselessly withdrew herself almost out of sight, to a low seat in a corner. So Mr. Randolph betook himself to his station in the doorway; and whether he slept or no, the hours of the night stole on quietly. The breeze died down; the moon and the stars shone steadily over the lower world; and Daisy slept, and her two watchers were still. By and by, another light began to break in the eastern horizon, and the stars grew pale. The morning had come.

The birds were twittering in the branches before Daisy awoke. At the first stir she made, her father and Mrs. Benoit were instantly at her side. Mr. Randolph bent over her and asked tenderly how she felt.

"I feel hot, papa."

"Everybody must do that," said Mr. Randolph. "The breeze has died away and the morning is very close."

"Papa, have you been awake all night?"

He stooped down and kissed her.

"You must go home and get some breakfast and go to sleep," Daisy said, looking at him lovingly with her languid eyes.

"Shall I bring you anything from home, Daisy?" he said, kissing her again.

The child looked a little wistfully, but presently said no; and Mr. Randolph left her to do as she had said. Mrs. Benoit was privately glad to have him out of the way. She brought water and bathed Daisy's face and hands, and gave her a delicate breakfast of orange; and contrived to be a long while about it all, so as to rest and refresh her as much as possible. But when it was all done, Daisy was very hot and weary and in much pain. And the sun was only in the tops of the trees yet. The black woman stood considering her.

"It will be a hot day, Miss Daisy—and my little lady is suffering already, when the dew is not dried off the grass. Can she say, 'Thank the Lord?'"

Daisy first smiled at her; then the little pale face grew grave, the eyelids fell, and the black woman saw tears gathering beneath them. She stood looking somewhat anxiously down at the child; till after a few minutes the eyelids were raised again and the eyes gave her a most meek and loving response, while Daisy said faintly, "Yes, Juanita."

"Bless the Lord!" said Juanita with all her heart. "Then my love can bear it, the hot day and the pain and all. When his little child trust him, Jesus not stay far off. And when he giveth quietness, then who can make trouble?"

"But I have a particular reason, Juanita. I am very glad of my hurt foot; though it does ache."

"The aching will not be so bad by and by," said the woman, her kindly face all working with emotion.

She stood there by Daisy's couch and prayed. No bathing nor breakfast could so soothe and refresh Daisy as that prayer. While she listened and joined in it, the feeling of yesterday came all back again; that wonderful feeling that the Lord Jesus loves even the little ones that love him; that he will not let a hair of their heads be hurt; that he is near, and keeps them, and is bringing them to himself by everything that he lets happen to them. Greatly refreshed and comforted, Daisy lay quiet looking out of the open window, while Juanita was busy about, making a fire and filling her kettle for breakfast. She had promised Daisy a cup of tea and a piece of toast; and Daisy was very fond of a cup of tea and did not ordinarily get it; but Mrs. Benoit said it would be good for her now. The fire was made in a little out-shed, back of the cottage, where it would do nobody any harm, even in hot weather. Daisy was so quieted and comforted, though her leg was still aching, that she was able to look out and take some pleasure in the sparkling morning light which glittered on the leaves of the trees and on the blades of grass; and to hearken to the birds which were singing in high feather all around the cottage. The robins especially were very busy whistling about in and under the trees; and a kildeer quite near from time to time sung its soft sweet song; so soft and tender, it seemed every time to say in Daisy's ears—"What if I am sick and in pain and weary? Jesus sends it—and he knows—and he is my dear Saviour." It brought the tears into Daisy's eyes at length; the song of the kildeer came so close home into her heart.

Juanita had gone to make the tea. While the kettle had been coming to a boil, she had put her little cottage into the nicest of order; and even filled a glass with some roses and set it on the little table. For, as she said to Daisy, they would have company enough that day, and must be in trim. She had gone now to make the tea, and Daisy lay contentedly looking out of the window, when she heard the swift tread of horses' feet again. Could her father be back from Melbourne already? Daisy could not raise herself up to look. She heard the feet stop in the road before the cottage; then listened for somebody's step coming up to it. She heard the step, but it was none of Mr. Randolph's; it was brisk and firm and measured. She guessed it was somebody's step whose feet had been trained.

Juanita came to open the door at the knock, and Daisy heard her saying something about the doctor's orders, and keeping quiet, and no excitement. Daisy could not stand that.

"O Capt. Drummond—come in! come in!" she cried. And in came the Captain. He looked wonderfully sober at his poor little playfellow. But Daisy looked all smiles at him.

"Is your furlough over? Are you going, Capt. Drummond?"

"I am off, Daisy."

"I am so glad you came to see me?" she said, putting out her little hand to him. The Captain took it and held it and seemed almost unable to speak.

"Daisy, I would have run the risk of being cashiered, rather than not have done it."

"What is that?"

"Cashiered? Having my epaulettes pulled off."

"Do you care a great deal for your epaulettes?" said Daisy.

The Captain laughed, with the water standing in his eyes. Yes, absolutely, his bright sparkling eyes had drops in them.

"Daisy, I have brought you our land fish—that we had such trouble for."

"The trilobite! O did you?" exclaimed Daisy as he placed it before her. "I wanted to see it again, but I was afraid you wouldn't have time before you went." She looked at it eagerly.

"Keep it Daisy; and keep a little bit of friendship for me with it—will you? in case we meet again some day."

"O Capt. Drummond—don't you want it?"

"No; but I want you to remember the conditions."

"When will you come to Melbourne again?

"Can't say, Daisy; I am afraid, not till you will have got the kingdom of England quite out of all its difficulties. We were just going into the battle of Hastings, you know; don't you recollect?"

"How nice that was!" said Daisy regretfully. "I don't think I shall ever forget about the Saxon Heptarchy, and Egbert, and Alfred."

"How about forgetting *me?*"

"You know I couldn't," said Daisy with a most genial smile. "O Capt. Drummond!"—she added, as a flash of sudden thought crossed her face.

"What now, Daisy?"

The child looked at him with a most earnest, inquisitive wistful gaze. The Captain had some difficulty to stand it.

"O Capt. Drummond," she repeated,—"are you going to be ashamed of Christ?"

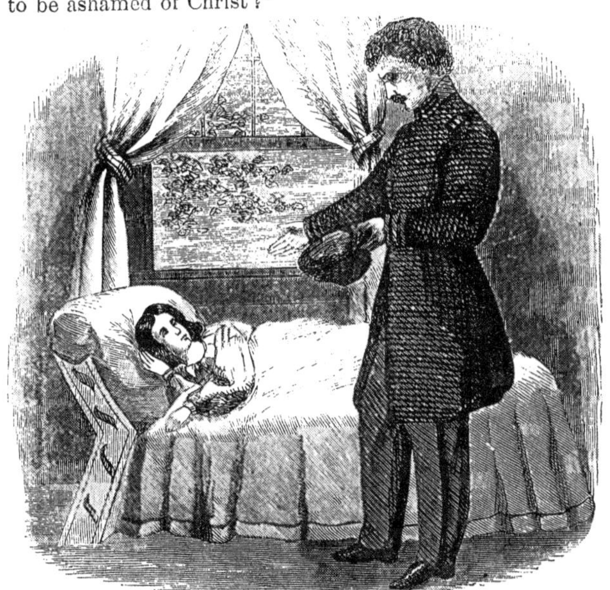

The young soldier was strangely enough confused by this simple question. His embarrassment was even evident. He hesitated for a reply, and it did not readily come. When it came, it was an evasion.

"That is right, Daisy," he said; "stand by your colours. He is a poor soldier that carries them behind his back in the face of the enemy. But whatever field you die in, I should like to be alongside of you!"

He spoke gravely. And he asked no leave this time, but clasping Daisy's hand he bent down and kissed her forehead twice and earnestly; then he did not say another word, but strode away. A little flush rose on Daisy's brow, for she was a very particular little lady as to who touched her; however she listened attentively to the sound of the retreating hoofs which carried the Captain off along the road; and when Juanita at last came in with her little tray and a cup of tea, she found Daisy's face set in a very thoughtful mood and her eyes full of tears. The face did not even brighten at her approach.

"Miss Daisy," said the black woman, "I thought you wanted a cup of tea?"

"So I do, Juanita. I want it very much."

Mrs. Benoit made remarks to herself upon the wise little face that met her with such a sober greeting. However she made none aloud; she supported Daisy nicely with one arm and set the little tray before her. The tea was excellent; the toast was in dainty, delicate, thin brown strips. Daisy took it soberly.

"Does it seem good to my love?"

"O yes, Juanita!" said the child looking up gratefully: "it is *very* good; and you make the prettiest toast I ever saw."

The black woman smiled, and bade her eat it and not look at it.

"But I think it tastes better for looking pretty, Juanita."

"The Lord knows," said the woman; "and he made the trees in the garden of Eden to be pleasant to the eyes, as well as good for food."

"I am glad he did," said Daisy. "How pleasant the trees have been to my eyes this morning. Then I was sick and could not do anything but look at them; but they are pleasant to my eyes too when I am well. It is very painful to have one's friends go away, Juanita."

"Has my love lost friends?" said Mrs. Benoit, wondering at this speech.

"Yes," said Daisy. "Mr. Dinwiddie is gone; and now Capt. Drummond. I have got hardly anybody left."

"Was Mr. Dinwiddie Miss Daisy's friend?"

Such a bright, warm, glad flash of a smile as Juanita got in answer! It spoke for the friendship on one side.

"But he is gone," said Daisy. "I wish I could see him again. He is gone, and I never shall!"

"Now Miss Daisy, you will lie still and be quiet, my love, until somebody else comes. The doctor says that's the way. Mr. Dinwiddie is about his Master's work, wherever he is; and you want to do the same?"

"How can I, Juanita, lying here? I cannot do anything."

"Does my love think the good Lord ever give his servants no work to do for him?"

"Why *here*, Juanita—I can only lie here and be still. What can I do?"

"My love pray the dear Master to shew her; and now not talk just now."

Daisy lay still. The next comer was the doctor. He came while the morning was still early; made his examinations; and Daisy made hers. He was a very fine-looking man. Thick locks of auburn hair, thrown back from his face; a noble and grave countenance; blue eye keen and steady; and a free and noble carriage; there was enough about Dr. Sandford to engage all Daisy's attention and interest. She gave him both, in her quiet way; while he looked not so much at her as at her condition and requirements.

"It is going to be a hot day," he remarked to Juanita who attended upon him. "Keep her quiet. Do not let more than one other person be here at once. Say I order it."

"Will his honour say it to Miss Daisy's father and mother?"

"I shal. not see them this morning. You are armed with my authority, Juanita. Nobody is to be here to talk and excite her; and only one at a time beside you. Have you got fruit for her? Let her live on that as much as she likes; and keep the house empty."

"I will tell papa——" said Daisy.

"How do you do?" said the doctor. It was the first question he had addressed to her; and the first attention he had given her otherwise than as a patient. Now the two looked at each other.

"I am better, a little, thank you," said the child. "May I ask something?"

"Ask it."

"Shall I be a long while here?"

"You will be a week or two—till your foot gets strong again."

"Will a week or two make it strong?"

The two pairs of eyes looked into each other. The thoughtful grey eyes of the child, and the impenetrable blue orbs of the man. There was mutual study; some mutual recognition.

"You must be a good child and try to bear it."

"Will you come and see me again?" said Daisy.

"Do you desire it?"

"You would not come unless it was necessary," said Daisy; "and if it is necessary, I should like to have you."

The lips of the young man curled into a smile that was very pleasant, albeit a little mocking in its character.

"I think it will be necessary, little one; but if I come to see you, you must be under my orders."

"Well, I am," said Daisy.

"Keep still, then; do not talk to anybody any more than is needful to relieve your impatience."

The doctor went away, and Daisy lay still musing. The morning had gone on a little further, wh n carriage wheels stopped at the gate.

"There's mamma——" said Daisy.

It was very unconsciously on her part that the tone of these two words conveyed a whole volume of information to Juanita's keen wits. It was no accent of joy, like that which had announced her father last night; neither was it fear or dread; yet the indefinable expression of the two words said that "mamma" had been a trouble in Daisy's life, and might be again. Juanita went to have the door open; and the lady swept in. Mr. Randolph was behind her. She came to Daisy's side and the mother and child looked at each other; Daisy with the tender, wistful eyes of last night, Mrs. Randolph with a vexed air of dissatisfaction. Yet after looking at her a moment she stooped down and kissed Daisy. The child's eye went to her father then. Mrs. Randolph stood in his way; he came round to the head of the couch, behind Daisy, and bent over her.

"Papa, I can't see you there."

"You can feel, Daisy——" said Mr. Randolph, putting his lips to her face. "How do you do?"

"This is a most maladroit arrangement of Capt. Drummond's!" said the lady. "What can we do to rectify it? A most stupid place for the child to be."

"She will have to bear the stupidity—and we too. Daisy, what would you like to have to help it along?"

"Papa, I am not stupid."

"You will be, my little daughter, I am afraid, before the weeks are over. Will you have June come to be with you?"

"Papa," said Daisy slowly,—"I think it would not be considerate."

"Are you comfortable?" said Mr. Randolph smiling, though his looks expressed much concern.

"No, papa."

"What is the matter?"

"It is hot, papa; and my leg aches; not so much as it did last night sometimes; but it aches."

"It is a cool, fresh morning," said Mrs. Randolph. "She is hot because she is lying in this place."

"Not very cool, with the mercury at eighty-four before eight o'clock You are cool because you have been driving fast."

"Mr. Randolph, this is no proper place for the child to be. I am convinced she might be moved with safety."

"I cannot risk the doctor's convictions against yours, Felicia. That question must be given up."

"He says I am under his orders, papa."

"Undeniable, Daisy. That is true doctrine. What orders does he give you?"

"To eat fruit, and keep quiet, papa. He says there must not be more than one person here at a time, besides Juanita."

"I suppose he does not mean to forbid your mother," said Mrs. Randolph, a good deal incensed. "I will see about that. Here, my good woman—where are you?—Will you let your cottage to me for the time that this child is confined here—and remove somewhere else yourself, that I may put the people here I want about her?"

"Oh mamma!——" said Daisy. But she stopped short; and Mrs. Randolph did not attend to her. Mr. Randolph looked round to see Juanita's answer.

"My lady shall put here who she will please," the woman said, standing before her visiters with the most unruffled face and demeanour.

"And you will leave me the house at once?"

"No, my lady. My lady shall have the house. Juanita will not be in the way."

"You do not seem to understand, my good woman, that I want to be here myself and have my people here. I want the whole house."

"My lady shall have it—she is welcome—nobody shall find Juanita trouble them," the black woman said with great sweetness.

"What will you do with yourself?"

"A little place be enough for me, my lady. My spirit lives in a large home."

Mrs. Randolph turned impatiently away. The manner of the woman was so inexpressibly calm and sweet, the dignity of her beautiful presence was so immovable, that the lady felt it in vain to waste words upon her. Juanita was a hopeless case.

"It is no use for me to be here then," she said. "Mr. Randolph, you may make your own arrangements."

Which Mr. Randolph did. He held a consultation with Juanita, as to what was wanting and what she would do; a consultation with which he was satisfied. Juanita was left in full charge, with authority to do for Daisy precisely according to Dr. Sandford's instructions, in all matters. Mrs. Randolph meanwhile had a talk with her poor pale little daughter, upon more or less the same subjects; and then the father and mother prepared to go home to breakfast.

"Shall I send you June?" said Mrs. Randolph.

"No, mamma; I think not."

"Be patient a little while, Daisy," said her father kissing her; "and you will be able to have books and company too. Now for a little while you must keep quiet."

"Juanita will keep me quiet, papa."

"I will come and see you again by and by."

"Papa, I want to tell you one thing. I want to speak to you and mamma before you go."

Mr. Randolph saw that the child's face flushed as if she were making some effort. He bent down over her again.

"Is it something of interest, Daisy?"

"Yes, papa. To me."

"Don't talk of it now then. Lie still and do not talk at all. By and by you will tell me what it is."

CHAPTER XVII.

Mr. and Mrs. Randolph departed.

"Daisy will be ruined forever!" So said the lady as soon as she was in the carriage.

"I hope not."

"You take it coolly, Mr. Randolph. That woman is exactly the sort to infect Daisy; and you have arranged it so that she will have full chance."

"What is the precise danger you apprehend?" said Mr. Randolph. "I have not heard it put into words."

"Daisy will be unmanageable. She is nearly that now."

"I never saw a more docile child in my life."

"That is because you take her part, Mr. Randolph. You will find it out in time, when it is too late; and it will be your own doing."

"What?"

"Daisy will be a confirmed piece of superstition. You will see. And you will not find her docile then. If she once takes hold of anything, she does it with great obstinacy."

"But what is she taking hold of now? After all, you do not tell me," said Mr. Randolph carelessly.

"Of every sort of religious fanatical notion, you will find, Mr. Randolph! She will set herself against everything I want her to do, after the fashion of those people, who think nothing is right but their own way. It will be a work of extreme difficulty, I foresee, to do anything with her after these weeks in this black woman's house.

I would have run any risk in removing her, rather than let it be so."

"Well, we shall see," said Mr. Randolph. "I cannot quite take your view of the matter. I would rather keep the child—even for my own private comfort—than lose her to prevent her from becoming religious."

Mrs. Randolph indignantly let this statement of opinion alone.

Little Daisy had a quiet day, meanwhile. The weather grew excessively hot; her broken ankle pained her; it was a day of suffering. Obliged to lie quite still; unable to change her position even a little, when the couch became very hot under her; no air coming in at the open window but what seemed laden with the heats of a furnace, Daisy lay still and breathed as well as she could. All day Juanita was busy about her; moistening her lips with orange juice, bathing her hands, fanning her, and speaking and singing sweet words to her, as she could attend to them. The child's eyes began to go to the fine black face that hovered near her, with an expression of love and trust that was beautiful to behold. It was a day that tried poor little Daisy's patience; for along with all this heat, and weary lying still in one position, there were shoots and twitches of pain that seemed to come from the broken ankle and reach every part of her body; and she could not move about or turn over to ease them by some change.

At last the weary hours began to grow less oppressive. The sun got low in the sky; the air came with a little touch of freshness. How good it was to see the sun lost behind the woods on the other side the road. Juanita kindled her fire again and put on the kettle; for Daisy was to have another cup of tea, and wanted it very much. Then, before the kettle had boiled, came the doctor.

It was a pleasant variety. Dr. Sandford's face was a good one to see come in anywhere, and in Daisy's case very refreshing. It was so noble a face; the features fine, manly, expressive; with a sedate gravity that spoke of a character above trifling. His calm, forceful eye was very imposing; the thick auburn locks of his hair, pushed back as they were from his face, were beautiful to Daisy's imagination. Altogether he fastened her attention whenever he came within reach of it; she could not read those grave lines of his face; she puzzled over them. Dr. Sandford's appearance was in some way bewitching to her. Truly many ladies found it so.

He examined now the state of her foot; gave rapid comprehensive glances at everything; told his orders to Mrs. Benoit. Finally, paused before going, and looked into the very wise little eyes that scanned him so carefully.

"Is there anything you want, Daisy?" he said with a physician's familiarity.

"No, sir,—I thank you."

"Mrs. Benoit takes good care of you?"

"Very good."

The manner of Daisy's speech was like her looks; childlike enough, and yet with a deliberate utterance unlike a child.

"What do you think about, as you lie there all day?" he said.

The question had been put with a somewhat careless curiosity; but at that he saw a pink flush rise and spread itself all over Daisy's pale face; the grey eyes looked at him steadily, with no doubt of some thoughts behind them. Dr. Sandford listened for her answer. What *was* the child thinking about? She spoke at last with that same sweet deliberateness.

"I have been thinking, Dr. Sandford, about what Jesus did for me."

"What was that?" said the doctor in considerable surprise.

"Because it was so hard for me to keep still to-day, I thought—you know—how it must have been——"

The flush deepened on the cheeks, and Daisy's eyes were swimming full of tears. Dr. Sandford looked, in much surprise; perhaps he was at some pains to comprehend what all this meant.

"How it must have been when?" said he, bending over Daisy's couch.

"You know, Dr. Sandford," she said tenderly. "When he was on the cross—and couldn't move——"

Daisy gave way. She put her hands over her face. The doctor stood erect, looking at her; glanced his grave eyes at Mrs. Benoit and at her again; then made a step towards Juanita.

"No excitement is permitted," he said. "You must keep her from it. Do you understand?"

"Yes, sir," Juanita said. But her face was all alight.

"Have you been reading some of those stories to her?"

"I have not been reading to her at all to-day, if his honour pleases."

"Daisy," said Dr. Sandford, coming back to the couch, "what put such thoughts into your head?"

"I felt so badly to-day." She spoke with her usual collectedness again.

"Well, try and not mind it. You will feel better in a day or two. Do you know when that happened that you were talking about?"

"Yes, sir."

"When was it?"

"More than eighteen hundred years ago."

"Do you think it is worth your while to be troubled for what happened eighteen hundred years ago?"

"I think it is just the same as if it happened now," said Daisy, without moving her eyes.

"Do you? By what power of reasoning?"

"I don't think I know how to reason," said Daisy. "It is feeling."

"How does feeling manage it?"

Daisy discerned the tone of the question, looked at her questioner, and answered with tender seriousness:

"I know the Lord Jesus did that for me; and I know he is in heaven now."

The doctor kept silence a minute. "Daisy," said he, "you are under my orders at present. You must mind me. You are to take a cup of tea, and a piece of toast, if you like; then you are to go to sleep and keep quiet, and not think of anything that happened more than an hour ago. Will you?"

"I will try to be quiet," said Daisy.

She and the doctor looked at each other in a dissatisfied manner, she wistfully, he disapprovingly, and then the doctor went out. Daisy's eyes followed, straining after him as long as they could; and when she could see him no longer they filled with tears again. She was looking as intent and wistful as if she might have been thirty years old instead of nine or ten, when Juanita came to her side with the tea she had been making.

The tea and toast did Daisy good; and she was ready to enjoy a visit from her father, who spent the evening with her. But he would not let her talk. The next day was hot again; however Daisy felt better. The heat was more bearable. It was a very quiet day.

Both she and Juanita obeyed orders and did not talk much; nevertheless Juanita sang hymns a great deal, and that was delightful to Daisy. She found Juanita knew one hymn in particular that she loved exceedingly; it was the one that had been sung in the little church the day she had heard Mr. Dinwiddie preach; it fell in with the course of Daisy's thoughts; and several times in the day she had Juanita sing it over. Daisy's eyes always filled when she heard it; nevertheless Juanita could not resist her pleading wish.

"O the Lamb! the loving Lamb!—
The Lamb on Calvary.

The Lamb that was slain, but lives again,
To intercede for me."

"I am so happy, Juanita," Daisy said after one of these times. "I am so happy!"

"What makes it so, my love?"

"O because that is true—because he lives up there to take care of me."

"Bless the Lord!" said the black woman.

Towards evening of that day, Juanita had left the room to make her fire and attend to some other things, when Daisy heard her own name hailed softly from the window. She turned her head, and there was Preston's bright face.

"My poor, poor little Daisy!"

"How do you do, Preston?" said Daisy, looking as clear as a moonbeam.

"There you are a prisoner!"

"It is a very nice prison."

"Don't, my dear Daisy! I'll believe you in anything else, you know; but in this I am unable. Tied by your foot for six weeks, perhaps! I should like to shoot Capt. Drummond."

"It was not Capt. Drummond's fault."

"Is it bad, Daisy?"

"My foot? It has been pretty bad."

"Poor Daisy! And that was all because you would not sing."

"Because I would not sing, Preston!"

"Yes, that is the cause of all the trouble that has been in the house. Now, Daisy, you'll give it up?"

"Give what up?"

"Give up your nonsense, and sing."

"*That?*" said Daisy, and a slight flush came into the pale cheeks.

"Aunt Felicia wants you to sing it, and she will make you do it, when you get well."

Daisy made no answer.

"Don't you see, my dear Daisy, it is foolish not to do as other people do?"

"I don't see what my broken ankle has to do with what you are saying, Preston."

"Daisy, what will become of you all these six weeks? We cannot go a fishing, nor have any fun."

"You can."

"What will you do?"

"I guess I can have books and read, by and by. I will ask Dr. Sandford."

"Suppose I bring some books, and read to you?"

"O Preston! how nice."

"Well, I'll do it then. What shall I bring?"

"I wish you could bring something that would tell about these things."

"These things? What is that?"

"It is a trilobite. Capt. Drummond got it the other day. It was a fish once, and now it is a stone; and I would like very much to know about it."

"Daisy, are you serious?"

"Why, yes, Preston."

"My dear little Daisy, do *not* you go and be a philosopher!"

"Why, I can't; but why shouldn't I?"

"Philosophers are not 'nice,' Daisy, when they are ladies," said Preston, shaking his head.

"Why not?"

"Because ladies are not meant to be philosophers."

"But I want to know about trilobites," said Daisy.

"I don't think you do. You would not find the study of fossils interesting."

"I think I should—if you would help me, Preston."

"Well, we will see, Daisy. I will do anything for you, if you will do one thing for me. O Daisy, do! Aunt Felicia has not given it up at all."

"Good bye, Preston," said Daisy. "Now you must go, and not talk to me any more this time."

Preston ran off. He was not allowed to come again for a day or two; and Daisy was not allowed to talk. She was kept very quiet, until it was found that the broken bone was actually healing and in a fair way to get well. The pains in it were no longer so trying; the very hot days had given place to a time of milder weather; and Daisy, under the care of the old black woman, enjoyed her solitary imprisonment well enough. Twice a day always her father visited her; once a day, Mrs. Randolph. Her stay was never very long; Juanita's house was not a comfortable place for her; but Mr. Randolph gave a large piece of his time and attention to his suffering little daughter, and was indeed the first one to execute Preston's plan of reading aloud for her amusement. A new and great delight to Daisy. She never remembered her father taking such pains with her before. Then, when her father and mother were gone, and the cottage was still, Juanita and Daisy had what the latter called their "good time." Juanita read the Bible and sang hymns and prayed. There was no time nor pleasure in all the day that Daisy liked so well.

She had gained strength and was in a good way to be well again. The first morning this was told her, Daisy said:

"Papa, may I speak to you now?"

"About something important, Daisy?"

"Yes, papa, I think so."

"Go on. What is it?"

Juanita was standing near by. The child glanced at her, then at her father.

"Papa," she said, speaking slowly and with some hesitation,—"I want you to know—I want to tell you—about me, so that you may understand."

"Are you so difficult to understand, Daisy?"

"No, papa; but I want you to know something. I want you to know that I am a Christian."

"Well, so are we all," said Mr. Randolph coolly.

"No, papa, but I don't mean that."

"What do you mean?"

"I mean, papa,—that I belong to the Lord Jesus, and must do what he tells me."

"What am I to understand by that, Daisy?"

"Nothing, papa; only I thought you ought to know."

"Do you understand what you are saying yourself, my child?"

"Yes, papa."

"What does it mean, Daisy?"

"Only, papa, I want you to know that I belong to the Lord Jesus."

"Does that imply that you will not belong to me any more?"

"O no, papa!"

"Why do you tell it me, then?"

"Papa, Jesus says he will be ashamed of those who are ashamed of him; I will not be ashamed of him; so I want you to know what I am."

"But, Daisy, you and I must come to an understanding about this," said Mr. Randolph, taking a chair. "Does this declaration mean that you are intending to be something different from what I like to see you?"

"I do not know, papa."

"You do not! Does it mean that you are proposing to set up a standard of action for yourself, independent of me?"

"No, papa."

"What then, Daisy?"

"Papa, I do not quite know what you mean by a *standard*."

"I will change the word. Do you mean that your purpose is to make, henceforward, your own rules of life?"

"No, papa; I do not mean that."

"What do you mean?"

"Papa," said Daisy, very deliberately, "if I belong to my Saviour,—you know,—I must follow his rules."

"Daisy, I shall not cease to require obedience to mine."

"No, papa,—but ——" said Daisy, colouring.

"But what?"

"I don't know very well how to say what I want, papa; it is difficult."

"Try."

"Papa, you will not be displeased?"

"That depends upon what you have to say, Daisy."

"Papa, I do not *mean* to displease you," said the child, her eyes filling with tears. "But—suppose——"

"Well,—suppose anything."

"Suppose *those* rules should be different from your rules?"

"I am to be the judge, Daisy. If you set up disobedience to me, on any pretext, you know the consequences."

Daisy's lip trembled; she put up her hands to her face and burst into tears. She could not bear that reminder. Her father took one of her hands down and kissed the little wet cheek.

"Where are you going to find these rules, Daisy," he said kindly, "which you are going to set up against mine?"

"Papa, I do not set them up."

"Where do you get them?"

"Only in the Bible, papa."

"You are a little child, Daisy; you are not quite old enough to be able to judge properly for yourself what the rules of that book are. While you are little and ignorant, I am your judge, of that and everything else; and your business is to obey me. Do you understand that?"

"But, papa——"

"Well—what?"

"Papa, I am afraid you will be angry."

"I do not think I shall. You and I had better come to an understanding about these matters Say on, Daisy."

"I was going to say, papa——"

Daisy was afraid to tell what. Mr. Randolph again stooped and kissed her; kissed her two or three times.

"Papa, I do not *mean* to make you angry," said the child with intense eagerness,—"but—suppose—papa, I mean,—are *you* a servant of the Lord Jesus?"

Mr. Randolph drew back. "I endeavour to do my duty, Daisy," he said coldly. "I do not know what you include in the terms you use."

"Papa, that is what I mean," said Daisy, with a very meek face. "Papa, if I *am*, and you are *not*, then perhaps you would not think the things that I think."

"If you are, and I am not, what?"

That, papa—which I wanted you to know I am. A servant of Jesus."

"Then, what?"

"Then, papa, if I am, and you are not,—wouldn't you perhaps not think about those rules as I must think of them?"

"You mean that our thoughts would disagree?"

"Papa—they might."

"What shall we do, then, Daisy?"

Daisy looked wistfully and somewhat sadly at him. There was more weight of thought under the little brow than he liked to see there. This would not do; yet matters must be settled.

"Do you want to be a different little person from what you have been, Daisy, hitherto?"

"I don't know, papa—I think so."

"How do you wish to be different?"

"I can't tell, papa. I might have to be."

"I want you just as you are, Daisy."

Mr. Randolph stooped his head down again to the too thoughtful little face. Daisy clasped her arms around his neck and held him close. It was only by her extraordinary self-command that she kept from tears; when he raised his head her eyes were perfectly dry.

"Will you be my good little Daisy—and let me do the thinking for you?" said Mr. Randolph tenderly.

"Papa—I *can't*."

"I will not have you different from what I like you, Daisy."

"Then, papa, what shall I do?"

"Obey me, and be satisfied with that."

"But, papa, I am a servant of the Lord Jesus Christ," said the child, looking unutterably sober.

"I do not intend my commands shall conflict with any of higher authority."

"Papa—suppose—they *might?*"

"I must be judge. You are a little child; you must take the law from my mouth, until you are older."

"But, papa, suppose I *thought* the Bible told me to do what you did not think it said?"

"I advise you to believe my judgment, Daisy, if you wish to keep the peace between us. I will not have any more calling of it in question."

Daisy struggled plainly, though she would not cry; her colour flushed, her lip quivered. She was entirely silent for a little while, and Mr. Randolph sat watching her. The struggle lasted some minutes; till she had overcome it somewhat she would not speak; and it was sharp. Then the child closed her eyes and her face grew calm. Mr. Randolph did not know what to think of her.

"Daisy——"

"What, papa?"

"I do not think we have settled this question yet."

"I do not think we have, papa."

"What is to be done? It will not answer, my little daughter, for you to set up your will against mine."

"Papa, it is not my will."

"What do you call it, then?"

"Papa, it is not my will at all. It is the will of God."

"Take care, Daisy," said her father. "You are not to

say that. My will will never oppose itself to that authority you speak of."

"Papa, I only want to obey that."

"But remember, I must be the judge."

"Papa," said Daisy, eagerly, "won't this do? If I think something is in the Bible, mayn't I bring it to you to see?"

"Yes."

"And if you think it *is* there, then will you let me do it?"

"Do what?"

"Do what the Bible says, papa."

"I think I may promise that, Daisy," said Mr. Randolph; though dubiously, as not quite certain what he was promising; "so long as I am the judge."

"Then that will do, papa! That is nice."

Daisy's countenance expressed such utter content at this arrangement, that Mr. Randolph looked grave.

"Now you have talked and excited yourself enough for to-day," he said. "You must be quiet."

"Mayn't I tell mamma when she comes?"

"What, Daisy?"

"I mean what I have told you, papa."

"No. Wait till to-morrow. Why do you wish to tell her, Daisy?"

"Papa, I think I ought to tell her. I want her to know."

"You have very uncompromising notions of duty. But this duty can wait till another day."

Daisy had to wait more than a day for her opportunity; her mother's next visits were too bustling and unsatisfactory, as well as too short, to promise her any good chance of being heard. At last came a propitious morning. It was more moderate weather; Daisy herself was doing very well and suffering little pain; and Mrs. Randolph looked in good humour and had sat down with her tetting-work as if she meant to make her daughter something of a visit.

Mr. Randolph was lounging at the head of the couch, out of Daisy's sight.

"Mamma," began the child, "there is something I wish to say to you."

"You have a favourable opportunity, Daisy. I can hear." Yet Daisy looked a minute at the white hand that was flying the bobbin about. That white hand.

"It isn't much, mamma. It is only—that I wish you to know—that I am a Christian."

"That you are *what?*" said Mrs. Randolph coldly.

"A Christian, mamma."

"Pray what does that mean?"

"That I am a servant of Christ, mamma."

"When did you find it out, Daisy?"

"Some time ago, mamma. Some time—a little while—before my birth-day."

"You did! What do you think *me?*"

Daisy kept silence.

"Well! why don't you speak? Answer me."

"Mamma, I don't know how to answer you," said Daisy, flushing for an instant. Her mother's eyes took note of her.

"I shall not ask you a third time, Daisy."

"Mamma," said the child low,—"I do not think you are what I mean by a Christian."

"You do not. I supposed that. Now you will go on and tell me what you mean by 'a Christian.'"

"It means," said Daisy, her eyes filling with tears, "it means a person who loves the Lord Jesus and obeys him."

"I hope you are gratified, Mr. Randolph," said the lady, "with this specimen of the new Christianity. Dutiful and respectful are happily united; along with a pleasant mixture of modesty. What do you expect me to do, Daisy, with this announcement of yours?"

"Nothing, mamma," said Daisy faintly.

"I suppose you think that my Christianity must accommodate itself to yours? Did you expect that?"

"No, mamma."

"It would be very foolish of you; for the fact will be the other way. Yours must accommodate itself to mine."

"I only wanted you to know what mine is, mamma."

"Yours is what mine is, Daisy. What I think right for you, that you are to do. I will not hear a whimper from you again about what you are—do you understand? Not again. I have listened to you this time, but this is the last. If I hear another syllable like this, about what you are or your Christianity, I shall know how to chastise it out of you. You are nothing at all, but my Daisy; you are a Jewess, if I choose to have it so."

Mr. Randolph made an uneasy movement; but the lady's white fingers flew in and out of her tetting-work without regarding him.

"What do you want to do, that you are asking my permission in this roundabout way? What do you want to do, that you think will not please me?"

Daisy at first hesitated; then Mr. Randolph was surprised to hear her say boldly—

"I am afraid, a great many things, mamma."

"Well, you know now what to expect. Mr. Randolph," said the lady letting fall her tetting-work, "if you please, I will go home. The sun will only be getting hotter, if I stay."

Mr. Randolph stood behind Daisy, bending down and holding her face in his two hands.

"What would you like me to send you from home, Daisy?"

"Nothing, papa."

"Would you like to have Preston come and see you?"

"If he likes to come, papa."

"He has been only waiting for my permission, and if you say so, I will give him yours."

"He may come. I should like to see him very much."

"You may have books too, now, Daisy. Do you not want some books?"

"I should like 'Sandford and Merton,' papa; and when Preston comes I'll tell him what else I want."

Mr. Randolph stood still, smoothing down the hair on each side of the little round head, while Mrs. Randolph was adjusting herself for her drive.

"Are you ready, Mr. Randolph?"

"Cannot say that I am," said the gentleman, stooping to kiss Daisy's forehead,—"but I will go with you. One thing I should like understood. For reasons which are sufficient with me, Daisy is to consider herself prohibited from making any music on Sundays henceforward, except she chooses to do it in church. I mention it, lest you should ask her to do what I have forbidden, and so make confusion."

Mrs. Randolph gave no sort of answer to this speech, and walked off to the door. Daisy, whose eyes had brightened with joy, clasped her arms around her father's neck when he stooped again and whispered with an energetic pressure,

"Thank you, papa!"

Mr. Randolph only kissed her, and went off after his wife. The drive home was remarkably silent.

CHAPTER XVIII.

It happened that day that Juanita had business on hand which kept her a good deal of the morning in the out-shed which formed part of her premises. She came in every now and then to see how Daisy was doing; yet the morning was on the whole spent by Daisy alone; and when Juanita at last came in to stay, she fancied the child was looking pale and worn more than usual.

"My love do not feel well?"

"Yes I do, Juanita—I am only tired. Have you done washing?"

"It is all done. I am ready for whatever my love pleases."

"Isn't washing very disagreeable work, Juanita?"

"I do not think what it be, while it is mine," the woman said contentedly. "All is good work that I can do for the Lord."

"But *that* work, Juanita? How can you do that work so?"

"When the Lord gives work, he give it to be done for him. Bless the Lord!"

"I do not understand, though, Juanita. Please tell me. How can you?"

"Miss Daisy, I don't know. I can do it with pleasure, because it is my Lord's command. I can do it with thanksgiving, because he has given me the strength and the power. And I can do it the best I can, so as nobody shall find fault in his servant. And then, Miss Daisy, I can do it to get money to send his blessed word to them that sit in darkness—where I come from. And I can do it with prayer, asking my Lord to make my heart clean for his glory; like as I make soiled things white again. And I do it with joy, because I know the Lord hear my prayer."

"I think you are very happy, Juanita," said Daisy.

"When the Lord leads to living fountains of waters, then no more thirsting,"—said the black woman expressively.

"Then, Juanita, I suppose—if I get tired lying here,—I can do patience work?"

"Jesus will have his people do a great deal of that work," said Mrs. Benoit tenderly. "And it is work that pleases him, Miss Daisy. My love is very weary?"

"I suppose, Juanita, if I was really patient, I shouldn't be. Should I? I think I am impatient."

"My love knows who carries the lambs in his bosom."

Daisy's tired face smoothed itself out at this. She turned her eyes to the window with a placid look of rest in them.

"Jesus knows where the trouble is," said the black woman. "He knows all. And he can help too. Now I am going to get something to do Miss Daisy good."

Before this could be done, there came a heavy clumping step up to the house and a knock at the door; and then a person entered whom Juanita did not know. A hard-featured woman, in an old-fashioned black straw bonnet and faded old shawl drawn tight round her. She came directly forward to Daisy's couch.

"Well I declare if it ain't true! Tied by the heels, ain't ye?"—was her salutation. Juanita looked, and saw that Daisy recognized the visiter; for she smiled at her, half pleasure, half assent to what she said.

"I heerd of it—that is, I heerd you'd gone up to the mountain and broke something; I couldn't find out what 'twas; and then Hephzibah she said she would go down to

Melbourne Sunday. I said to her, says I, 'Hephzibah, I wouldn't go all that ways, child, for to do nothing; 'tain't likely but that some part of the story's true, if you and me can't find out which;' but Hephzibah she took her own head and went; and don't you think, she came back a cryin'?"

"What was that for?" said Daisy, looking very much interested.

"Why she couldn't find you, I guess; and she thought you was killed. But you ain't, be you?"

"Only my foot and ankle hurt," said Daisy smiling; "and I am doing very well now."

"And was you broke anywheres?"

"My ankle was broken."

"I declare! And you couldn't be took home?"

"No."

"So the folks said; only they said that young soldier had killed you. I hope he got hurted himself?"

"Why Mrs. Harbonner, *he* did not do it. It was an accident. It wasn't anybody's fault."

"It wouldn't ha' happened if *I* had been there, I can tell you!" said Hephzibah's mother. "I don't think much of a man if he ain't up to taking care of a woman;—and a child above all. Now how long are you goin' to be in this fix?"

"I don't know. I suppose I shall have to lie still for four or five weeks more, before my foot is well."

"It's tiresome, I guess, ain't it?"

"Yes—sometimes."

"Well I used to think, if folks was good, things wouldn't happen to 'em. That's what I thought. That was my study of divinity. And when everything on earth happened to me, I just concluded it was because I warn't a bit too good to deserve it. Now I'm beat—to see you lie there. I don't see what is the use of being good, if it don't get none."

"O Mrs. Harbonner!" said Daisy—"I am glad my foot was broken."

"Well, I'm beat!" was all Mrs. Harbonner could say. "You air, be you?"

"It hasn't done me any harm at all; and it has done me a great deal of good."

Mrs. Harbonner stood staring at Daisy.

"The promise is sure," said Mrs. Benoit. "All things shall work together for good to them that love God!"

The other woman wheeled about and looked at her for an instant with a sharp keen eye of note-taking; then she returned to Daisy.

"Well I suppose I'll tell Hephzibah she won't see you again till summer's over; so she may as well give over thinking about it."

"Do you think Hephzibah wants to learn, Mrs. Harbonner?"

"Well, I guess she does."

"Wouldn't she come here and get her lessons? Couldn't she come to see me every day while I am here?"

"I 'spose she'd jump out of her skin to do it," said Mrs. Harbonner. "Hephzibah's dreadful sot on seeing you."

"Mrs. Benoit," said Daisy, "may I have this little girl come to see me every day, while I am here?"

"Miss Daisy shall have all, who she will," was the answer; and it was arranged so; and Mrs. Harbonner took her departure. Lingering a minute at the door, whither Juanita attended her, she made one or two enquiries and remarks about Daisy, answered civilly and briefly by Mrs. Benoit.

"Poor little toad!" said Mrs. Harbonner, drawing her shawl tight round her for the last time. "But ain't she little *queer?*"

These words were spoken in a low murmur, which just served to draw Daisy's attention. Out of sight behind the moreen curtain, Mrs. Harbonner forgot she was not beyond hearing; and Daisy's ears were good. She noticed that Juanita made no answer at all to this question, and presently shut the door.

The business of giving Daisy some fruit was the next thing attended to; in the course of eating which Daisy marvelled a little to herself what possible likeness to a *toad* Mrs. Harbonner could have discovered in her. The comparison did not seem flattering; also she pondered somewhat why it could be that anybody found her queer. She said nothing about it; though she gave Mrs. Benoit a little account of Hephzibah and the reason of the proposed series of visits. In the midst of this came a cheery "Daisy"—at the other side of her; and turning her head, there was Preston's face at the window.

"O Preston!"—Daisy handed to Mrs. Benoit her unfinished saucer of strawberries—"I am so glad! I have been waiting for you. Have you brought my books?"

"Where do you think I have been, Daisy?"

"I don't know. Shooting!—Have you?"

Daisy's eye caught the barrel of a fowling-piece shewing its end up at the window. Preston without replying lifted up his game bag and let her see the bright feathers of little birds which partly filled it.

"You have!—Shooting!"—Daisy repeated, in a tone between disapprobation and dismay. "It isn't September!"

"Capital sport, Daisy," said Preston, letting the bag fall.

"I think it is very poor sport," said Daisy. "I wish they were all alive and flying again."

"So do I—if I might shoot them again."

"It's cruel, Preston!"

"Nonsense, Daisy. Don't you be too tender. Birds were made to kill. What are they good for?"

With a wit that served her instead of experience, Daisy was silent, looking with unspoken abhorrence at the wicked muzzle of the fowling-piece.

"Did you bring me 'Sandford and Merton,' Preston?" she said presently.

"'Sandford and Merton'! My dear Daisy, I have been going all over the world, you know—this part of it—and I was too far from Melbourne to go round that way for your book; if I had, it would have been too late to get here. You see the sun's pretty well down."

Daisy said no more; but it was out of her power not to look disappointed. She had so counted upon her book; and she was so weary of lying still and doing nothing. She wanted very much to read about the house that Harry and Tommy built; it would have been a great refreshment.

"Cheer up, Daisy," said Preston; "I'll bring you books to-morrow—and read to you too, if you like it. What shall I bring?"

"O Preston, I want to know about trilobites!"

"Daisy, you might as well want to know about the centre of the earth! That's where they belong."

"I should like to know about the centre of the earth," said Daisy. "Is there anything there?"

"Anything at the centre of the earth? I suppose so."

"But I mean, anything *but* earth," said Daisy.

Preston burst out laughing. "O Daisy, Daisy!—Hadn't you better learn about what is on the outside of the earth, before we dig down so deep into it?"

"Well, Preston, my trilobite was on the outside."

"Daisy, it wouldn't interest you," said Preston seriously; "you would have to go deep into something else besides the earth—so deep that you would get tired. Let the trilobite alone, and let's have Grimm's Tales to-morrow—shall we? or what will you have?"

Daisy was patiently silent a minute; and then in came Dr. Sandford. In his presence Preston was mute; attending to the doctor's manipulations as gravely as the doctor himself performed them. In the midst of the general stillness, Dr. Sandford asked,

"Who was speaking about trilobites as I came up?"

"Preston was speaking," said Daisy, as nobody else seemed ready to answer.

"What about them?"

"He thinks they would not interest me," said Daisy.

"What do you know about trilobites?" said Dr. Sandford, now raising his blue eyes for a good look into the child's face. He saw it looked weary.

"I have got a beautiful one. Juanita, will you bring it here, please?"

The doctor took it up and handled it with an eye that said, Daisy knew, that it was a fine specimen. The way he handled it gratified her.

"So this is one of your playthings, is it, Daisy?"

"No, sir; it is not a plaything, but I like to look at it."

"Why?"

"It is so wonderful, and beautiful, I think."

"But do tell Daisy, will you, doctor," said Preston, "that it is a subject she cannot understand yet. She wants me to bring her books about trilobites."

"Time hangs heavy, Daisy?" said the doctor.

"No, sir—only when I have nothing to do."

"What have you done to-day?"

"Nothing, sir; except talking to papa and mamma,—and some business about a little girl."

The sedateness of this announcement was inexpressible, coming as it did after a little thoughtful pause. Preston burst out laughing. Dr. Sandford did not so far forget himself. He only gave Daisy a rapid look of his grave blue eyes.

"It would be a charity to give you more employment than that," he said. "You like wonderful things, Daisy?'

"Very much, when I understand about them."

"I will agree to tell you anything you please—that I know—about any wonderful things you can see to-morrow, looking from your window."

The Doctor and Preston went off together, and left Daisy, though without books, in a high state of excitement and gratification. The rest of the evening her little head was busy by turns with fancying the observations of the next day, and wondering what she could possibly find from her window to talk to the doctor about. A very unpromising window Daisy considered it. Nothing was to be seen beside trees and a little strip of road; few people passed by that way; and if there had, what wonder could there have been in that. Daisy was half afraid she should find nothing to talk to the doctor about; and that would be a mortification.

Daisy and Juanita were both apt to be awake pretty early. Lying there on her back all day, without power to run about and get tired, Daisy's sleep was light; and her eyes were generally open before the sun got high enough to look at them. Juanita was always up and dressed earlier even than that; how much earlier Daisy had no means of knowing; but she was sure to hear the murmur of her friend's voice at her prayers, either in the other room or outside of the house. And Juanita did not come in to see Daisy till she had been awake a good while, and had had leisure to think over a great many things. Daisy found that was a good time for her own prayers; there was nothing to disturb her, and nothing to be heard at all, except that soft sound of Juanita's voice and the clear trills and quavers of the little birds' voices in the trees. There was no disturbance in any of those sounds; nothing but joy and gladness and the voice of melody from them all.

By and by, when the light began to kindle in the tops of the trees, and Daisy was sure to be watching it and trying to get sight of some of the bird singers which were so merry up there, she would hear another sound by her bedside, or feel a soft touch; and there would be Juanita, as bright as the day, in her way of looking bright, bending over to see and find out how Daisy was. Then, having satisfied herself, Juanita would go about the business of the morning. First her fire was made, and the kettle put on for breakfast. Daisy used to beg her to leave the door open, so that though she could not follow her with her eyes and see, she could yet hear what Juanita was doing. She used to listen to hear the kindling put in the stove, and the wood ; she knew the sound of it ; then when the match was lit and applied she liked the rushing sound of the blaze and kindling fire ; it gave pleasant token that the kettle would be boiled by and by. But first she listened to Juanita's feet brushing through the grass to get to the well ; and Daisy listened so hard she could almost tell after a while whether the grass was dry or whether it was heavy with dew. Juanita always carried the kettle to the well ; and when she came back Daisy could hear the iron clink of the stove as the kettle was put on. Presently Juanita came in then from her kitchen, and began the work of putting the house in order. How nicely she did it ! like the perfection of a nurse, which she was. No dust, no noise, no bustle ; still as a mouse, but watchful as a cat, the alert old woman went round the room and made all tidy and all clean and fresh. Very likely Juanita would change the flowers in a little vase which stood on the mantelpiece or the table, before she felt that everything was as it ought to be.

When all that was done, her next attention was to Daisy herself ; and Daisy never in her life had nicer tending than now. If Juanita was a nurse, she was a dressing-maid too, of first-rate qualifications. It was a real pleasure to have her ministering about the couch ; and for that matter, the whole work of the morning, as Juanita managed it, was a regular and unfailing piece of amusement to Daisy. And in the midst of it, every look at the black woman's noble, sweet face, warmed Daisy's heart with something better than amusement. Daisy grew to love her very much.

This morning all these affairs had been gone through as usual; and leaving Daisy in a happy, refreshed state, Mrs. Benoit went off to prepare her breakfast. Like everything else, that was beautifully done. By and by, in she came with a tray and white napkin, white as napkin could be, and fine damask too. For Juanita had treasures of various sorts, besides old moreen curtains. On this tray for instance, there was not only a fine napkin of damask; there was a delicate cup and saucer of fine china, which Daisy thought very beautiful. It was as thin and fine as any cup at Melbourne House, and had a dainty vine of leaves and flowers running round it, in a light red brown colour. The plate was not to match; it was a common little white plate; but that did not matter. The tea was in the little brown cup, and Daisy's lips closed upon it with entire satisfaction. Juanita had some excellent tea too; and if she had not, there was a sufficient supply sent from Melbourne; as well as of everything else. So today there was not only the brown toast in strips, which Daisy fancied; but there were great red Antwerp raspberries for her; and that made, Daisy thought, the very best breakfast that could be eaten. She was very bright this morning.

"Juanita," she said, "I have found something for Dr Sandford already."

"What does Miss Daisy mean?"

"Don't you know? Didn't you hear him yesterday? He gave me something to do. He said he would tell me about anything wonderful I could see in the course of the day; and I have found something already."

"'Seems to me as all the Lord has made is wonderful," said the black woman. "Does Miss Daisy think Dr. Sandford can tell her all about it?"

"Why I suppose he knows a great deal, Juanita."

"If he knowed one thing more,"—said the black woman. "Here he is, Miss Daisy. He's early."

Certainly he was; but Dr. Sandford had a long ride to take that morning, and could only see Daisy then on his way. In silence he attended to her, and with no delay; smiled at her; put the tips of his fingers to her raspberry dish and took out one for his own lips; then went quick away. Daisy smiled curiously. She was very much amused at him. She did not ask Juanita what she meant by the "one thing more." Daisy knew quite well; or thought she did.

All that day she was in an amused state, watching to see wonderful things. Her father's and mother's visits came as usual. Preston came and brought her some books. Hephzibah came too and had a bit of a lesson. But Hephzibah's wits were like her hair, straying all manner of ways. It was very difficult to make her understand the difference between a, b, ab,—and b, a, ba; and that was discouraging. Daisy toiled with her till she was tired; and then was glad to lie still and rest without even thinking of wonderful things, till Juanita brought her her dinner.

As the doctor had been early, so he was late to-day. It was near sunset when he came, and Daisy was a little disappointed, fancying that he was tired. He said nothing at first; attended to Daisy's foot in the profoundest gravity; but in the midst of it, without looking up, he asked,

"What wonderful things have you seen to-day?"

"I am afraid you are tired, Dr. Sandford," said Daisy very gently.

"What then?"

"Then it might tire you more to talk to me."

"You have seen something wonderful, have you?" said he doctor glancing at her.

"Two or three things, sir."

"One at a time," said the doctor. "I *am* tired. I have ridden nearly seventy miles to-day, one way and another. Have you got a cup of milk for me, Mrs. Benoit?"

Daisy eagerly beckoned Juanita and whispered to her, and the result was that with the cup of milk came a plate of the magnificent raspberries. The doctor opened his grave eyes at Daisy, and stood at the foot of her couch picking up raspberries with his finger and thumb, as he had taken that one in the morning.

"Now what are the wonderful things?" said he.

"You are too tired to-night, Dr. Sandford."

"Let us have number one. Promises must be kept, Daisy. Business is business. Have you got such hard work for me? What was the first thing?"

"The first wonderful thing that I saw—or at least that I thought of—" said Daisy, "was the sun."

The doctor eat half a dozen raspberries without speaking, giving an odd little smile first in one corner of his mouth and then in the other.

"Do you expect me to tell you about *that?*" said he.

"You said business was business," Daisy replied with equal gravity to his own.

"I am glad the idea of the universe did not occur to you," said the doctor. "That might have been rather inconvenient for one evening's handling. What would you like me to tell you about the sun?"

"I do not know anything at all about it," said Daisy. "I would like to know everything you can tell me."

"The thought that first comes to me," said the doctor, "is, that it ripened these raspberries."

"I know *that*," said Daisy. "But I want to know what it *is*."

"The sun! Well," said the doctor, "it is a dark, round thing, something like this earth, only considerably bigger."

"*Dark!*" said Daisy.

"Certainly. I have no reason to believe it anything else."

"But you are laughing at me, Dr. Sandford," said Daisy, feeling very much disappointed and a little aggrieved.

"Am I? No, Daisy—if you had ridden seventy miles to-day, you might be tempted, but you would not feel like laughing. Business is business, I must remind you again."

"But you do not *mean* that the sun is dark?" said Daisy.

"I mean precisely what I say, I assure you."

"But it is so bright we cannot look at it," said Daisy.

"Something is so bright you cannot look at it. The something is not the body of the sun."

"Then it is the light that comes from it."

"No light comes from it, that I know. I told you, the sun is a dark body."

"Not laughing?"

"No," said Dr. Sandford, though he did laugh now;—"the sun, you see, is a more wonderful thing than you imagined."

"But sir, may I ask any question I have a mind to ask?"

"Certainly! All in the course of business."

"How do you know that it is dark, sir?"

"Perfectly fair. Suppose that Mrs. Benoit stood behind your curtain there, and that you had never seen her; how could you know that she has a dark skin?"

"Why I could not."

"Yes, you could—if there were rents in the curtain."

"But what are you talking of, sir?"

"Only telling you, in answer to your question, how I know the sun to be a dark body."

"But there is no curtain over the sun."

"That proves you [illegible] no philosopher, Daisy. If you were a philosopher, you would not be so certain of anything. There is a curtain over the sun; and there are rents or holes in the curtain sometimes,—so large that we can see the dark body of the sun through them."

"What is the curtain? Is *that* the light?"

"Now you are coming pretty near it, Daisy," said the doctor. "The curtain, as I call it, is not light, but it is what the light comes from."

"Then what *is* it, Dr. Sandford?"

"That has puzzled people wiser than you and I, Daisy. However, I think I may venture to say, that it is something like an ocean of flame, surrounding the dark body of the sun."

"And there are holes in it?"

"Sometimes."

"But they must be very large holes to be seen from this distance?"

"Very," said the doctor. "A great many times bigger than our whole earth."

"Then how do you know but they are dark islands in the ocean?"

"For several reasons," said the doctor looking gravely funny; "one of which reasons is, that we can see the deep ragged edges of the holes, and that these edges join together again."

"But there could not be holes in *our* ocean?" said Daisy.

Dr. Sandford gave a good long grave look at her, set aside his empty plate which had held raspberries, and took a chair. He talked to her now with serious quiet earnest, as if she had been a much older person.

"Our ocean, Daisy, you will remember, is an ocean of fluid matter. The ocean of flame which surrounds the sun is gaseous matter—or a sort of ocean of air, in a state of incandescence. This does not touch the sun, but floats round it, upon or above another atmosphere of another kind—like the way in which our clouds float in the air over our heads. You know how breaks come and go in the clouds; so you can imagine that this luminous covering of the sun parts in places, and shews the sun through, and then closes up again."

"Is *that* the way it is?" said Daisy.

"Even so."

"Dr. Sandford, you said a word just now I did not understand."

"Only one?" said the doctor.

"I think there was only one I did not know in the least."

"Can you direct me to it?"

"You said something about an ocean of air in a state—what state?"

"Incandescence?"

"That was it."

"That is a state where it gives out white heat."

"I thought everything at the sun must be on fire," said Daisy looking meditatively at the doctor.

"You see you were mistaken. It has only a covering of clouds of fire—so to speak."

"But it must be very hot there."

"It is pretty hot *here*," said the doctor shrugging his shoulders,—"ninety five millions of miles away; so I do not see that we can avoid your conclusion."

"How much is ninety five millions?"

"I am sure I don't know," said Dr. Sandford gravely. "After I have gone as far as a million or so, I get tired."

"But I do not know much about arithmetic," said Daisy humbly. "Mamma has not wanted me to study. I don't know how much one million is."

"Arithmetic does not help one on a journey, Miss Daisy," said the doctor pleasantly. "Counting the miles did not comfort me to-day. But I can tell you this. If you and I were to set off on a railway train, straight for the sun, and go at the rate of thirty-two miles an hour,—you know that is pretty fast travelling?"

"How fast do we go on the cars from here to New York?"

"Thirty miles an hour."

"Now I know," said Daisy.

"If we were to set off and go straight to the sun at that rate of speed, keeping it up night and day, it would take us—how long do you guess? It would take us three hundred years and more; nearly three hundred and fifty years, to get there."

"I cannot imagine travelling so long," said Daisy gravely. At which Dr. Sandford laughed; the first time Daisy had ever heard him do such a thing. It was a low, mellow laugh now; and she rather enjoyed it.

"I should like to know what a million is," she observed.

"Ten hundred thousand."

"And how many million miles did you say the sun is?"

"Ninety-five millions of miles a ay."

Daisy lay thinking about it.

"Can you imagine travelling faster? And then we need not be so long on the journey," said Dr. Sandford. "If we were to go as fast as a cannon ball, it would take us about seven years—not quite so much—to get to the sun."

"How fast does a cannon ball go?"

"Fifty times as fast as a railway train."

"I cannot imagine that either, Dr. Sandford."

"Give it up, Daisy," said the doctor, rising and beginning to put himself in order for travelling.

"Are you going?" said Daisy.

"Not till you have done with me!"

"Dr. Sandford, have you told me all there is to tell about the sun?"

"No."

"Would it take too long this evening?"

"Considering that the sun will not stay to be talked about, Daisy," said the doctor glancing out of the window, "I should say it would."

"Then I will ask only one thing more. Dr. Sandford, how can you tell so exactly how long it would take to go to the sun? how do you know?"

"Quite fair, Daisy," said the doctor surveying her gravely. "I know, by the power of a science called mathematics, which enables one to do all sorts of impossible things. But you must take that on my word; I cannot explain so that you would understand it."

"Thank you, sir," said Daisy.

She wanted further to ask what sort of a science mathematics might be; but Dr. Sandford had answered a good many questions, and the sun was down, down, behind the trees on the other side of the road. Daisy said no more. The doctor seeing her silent, smiled, and prepared himself to go.

"Shall we finish the sun to-morrow, Daisy?"

"O, if you please."

"Very well. Good bye."

The doctor went, leaving Daisy in a very refreshed state; with plenty to think of. Daisy was quite waked out of her weariness and disappointment, and could do well enough without books for one day longer. She took her own raspberries now with great spirit.

"I have found two more wonderful things to talk to Dr. Sandford about, Juanita; that is three to-day."

"Does Miss Daisy think the doctor can tell her all?"

"I don't know. He knows a great deal, Juanita."

"'Seems he knows more than Job did," said Mrs. Benoit, who had her private misgivings about the authenticity of all Dr. Sandford's statements. Daisy thought a little.

"Juanita, Job lived a great while ago."

"Yes, Miss Daisy."

"How much did he know about the sun? does the Bible tell?"

"It tells a little what he didn't know, Miss Daisy."

"O, Juanita, after I get through my tea and when you have had yours, won't you read me in the Bible all about Job and the sun?"

Mrs. Benoit liked nothing better; and whatever other amusements failed, or whatever other parties anywhere in the land found their employments unsatisfactory, there was one house where intent interest and unflagging pleasure went through the whole evening; it was where Daisy and Mrs. Benoit read "about Job and the sun." Truth to tell, as that portion of Scripture is but small, they extended their reading somewhat.

Daisy's first visiter the next day was her father. He came with fresh flowers and fresh fruit, and with "Sandford and Merton" too, in which he read to her; so the morning went well.

"Papa," said Daisy when he was about leaving her, "do you not think Dr. Sandford is a very interesting man?"

"It is the general opinion of ladies, I believe, Daisy; but I advise you not to lose your heart to him. I am afraid he is not to be depended on."

"O papa," said Daisy, a little shocked, "I do not mean that he is a man one would get *fond of.*"

"Pray who do you think is, Daisy?" said Mr. Randolph, maintaining his gravity admirably.

"Papa, don't you think Capt. Drummond is—and—

"And who, Daisy?"

"I was thinking—Mr. Dinwiddie, papa." Daisy did not quite know how well this last name would be relished, and she coloured a little apprehensively.

"You are impartial in your professional tastes, I am glad to see," said Mr. Randolph. Then observing how innocent of understanding him was the grave little face of Daisy, he bent down to kiss her.

"And you are unfortunate in your favourites. Both at a distance! How is Gary McFarlane?"

"Papa, I think he has good nature; but I think he is rather frivolous."

Mr. Randolph looked soberly at the little face before him, and went away thinking his own thoughts. But he had the cruelty to repeat to Dr. Sandford so much of this conversation as concerned that gentleman; in doing so he unwittingly laid the foundation of more attention to Daisy on the doctor's part, than he probably would ever otherwise have given her. To say truth—the idea propounded by Daisy was so very novel to the doctor that it both amused and piqued him.

Mr. Randolph had hardly gone out, when Hephzibah came in. And then followed a lesson the like of which Daisy had not given yet. Hephzibah's attention was on everything but the business in hand. Also, she had a little less awe of Daisy lying on Mrs. Benoit's couch in a loose gown, than when she met her in the Belvidere at Melbourne, dressed in an elegant cambrick frock with a resplendent sash.

"C, a, spells ca, Hephzibah. Now what is that?"

"Over your finger?"

"Yes."

"That's—C."

"C, a. And what does it spell?"

"Did the stone fall right onto your foot?"

"Yes—partly on."

"And was it broke right off?"

"No. O no. Only the bone of my ankle was broken."

"It smarted some, I guess; didn't it?"

"No. Now Hephzibah, what do those two letters spell?"

"C, a, ca. That don't mean nothin'."

"Now the next. D, a—"

"What's D, a?"

"D, a, da."

"What's that?"

"Nothing; only it spells that."

"How soon'll you be up again?"

"I do not know. In a few weeks."

"Before the nuts is ripe?"

"O yes, I hope so."

"Well, I'll shew you where there's the biggest hickory nuts you ever see! They're right back of Mr. Lamb's barn—only three fields to cross—and there's three hickory trees; and the biggest one has the biggest nuts, mother says, she ever see. Will you go and get some?"

"But, Hephzibah, those are Mr. Lamb's nuts, aren't they?"

"I don't care."

"But," said Daisy, looking very grave, "don't you know, Hephzibah, it is wrong to meddle with anything that belongs to other people?"

"He hain't no right to 'em, I don't believe."

"I thought you said they were in Mr. Lamb's field?"

"So they be."

"Then they are his nuts. You would not like anybody to take them, if they belonged to you."

"It don't make no odds," said Hephzibah sturdily, but looking down at the same time. "He'll get it out of us some other way."

"Get it out of you?" said Daisy.

"Yes."

"What do you mean?"

"He gets it out of everybody," said Hephzibah. "Tain't no odds."

"But Hephzibah, if those trees were yours, would you like to have Mr. Lamb come and take the nuts away?"

"No. I'd get somebody to shoot him."

Daisy hardly knew how to go along with her discourse; Hephzibah's erratic opinions started up so fast. She looked at her little rough pupil in absolute dismay. Hephzibah shewed no consciousness of having said anything remarkable. Very sturdy she looked; very assured in her judgment. Daisy eyed her rough bristling hair, with an odd kind of feeling that it would not be more difficult to comb down into smoothness than the unregulated thoughts of her mind. She must begin gently. But Daisy's eyes grew most wistfully earnest.

"Would you shoot Mr. Lamb for taking away your nuts?"

"Just as lieves."

"Then how do you think he would feel about your taking his nuts?"

"I don't care!"

"But, Hephzibah, listen. Do you know what the Bible says? It says, that we must do to other people just what we would like to have them do to us in the same things."

"Then he oughtn't to have sot such a price on his meat," said Hephzibah.

"But then," said Daisy, "what would it be right for you to do about his nuts?"

"I don't care," said Hephzibah. "'Tain't no odds. I'm a going to get 'em. I guess it's time for me to go home."

"But Hephzibah,—you have not done your lesson yet. I want you to learn all this row to-day. The next is, f, a, fa."

"That don't mean nothin'," said Hephzibah.

"But you want to learn it, before you can go on to what does mean something."

"I don't guess I do," said Hephzibah.

"Don't you want to learn to read?"

"Yes, but that ain't readin'."

"But you cannot learn to read without it," said Daisy.

Under this urging, Hephzibah did consent to go down the column of two-letter syllables.

"Ain't you going with me after them nuts?" she said as soon as the bottom of the page was reached. "I'll shew you a rabbit's nest. La! it's so pretty!"

"I hope you will not take the nuts, Hephzibah, without Mr. Lamb's leave."

"I ain't going to ask his leave," said Hephzibah. "He wouldn't give it to me, besides. It's fun, I tell you."

"It is wrong," said Daisy. "I don't think there's any fun in doing what's wrong."

"It is fun, though, I tell you," said Hephzibah. "It's real sport. The nuts come down like rain; and we get whole baskets full. And then, when you crack 'em, I tell you, they are sweet!"

"Hephzibah, do you know what the Bible says?"

"I don't want to learn no more to-day," said the child. "I'm going. Good bye, Daisy."

She stayed no further instruction of any kind; but caught up her calico sunbonnet and went off at a jump, calling out "Good bye, Daisy!" when she had got some yards from the house. Daisy lay still, looking very thoughtful.

"The child has just tired you, my love!" said the black woman.

"What shall I do, Juanita? She doesn't understand."

"My love knows who opened the eyes of the blind," said Juanita.

Daisy sighed. Certainly teaching seemed to take very small hold on her rough little pupil. These thoughts were suddenly banished by the entrance of Mrs. Randolph.

The lady was alone this time. How like herself she looked, handsome and stately, in characteristic elegance of attire and manner both. Her white morning dress floated off in soft edges of lace from her white arms; a shawl of precious texture was gathered loosely about them; on her head a gossamer web of some fancy manufacture fell off on either side, a mock covering for it. She came up to Daisy and kissed her, and then examined into her various arrangements, to see that she was in all respects well and properly cared for. Her mother's presence made Daisy feel very meek. Her kiss had been affectionate, her care was motherly; but with all that there was not a turn of her hand nor a tone of her calm voice that did not imply and express absolute possession, perfect control. That Daisy was a little piece of property belonging to her in sole right, with which she did and would do precisely what it might please her, with very little concern how or whether it might please Daisy. Daisy was very far from putting all this in words, or even in distinct thoughts; nevertheless she felt and knew every bit of it; her mother's hand did not touch Daisy's foot or her shoulder, without her inward consciousness what a powerful hand it was. Now it is true that all this was in one way no new thing; Daisy had always known her mother's authority to be just what it was now; but it was only of late that a question had arisen about the bearing of this authority upon her own little life and interests. With the struggle that had been, and the new knowledge that more struggles in the future were not impossible, the consciousness of her mother's power over her had a new effect. Mrs. Randolph sat down and took out her tetting work; but she only did a few stitches.

"What child was that I met running from the house as I came up?" she asked, a little to Daisy's discomfiture.

"It was a little girl who belongs in the village, mamma."

"How comes she to know you?"

"It happened by accident partly, in the first place."

"What accident?"

"Mamma, I will tell you another time, if you will let me." For Daisy knew that Juanita was not far off. But Mrs. Randolph only said, "Tell me now."

"Mamma—it was partly an accident," Daisy repeated. "I found out by accident that they were very poor—and I carried them something to eat."

"Whom do you mean by 'them?'"

"That little girl and her mother—Mrs. Harbonner."

"When did you do this?"

"About the time of my birthday."

"And you have kept up the acquaintance since that time?"

"I carried the woman work once, mamma. I had papa's leave to go."

"Did you ask mine?"

"No, mamma. It was papa who had forbidden me to go into any house without leave; so I asked him to let me tell her about the work."

"What was this child here for to-day?"

"Mamma—she is a poor child and could not go to school; and—I was trying to teach her something."

"What were you trying to teach her?"

"To read, mamma—and to do right."

"Have you ever done this before?"

"Yes, mamma—a few times."

"Can it be that you have a taste for low society, Daisy?"

Mrs. Randolph had been asking questions calmly while going on with her tetting work: at this one she raised her eyes and bent them full, with steady cold inquiry, on Daisy's face. Daisy looked a little troubled.

"No, mamma—I do not think I have."

"Is not this child very rude and ill-mannered?"

"Yes, ma'am, but—"

"Is she even a clean child?"

"Not *very*, mamma."

"You are changed, Daisy," said Mrs. Randolph, with a slight but keen expression of disdain. The child felt it, yet felt it not at all to the moving of her steadfastness.

"Mamma—it was only that I might teach her. She knows nothing at all, almost."

"And does Daisy Randolph think such a child is a fit companion for her?"

"Not a *companion*, mamma."

"What business have you with a child who is not a fit companion for you?"

"Only, mamma, to try to be of some benefit to her."

"I shall be of some benefit to you, now. Since I cannot trust you, Daisy—since your own delicacy and feeling of what is right does not guide you in such matters, I shall lay my commands on you for the future. You are to have nothing to do with any person, younger or older, without finding out what my pleasure is about it. Do you understand me?"

"Yes, mamma."

"You are to give no more lessons to children who are not fit companions for you. You are not to have anything to do with this child in particular. Daisy, understand me —I forbid you to speak to her again."

"O mamma——"

"Not a word," said Mrs. Randolph.

"But mamma, please! just this. May I not tell her once, that I cannot teach her? She will think me so strange!"

Mrs. Randolph was silent.

"Might I not, just that once, mamma?"

"No."

"She will not know what to think of me," said Daisy; her lip trembling, her eye reddening, and only able by the greatest self-control to keep from bursting into tears.

"That is your punishment"—replied Mrs. Randolph, in a satisfied, quiet sort of way. Daisy felt crushed. She could hardly think.

"I am going to take you in hand and bring you into order," said Mrs. Randolph with a smile, bending over to kiss Daisy, and looking at her lips and eyes in a way Daisy wished she would not. The meek little face certainly promised small difficulty in her way, and Mrs. Randolph kissed the trembling mouth again.

"I do not think we shall quarrel," she remarked. "But if we do, Daisy, I shall know how to bear my part of it."

She turned carelessly to her tetting again, and Daisy lay still; quiet and self-controlled, it was all she could do. She could hardly bear to watch her mother at her work; the thought of "quarrels" between them was so inevitable and so dreadful. She could hardly bear to look out of her window; the sunshine and bright things out there seemed to remind her of her troubles; for they did not look bright now as they had done in the early morning. She lay still and kept still; that was all; while Mrs. Randolph kept at her work amusing herself with it an uncommonly long time. At last she was tired; threw her shawl round her shoulders again, and stood up to go.

"I think we can soon have you home, Daisy," she said as she stooped to kiss her. "Ask Dr. Sandford when he comes, how soon it will do now to move you; ask him to-night; will you?"

Daisy said "Yes, mamma," and Mrs. Randolph went.

CHAPTER XIX.

The day was a heavy one to Daisy and Juanita after that. The little cottage was very silent. Daisy lay still, saying nothing, and generally keeping her face turned towards the window so that her friend could not see it; and when Mrs. Benoit proposed, as she several times did, to read to Daisy or sing to her, she was always answered by a gentle, "No, Juanita," which was as decided as it was gentle. The last time indeed, Daisy had yielded and given assent to the proposition; but Mrs. Benoit did not feel sure that she gave anything else; either attention or approbation. Daisy's dinner she had prepared with particular care; but it was not enjoyed; Mrs. Benoit knew that. She sighed to herself, and then sang to herself, in a softly kind of way; Daisy gave no heed, and only lay still with her face turned to the window. By and by, late in the afternoon, the doctor came in. He was not a favourite of Mrs. Benoit, but she was glad to see him now. She withdrew a little out of the way and watched to see what he would say.

The doctor's first care as usual was the foot. That was going on well. Having attended to that, he looked at Daisy's face. It did not seem to him satisfactory, Mrs. Benoit saw; for his next move was to the head of the couch, and he felt Daisy's hand, while his eyes studied her.

"How do you do to-day?"

"I am getting better," said Daisy.

"Are you? Your voice sounds weak to-night."

"I do not suppose I am very strong."

"How many wonderful things have you found to-day?"

"I have not thought about them—I have not found any."

Doctor Sandford bent a little over Daisy's couch, holding her hand still and examining her.

"What is the matter, Daisy?" said he.

Daisy fidgeted. The doctor's fine blue eyes were too close to her and too steady to be escaped from. Daisy turned her own eyes uneasily away, then brought them back; she could not help it. He was waiting for her to speak.

"Dr. Sandford," she said humbly, "won't you please excuse me?"

"Excuse you what, Daisy?"

"From telling you what you want to know."

"Pray why should I?"

"It is something that is quite private to myself."

If the doctor's lips remained perfectly still for some moments, it was because they had a private inclination to smile, in which he would not indulge them. Daisy saw nothing but the most moveless gravity.

"Private from all but your physician, Daisy," he said at last. "Do not you know he is an exception to general rules?"

"Is he?" said Daisy.

"Certainly. I always become acquainted with people's private affairs."

"But I do not want that you should be acquainted with mine."

"No matter. You are under my care," said the doctor. Then after a minute he added in a lower tone, "What have you been shedding tears about to-day?"

Daisy's face looked intensely grave; wise and old beyond her days, though the mouth was also sweet. So she faced the doctor and answered him with the sedateness of fifty years—"I can't very well tell you, Dr. Sandford."

"You have been shedding tears to-day?"

"Yes, sir—" said Daisy softly.

"A good many of them? You have been lying nere with your face to the window, crying quietly, a good part of the afternoon—have you not?"

"Yes, sir," said Daisy, wondering at him.

"Now I am your physician and must know what was the matter."

"It is something I cannot tell about, Dr. Sandford."

"Yes, Daisy, you are mistaken. Whatever concerns you, concerns me; if it is the concern of nobody else. Were you tired of lying here so long, day after day?"

"O no, sir! I don't mind that at all. I mean—I don't mind it at all much."

"You do not?" said the doctor. "Have you lost a pet kitten, or a beloved lap-dog?"

"I haven't any, either a kitten or a dog," said Daisy.

"Has that young cavalier, Preston Gary, neglected you?"

"He would not do that," said Daisy; "but he is very fond of shooting."

"He is!" said Dr. Sandford. "Most boys are. You have not felt lonely, then, Daisy?"

"O no, sir."

"I believe I should, in your place. What is the matter, then? I ask as your friend and physician; and you must tell me, Daisy. Who has been to see you to-day?"

"Papa—he came and read to me. Then a little girl—and mamma."

"Did the little girl trouble you?"

"Not much—" said Daisy hesitatingly.

"In what way?"

"She only would not learn to read as fast as I wanted."

"You were the teacher?"

"Yes sir—I was trying—I wanted to teach her."

"And has her obduracy or stupidity caused all this sorrow and annoyance?"

"O no, sir —" But Daisy's eyes filled.

"Then has Mrs. Randolph been the trouble-maker?"

Now Daisy flushed, her lip worked tremblingly; she turned her little head to one side and laid her hand over her brow, to baffle those steady blue eyes of the doctor's. But the doctor left the side of the couch and took a step or two towards where Juanita was sitting.

"Mrs. Benoit," said he, "has this little patient of yours had her tea?"

No, sir. His honour knows, it's early yet in the afternoon."

"Not so very. Do you mean she took enough for dinner to last her till to-morrow?"

"No, sir; her dinner was little better than nothing."

"Then make a cup, in your best style, Mrs. Benoit—and perhaps you will give me one. And have you got any more of those big raspberries for her? bring them and a bit of toast."

While Juanita was gone on this business, which took a little time, the doctor slowly paced back and forth through the small cottage room, with his hands behind him and a thoughtful face. Daisy fancied he was considering her affair; but she was very much mistaken; Dr. Sandford had utterly forgotten her for the moment, and was pondering some difficult professional business. When Juanita appeared with her tea tray, he came out of his abstraction; and though still with a very unrelaxed face, he arranged Daisy's pillows so that she might be raised up a little and feel more comfortable. His hands were strong and skilful, and kind too; there was a sort of pleasure in having them manage her; but Daisy looked on with a little wonder to see him take the charge of being her servitor in what came afterwards. He made her a cup of tea; let her taste it from his hands; and gave the plate of raspberries into her own.

"Is it good?" he asked her.

"Very good!" Daisy said, with so gentle and reverential a look at him that the doctor smiled. He said nothing however at present but to take care that she had her supper; and looked meanwhile to see the colour of Daisy's cheeks change a little, and the worn, wearied lines of her face take a more natural form. His own ministrations were more effectual than the eating and drinking; it was so very odd to have Dr. Sandford waiting upon her that Daisy was diverted, and could not help it.

"Will you take some tea too, Dr. Sandford?" she said in the midst of this. "Won't you take it now, while it is hot?"

"I take my tea cold, Daisy, thank you. I'll have it presently."

So he poured out his own cup and left it to cool while he attended to Daisy; and when she would have no more, he took the cup from the tray and sent Mrs. Benoit off with the rest of the things.

"Now Daisy," said he as he took away her bolstering pillows and laid her nicely down again, "now, Daisy, I am your confidential friend and physician, and I want to know what command Mrs. Randolph has given to trouble you. It is my business to know, and you must tell me."

He was so cool about it, and so determined, that Daisy was staggered. He stood holding her hand and waiting for her answer.

"Mamma——"

Daisy came to a great stop. The doctor waited.

"It was about the little girl."

"Very well. Go on, Daisy."

He took up his cup of tea now and began to sip it. Poor Daisy! She had never been more bewildered in her life.

"What about the little girl?"

"Mamma—doesn't want me to teach her."

"Is it so favourite an amusement?"

"No, sir—" said Daisy hesitatingly.

"Was that all the trouble?"

"No, sir."

The doctor sipped his cup of tea and looked at Daisy. He did not say anything more; yet his eyes so steadily waited for what further she had to say, that Daisy fidgeted; like a fascinated creature, obliged to do what it would not. She could not help looking into Dr. Sandford's face, and she could not withstand what she saw there.

"Dr. Sandford," she began in her old-fashioned way, "you are asking me what is private between my mother and me."

"Nothing is private from your physician, Daisy. I am not Dr. Sandford; I am your physician."

"But you are Dr. Sandford to mamma."

"The business is entirely between you and me."

Daisy hesitated a little longer, but the power of fascination upon her was irresistible.

"I was sorry not to teach the little girl," she said at length; "but I was particularly troubled because—because—"

"Mrs. Randolph was displeased with your system of benevolence?"

"No—not that. Yes, I was troubled about that too. But what troubled me most was—that mamma would not let me speak to her, to tell her why I must not teach her. I must not say anything to her again, at all."

Dr. Sandford's eyes, looking, saw that Daisy had indeed spoken out her trouble now. Such a cloud of sorrow came over her brow; such witnessing redness about her eyelids, though Daisy let the witness of tears get no further.

"What do you suppose was your mother's purpose in making that last regulation?" he went on in a cool business tone.

"I don't know—I suppose to punish me,"—Daisy said faintly.

"Punish you for what?"

"Mamma did not like me to teach that little girl—and I had done it, I mean I had begun to do it, without asking her."

"Was it a great pleasure?" said the doctor.

"It would have been a great pleasure if I could have taught her to read," Daisy said, with her face brightening at the idea.

"I presume it would. Well Daisy, now you and I will arrange this affair. I do not consider it wholesome for you to engage in this particular amusement at this particular time; so I shall endorse Mrs. Randolph's prohibition; but I will go round—— Where does this girl live, and who is she?"

"Her name is Hephzibah Harbonner; she lives in the village, on the road where the Episcopal church is—you know;—a little way further on. I guess it's a quarter of a mile."

"South, eh? Well, I will go round by her house and tell the girl that I cannot let you do any such kindnesses just now, and that till I give her leave she must not come to see you. How will that do, Daisy?"

"Thank you, Dr. Sandford!"

He saw it was very earnestly spoken and that Daisy's brow looked clearer.

"And instead of that amusement, you must study wonderful things to morrow. Will you?"

"O yes, Dr. Sandford! But we have not finished about the sun yet."

"No. Well—to-morrow, then, Daisy."

"Thank you, sir. Dr. Sandford, mamma wanted me to ask you a question before you go."

"Ask it."

"How soon I can be moved home?'

"Are you in a great hurry?"

"No, sir, but I think mamma is."

"You can bear to wait a little longer and study wonderful things from your window?"

"O yes, sir! I think I can do it better here than at home, because my bed is so close to the window, I can look right out."

"I shall not let you be moved just yet, Daisy. Good night. I will see—what's her name?"

"Harbonner—Hephzibah Harbonner."

"Good night."

And Daisy watched the doctor as he went down the path, mounted his horse and rode away, with great admiration; thinking how handsome and how clever and how chivalric he was. Daisy did not use that word in thinking of him; nevertheless his skilful nursing and his taking up her cause so effectually had made a great impression upon her. She was greatly comforted. Juanita, watching her face, saw that it looked so; there was even a dawning smile upon Daisy's lips at one time. It faded however into a deep gravity; and one or two long drawn breaths told of heavy thoughts.

"What troubles has my love?" said the old woman.

Daisy turned her head quick round from the window, and smiled a very sweet smile in her face.

"I was thinking, Juanita."

"My little lady has a cloud come over her again."

"Yes, Juanita, I think I have. O Juanita, I might tell you! What shall I do, when everybody wants me to do what—what I don't think is right? What shall I do, Juanita? I don't know what I shall do."

"Suppose Miss Daisy take the Bible to her pa'—Miss Daisy knows what her pa' promised."

"So he did, Juanita! thank you. I had forgotten that."

In five minutes more Daisy was fast asleep. The black woman stood looking at her. There was no cloud on the little face now, but the signs of the day's work were there. Pale cheeks, and weary features, and the tokens of past tears. Juanita stood and looked, and twinkled away one or two from her own eye-lashes; and then knelt down at the head of the bed and began a whispered prayer. A prayer for the little child before her, in which her heart poured itself out, that she might be kept from evil, and might walk in the straight path, and never be tempted or driven from it. Juanita's voice grew louder than a whisper in her earnestness; but Daisy slept on.

CHAPTER XX.

The next day was an exceedingly hot and sultry one. Daisy had no visiters until quite late in the afternoon; however it was a peaceful day. She lay quiet and happy, and Juanita was quite as well contented that the house should be empty and they two alone. Late in the afternoon, Preston came.

"Well my dear little Daisy! so you are coming home?"

"Am I?" said Daisy.

"To be sure; and your foot is going to get well, and we are going to have all sorts of grand doings for you."

"My foot *is* getting well."

"Certainly. Don't be a Quaker, Daisy."

"What sort of doings are you going to have, Preston?"

"First thing—as soon as you are well enough for it—we are going to have a grand pic-nic party to Silver Lake."

"Silver Lake? what, on the other side of the river?"

"Yes."

"O how delightful! But I shall not be able to go in a long time, Preston."

"Yes, you will. Aunt Felicia says you are coming back to Melbourne now; and once we get you there, we'll cure you up. Why you must have moped half your wits away by this time. I don't expect to find more than two-thirds of the original Daisy left."

"I haven't moped at all."

"There! that is proof the first. When people are moping and do not know they are moping, that is the sign their wits are departing. Poor Daisy! I don't wonder. We'll get you to rights at Melbourne."

"Doctor Sandford will not let me be moved."

"Doctor Sandford cannot help himself. When aunt Felicia says so, he will find ways and means."

"Preston," said Daisy, "I do not think you understand what sort of a man Dr. Sandford is."

"Pray enlighten me, Daisy. I thought I did."

But Daisy was silent.

"What sort of a man is he?"

"Preston," said Daisy abruptly, "I wish you would bring me from Melbourne that tray filled with something,—plaster,—I don't know what it is,—on which Capt. Drummond and I studied geography, and history."

"Geography and history on a tray!" said Preston. "That would be one's hands full to carry!"

"Well, but it was," said Daisy. "The tray was smooth filled with something, something a little soft, on which you could mark; and Capt. Drummond drew the map of England on it; and we were just getting into the battle—what battle was it?—when William came over from France and King Harold met him?"

"Hastings?"

"We were just come to the battle of Hastings, before Capt. Drummond went away; and I should like so much to go on with it!"

"But was the battle of Hastings on the tray?"

"No, Preston, but the place was; and Capt. Drummond told me about the battles."

"Who is here to tell you about them now, Daisy?"

"Couldn't you?—sometimes, now and then?"

"I might; but you see, Daisy, you are coming to Melbourne now, and there will be Silver Lake and lots of other things to do. You won't want the tray here."

Daisy looked a little wistfully at her cousin. She said nothing. And Preston turned sharply, for he heard a soft rustle coming up the path, and was just in time to spring to the door and open it for his aunt.

"'How insufferably hot!" was Mrs. Randolph's remark. "How do you do, Daisy?"

"I think she is bewitched to stay in banishment, aunt Felicia; she will have it she is not coming home."

Mrs. Randolph's answer was given to the doctor, who entered at the instant behind Preston.

"How soon can Daisy be moved, doctor?"

The doctor took a leisurely view of his little patient before he replied.

"Not at present."

"How soon?"

"If I think her fit for it, in a fortnight; possibly earlier."

"But that is, not till September!"

"I am afraid you are correct," said the doctor coolly. Mrs. Randolph stood pondering the question, how far it was needful to own his authority.

"It is dreadfully hot here, in this little place! She would be much better if she were out of it."

"How have you found it at Melbourne to-day?"

"Insufferable!"

"How has it been with you, Daisy?"

"It has been a nice day, Dr. Sandford."

The contrast was so extreme between the mental atmosphere of one speaker and of the other, that Dr. Sandford smiled. It was ninety degrees of Fahrenheit—and the fall of the dew.

"I have heard nobody say as much for the day before," he remarked.

"But she would be much better at Melbourne."

"As soon as I think that, she shall go."

The doctor was absolute in his sphere, and Mr. Randolph moreover, she knew, would back him; so Mrs. Randolph held her peace, though displeased. Nay, she entered into a little conversation with the doctor on other subjects, as lively as the day would admit, before she de parted. Preston stayed behind, partly to improve his knowledge of Dr. Sandford.

"All has gone well to-day, Daisy?" he asked her pleasantly.

"O yes. And Dr. Sandford, shall we finish the sun?"

"By all means. What more shall I tell you?"

"How much more do you know, sir?"

"I know that it is globe-shaped—I know how big it is—I know how heavy it is; and I know that it turns round and round continually."

"O sir, do you *know* all these things?"

"Yes."

"Please, Dr. Sandford, how can you?"

"You would mature into a philosopher, in time, Daisy."

"I hope not," muttered Preston.

"I know that it is globe-shaped, Daisy, because it turns round and lets me see all sides of it."

"Is one side different from another?"

"Only so far, as that there are spots here and there," Dr. Sandford went on, looking at the exceeding eagerness in Daisy's eyes. "The spots appear at one edge—pass over to the other edge, and go out of sight. After a certain time I see them come back again where I saw them first."

"O I should like to see the spots on the sun!" said Daisy. "You said they were holes in the curtain, sir?"

"Yes."

"What curtain?" said Preston.

"You are not a philosopher," said the doctor.

"How long does it take them, the spots, Dr. Sandford, to go round and come back again?"

"A little more than twenty-five days."

"How very curious!" said Daisy. "I wonder what it turns round for—the sun, I mean?"

"You have got too deep there," said the doctor. "I cannot tell you."

"But there must be some reason," said Daisy; "or it would stand still."

"It is in the nature of the thing, I suppose," said Dr. Sandford; "but we do not fully know its nature yet. Only what I am telling you."

"How came people to find these things out?"

"By watching—and experimenting—and calculating."

"Then how big is the sun, Dr. Sandford?"

"How big does it look?"

"Not very large—I don't know—I can't think of anything it looks like."

"It looks just about as big as the moon does."

"Is it just the same size as the moon? But Dr. Sandford, it is a great deal further off, isn't it?"

"Four hundred times as far."

"Then it must be four hundred times as large, I should think."

"It is just about that."

"But I do not know how large that would be. I cannot think."

"Nor can I, Daisy. But I can help you. Suppose we, and our earth, were in the centre of the sun; and our moon going round us at the same distance from us that she is now; there would be room enough for the whole concern, as far as distances are concerned."

"In the sun, Dr. Sandford?"

"In the sun."

"And the moon as far off as she is now?"

"Yes."

"But the *moon* would not be in the sun too?"

"Plenty of room, and to spare."

Daisy was silent now. Preston looked from her face to the doctor's.

"Not only that, Daisy; but the moon then would be

two hundred thousand miles within the circumference of the sun; the sun's surface would be two hundred thousand miles beyond her."

"Thank you, Dr. Sandford!"

"What for, Daisy?"

"I am so glad to know all that."

"Why?"

Daisy did not answer. She did not feel ready to tell her whole thought, not to both her friends together, at least; and she did not know how to frame her reply. But then perceiving that Dr. Sandford was looking for an answer, and that she was guilty of the rudeness of withholding it, she blushed and spoke.

"It makes me understand some things better."

"What, for instance?" said the doctor, looking as grave as ever, though Preston was inclined to laugh. Daisy saw it; nevertheless she answered,

"The first chapter of Genesis."

"O you are there, are you?" said the doctor. "What light have I thrown upon the passage, Daisy? It has not appeared to myself."

Now Daisy hesitated. A sure though childish instinct told her that her thoughts and feelings on this subject would meet with no sympathy. She did not like to speak them.

"Daisy has peculiar views, Dr. Sandford," said Preston. But the doctor paid him no attention. He looked at Daisy, lifted her up and arranged her pillows; then as he laid her back said, "Give me my explanation of that chapter, Daisy."

"It isn't an explanation, sir;—I did not know there was anything to explain."

"The light I have thrown on it then—out of the sun."

Preston was amused, Daisy saw; she could not tell whether the doctor was; his blue eyes gave no sign, except of a will to hear what she had to say. Daisy hesitated, and hesitated, and then with something very like the old diplomacy she had partly learned and partly inherited from her mother, she said,

"If you will read the chapter, I will tell you."

Now Daisy did not think Dr. Sandford would care to read the chapter, or perhaps have the time for it; but with an unmoved face he swung himself round on his chair and called on Mrs. Benoit for a Bible. Preston was in a state of delight, and Mrs. Benoit of wonder. The Bible was brought, Dr. Sandford took it, and opened it.

"We have only time for a short lecture to-day," he remarked, "for I must be off. Now Daisy, I will read, and you shall comment."

Daisy felt worried. She turned uneasily and rested her face on her hand, and so lay looking at the doctor; at his handsome calm features and glittering blue eye. What could *she* say to him? The doctor's eye saw a grave sweet little face, a good deal flushed, very grave, with a whole burden of thought behind its unruffled simplicity. It may be said, that his curiosity was as great as Daisy's unwillingness. He began, facing her as he read. Juanita stood by, somewhat anxious.

'"In the beginning God created the heaven and the earth."'——

The doctor stopped and looked down at that face of Daisy looking up at him. He waited.

"I did not use to think how much all that meant," said Daisy humbly. The doctor went on.

He went on with the grand, majestic words of the story, which sounded very strange to Daisy from his lips, but very grand; till he came to the fourteenth verse. '"And God said, Let there be lights in the firmament of the heaven to divide the day from the night; and let them be for signs, and for seasons, and for days and years: and let them be for lights in the firmament of the heaven, to give light upon the earth: and it was so."' The doctor looked at Daisy again.

"There," said she, "that is very different now from what it used to be—I didn't know what sort of lights those were; it's a great deal more wonderful now. Won't you read on a little further?"

'"And God made two great lights; the greater light to rule the day, and the lesser light to rule the night; he made the stars also. And God set them in the firmament of the heaven, to give light upon the earth, and to rule over the day, and over the night, and to divide the light from the darkness: and God saw that it was good."'

"That is what I mean," said Daisy, as the doctor paused. "I never knew before what those 'lights' meant—I thought the sun was—I don't know what; I didn't think much about it; but now I never shall forget again. I know now what sort of a light was made to rule the day; and I don't wonder——"

"Do not wonder what, Daisy?

"I do not wonder that God said that it was good. I am so much obliged to you for telling me about it."

"Never heard a more satisfactory application of knowledge in my life,"—the doctor remarked with a smile as he handed back the Bible to Mrs. Benoit. And then he and Preston went off; but Daisy lay long very thoughtfully looking after them out of her window. Till the sound of the horses' feet was far out of hearing Daisy lay there looking into the evening. She did not stir till Mrs. Benoit brought her supper.

"Isn't it wonderful, Juanita," she said with a long drawn breath, "how the sun divides the light from the darkness!"

"Most things is wonderful, that the Lord makes," answered the black woman.

"Are they?" said Daisy.

"But what makes my love sigh?" said Juanita anxiously; for Daisy's face had not brightened up, though she was taking her tea. Daisy looked at her.

"O Juanita!" she said,—"I am afraid that Dr. Sandford is in the darkness!"

"Where the sun don't shine it be darkness, sure!" said Juanita. "And he do not see the Light of the world, Miss Daisy."

Daisy's eyes filled, filled. She liked Dr. Sandford very much. And then who else that she loved had never seen that Light! Daisy pushed aside her tears and tried to drink her tea; but at last she gave it up. Her spoon fell into her saucer and she lay down and hid her face in the pillow. The black woman stood with a strange grave look and with watering eyes, silent for a little time; holding Daisy's tray in her hands and waiting.

"Miss Daisy——"

"What, Juanita?"

"My love take her tea, to be strong; and then see how many she can bring out of the darkness."

"I, Juanita?" said Daisy rousing up.

"Maybe the Lord send his message by little hands. What hinder?"

"But, Juanita, *I* can't do anything?"

"Carry the Lord's message, Miss Daisy."

"Can I?"

"Why not, my love? The dear Lord, he do all. And Miss Daisy knows, he hear the prayer of his servants."

The child looked at the black woman, with a wistful, earnest, searching look that it was curious to see. She said nothing more; she eyed Juanita as if she were searching into the depth of something; then she went on with her supper. She was thoughtful all the evening; busy with cogitations which she did not reveal; quiet and absent minded. Juanita guessed why; and many a prayer went up from her own secret heart.

But from about this time Daisy began to grow well again. She could not be moved, of course; Dr. Sandford would not permit that; neither to be carried home, nor to change her place and position in the cottage. But she was getting ready for it. The latter half of August cooled off from its fierce heats and was pleasantly warm. Daisy took the benefit of the change. She had rather a good time, those last weeks at Juanita's house; and perhaps that was one reason why Dr. Sandford, seeing it, chose to let well alone and would not have anybody take Daisy home. Daisy had a very good time. She had the peace of Juanita's house; and at home she knew there would be things to trouble her. She had books and could read now as much as she liked; and she was very fond of reading. Preston did not find it expedient to bring the geography tray; on the other hand, Mr. Randolph thought it good to come every day and spend a piece of time with his little daughter; and became better acquainted with her than ever he had been in his life before. He discovered that Daisy was very fond of knowledge; that he could please her no way better than by taking up the history of England and reading to her and stopping to explain everything by the way which Daisy did not understand. English history was certainly an old story to Mr. Randolph; but to discuss it with Daisy was a very new thing. He found her eager, patient, intelligent, and wise with an odd sort of child-wisdom which yet was not despicable for older years. Daisy's views of the feudal system, and of the wittenagemot, and of trial by jury, and of representative legislation, were intensely amusing to Mr. Randolph; he said it was going back to a primitive condition of society, to talk them over with her; though there I think he was mistaken. If Daisy had read those pages of history to herself, she would have passed over some of these matters at least with little heed; she would not have gone to anybody with questions. But Mr. Randolph reading to her, it was an easy thing to ask the meaning of a word as they passed; and that word would draw on a whole little bit of talk. In this intercourse Mr. Randolph was exceedingly gentle, deliberate, and kind. Daisy had nothing to fear, not even that she might weary him; so those were hours of real enjoyment to both parties.

Preston not very seldom came and made himself agreeable; playing an occasional game of chess, and more often regaling Daisy with a history of his expeditions. Other visiters Daisy had from Melbourne, now and then; but her best friend for real service, after her father and Juanita, was Dr. Sandford. He took great care of his little patient's comfort and happiness; which was a pretty thing in him, seeing that he was a young man, busy with a very good country practice, and furthermore busy with the demands made upon him as an admired pet of society. For that was Dr. Sandford, and he knew it perfectly well. Nevertheless his kind care of Daisy never abated.

It was of course partly his professional zeal and care that were called for; but it could not have been those that made him keep up his lectures to Daisy on the wonderful things she found for him, day by day. In professional care those lectures certainly began; but Daisy was getting well now; had nothing more to trouble her, and shewed an invariably happy as well as wise little face. Yet Dr. Sandford used to sit down and tell her of the things she asked about, with a sort of amused patience—if it was no more; at any rate he was never impatient. He talked to Daisy of the stars, which, with the moon, were very naturally the next subjects of investigation after the sun.

At last Daisy got him upon the subject of trilobites. It was not difficult. Dr. Sandford was far more easy to move than Preston—in this matter at least. He only smiled, and slid into the story very simply; the story that Daisy was so eager to hear. And it did not seem less worth hearing than she had expected, nor less wonderful, nor less interesting. Daisy thought about it a great deal, while Juanita listened and doubted; but Daisy did not doubt. She believed the doctor told her true. That the family to which her little fossil trilobite belonged—the particular family—for they were generally related, he said to the lobster and crab, were found in the very oldest and deepest down rocks in which any sort of remains of living things have been found; therefore it is likely they were among the earliest of earth's inhabitants. There were a great many of them, the doctor said, and many different species; for great numbers of them are found to this day in those particular rocks. The rocks must have been made at the time when the trilobites lived, and have somehow shut them in. And the doctor thought it likely that at the time when they lived, there was no dry land in existence, but all covered by the sea. He would not take it upon him to be positive; but this he could tell Daisy; there was never a stick or a leaf to be found in those old rocks that ever lived and grew on dry ground, though there were plenty that grew in the sea, until in the very topmost or latest of those rocks some few bits of fern growth began to appear.

"But what plants live under water?" said Daisy.

"Sea weeds."

"Oh! So many of them?"

"So many, that the rocks are sometimes darkened by their fossil remains, and in some places those remains form beds of coal several feet thick."

"And are there a great many remains of the trilobites?"

"There are whole rocks, Daisy, that are formed almost entirely of trilobites."

"Sea weeds and trilobites—what a strange time!" said Daisy. "Was that all that was living?"

"No; there were other sea creatures of the lower kind, and at last fishes. But when the fishes became very numerous, the trilobites died out and passed away."

That old time had a wonderful charm for Daisy; it was, as she thought, better than a fairy tale. The doctor at last let her into the secret that *he* had a trilobite too; and the next time he came he brought it with him. He was good enough to leave it with Daisy a whole day; and Daisy's meditations over it and her own together were numberless and profound.

The next transition was somewhat sudden; to a wasp or two that had come foraging on Daisy's window-sill. But Dr. Sandford was at home there; and so explained the wasp's work and manner of life, with his structure and fitness for what he had to do, that Daisy was in utter delight; though her eyes sometimes opened upon Dr. Sandford with a grave wistful wonder in them, that he should know all this so well and yet never acknowledge the hand that had given the wasp the tools and instinct for his work, one so exactly a match for the other. But Dr. Sandford never did. He used to notice those grave looks of Daisy, and hold private speculation with himself what they might mean; private amused speculation; but I think he must have liked his little patient as well as been amused at her, or he would hardly have kept up as he did this personal ministering to her pleasure, which was one of the great entertainments of Daisy's life at this period. In truth only to see Dr. Sandford was an entertainment to Daisy. She watched even the wave of his long locks of hair. He was a fascination to her.

"Are you in a hurry to get home?" he would ask her every now and then. Daisy always said, "No sir; not till you think it is time;" and Dr. Sandford never thought it was time. No matter what other people said, and they said a good deal; he ordered it his own way; and Daisy was almost ready to walk when he gave permission for her to be taken home in the carriage. However, the permission was given at last.

"To-morrow night I shall not be here, Juanita," Daisy remarked as she was taking her supper.

"No, Miss Daisy."

"You will be very quiet when I am gone."

It had not been a bustling house, all those weeks! But the black woman only answered,

"My love will come to see Juanita sometimes?"

"O yes. I shall come very often, Juanita—if I can. You know when I am out with my pony, I can come very often,—I hope."

Juanita quite well understood what was meant by the little pauses and qualifying clauses of this statement. She passed them over.

But Daisy shed a good many tears during Juanita's prayer that night. I do not know if the black woman shed any; but I know that some time afterwards and until late in the night, she knelt again by Daisy's bedside, while a whisper of prayer, too soft to arouse the child's slumbers, just chimed with the flutter and rustle of the leaves outside of the window moving in the night breeze.

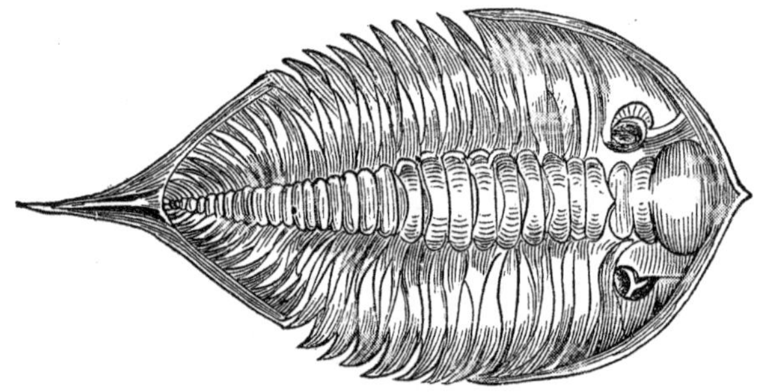

THE DOCTOR'S TRILOBITE.

www.ingramcontent.com/pod-product-compliance
Lightning Source LLC
LaVergne TN
LVHW010210110826
845151LV00004B/1043
9781425529017